The Killing

Frank Maney

First published in 2023 by Sharpe Books.

For Carole and Michael

'Now I am become Death, the destroyer of worlds.'

J. Robert Oppenheimer reciting Hindu scripture on witnessing the first detonation of a nuclear weapon on July 16th, 1945.

1

Sweat dripped from his brow, a film of foam smeared his lips. The poison was scorching through the cells of his body, searching out internal organs.

Soon, it would paralyse limbs, shutting down his brain. There was no escape. Already his eyes were blurry, the huge oil portrait of Horatio Nelson on the wall before him assuming a dreamy quality.

"Miss Volkov, I think we'll have to … I don't feel … well." Sir Robert Bellingham spluttered, slumping in his chair.

The woman across the desk smiled. "Don't struggle, it won't take long." Her tone was soft, but not with concern.

Sir Robert, First Sea Lord and Chief of Naval Staff, could not place the accent. It had challenged him for more than an hour. It could have been British. North London even, although he knew that was unlikely as she had not recognised his reference to 'Ally Pally', or Alexandra Palace, the famous entertainment venue, home of the BBC's first regular public television service.

He detected a hint of American, but knew many non-English speakers learned the language from Hollywood films. She was a subtle, intriguing mix. But she knew her stuff. He had agreed to the interview at his country home because her credentials seemed impeccable.

A degree from Oxford University. A trainee assignment with the Financial Times. A contributor to Navy News, the official magazine of the Royal Navy. Two years with the Washington Post, after which she went off the radar for several years, turning up as a freelancer 18 months ago. Even so, the media department and security had insisted on checking out Nina Volkov, as was the case with all journalists requesting exclusive articles about the UK's defence policy.

Now, as he attempted to stem the swirling sensation in his brain, the gripe at the pit of his stomach sharpening, for the first time Sir Robert sensed a slight Slavic edge to her tone. The recent warnings in the British Press, as well as the corridors of Whitehall, suggesting third parties were actively seeking high-profile targets in the war on democracy, came to mind.

"Goodbye, Admiral." The woman spat the sentiment across the desk with callous disregard, leaving no doubt of her intention. "They say old men are wise, but obviously not all of them. This is not a game for old men."

With military composure she watched Sir Robert, unable to speak, slowly slide off the captain's chair, collapsing prostrate on the carpet. His legs felt like iron girders, paralysis biting deep into his limbs.

Crossing to the front of the desk, Volkov immediately rifled through the drawers, flicking over files, stuffing papers, especially those containing relevant buzzwords, into her bag.

Hearing voices, she paused for a moment before walking over to the big sash window overlooking the admiral's garden.

Her parked car pointed down the sweeping driveway, positioned for a speedy exit. The admiral's two protection officers, dark suits stark against the green background, were chatting, laughing with the gardener, their conversation muffled by the distant whine of a hedge-trimmer. Volkov was sure they would pay no heed when she left. One of the officers had frisked her before she entered the admiral's home. Frisked her roughly at that, the bodyguard smirking, enjoying his work. He found nothing, the tiny lethal vial sunk deep inside a tube of lipstick.

She afforded the admiral's body not even the merest glance as she returned to her search at the desk. She'd used this poison before, fast-acting, virtually undetectable five minutes after deployment. When the pathologist performed the autopsy he would find no trace. A massive heart attack, triggered by a combination of stress, alcohol, too much tobacco and not enough exercise, would be the likely verdict.

Flicking through more papers, a scraping noise drew her attention. She half-turned to discover a Glock 17 navy-issue pistol thrust in her direction. Stumbling back against a filing cabinet, her first thought was of reproach. She had underestimated the admiral. Miscalculated the poison dosage. That was the only explanation.

A big man, perhaps on the high side of 18 stones, his bulk must have slowed the rate of absorption.

For the admiral there were no such thoughts. For him, it was simpler. His ego, perhaps also the fact that Nina Volkov was a fragrant, successful woman, had rendered himself and his nation vulnerable to attack. His dying breaths held a single focus. What a fool, he thought. He never did interviews. Why did he agree? She must have slipped something into the cup of tea. He couldn't let this happen. His legs would no longer bear his weight, but as Volkov searched his drawers, her attention distracted, the admiral had stretched an arm where he had fallen, inching forward, curling the stiffening fingers of his right hand around the weapon he kept under the desk.

No feel. No balance. Instead, terror mixed with rage directed his last shreds of lucidity, summoning the strength and will to lift and point the gun. As Volkov stared, the admiral's final act of redemption before his world turned black was to pull the trigger. For a few seconds she gazed at him in disbelief, a crimson patch swelling on her white linen blouse directly over her heart. A gurgle sounded in her throat. Horatio Nelson looked on. A stern expression.

Then she was gone, collapsing on the floor, eyes open but unseeing, both she and Sir Robert Bellingham victims of a deadly game that, unknown to them and depending how it played out, could determine the future of mankind.

2

A buzz, tinny and grating, jerked her awake, sleepy brain struggling to compute the unfamiliar sound.

She sat up, rubbed her eyes, reaching across the bedside table where her mobile phone vibrated on top of a row of discarded coins.

The screen illuminated. She clocked the time, 2.15am. *That's strange. No-one phones at this time. Unless it's that dodgy taxi company whose customers somehow keep dialling the wrong number.*

Beside her, she could hear the low, comforting, snores of her boyfriend, Al. For a moment, she contemplated ending the call unanswered. Then she saw the caller's name.

Mind still fuzzy, she clicked. "Hello, Miles."

"Emily, we have a situation." No apology for the late call. The voice contained flat vowels, rough as sandpaper, but with natural authority. It belonged to Miles Dent, section chief at the Secret Intelligence Service in London's head office.

"What sort of situation?"

"Can't say on the phone. Tell you later."

"I'm due in at seven-thirty."

"Now, Emily. We need you now."

"But ..."

"Now. This won't wait."

The line went dead. There were times when Emily Stearn loved her job as an analyst cum expert cryptographer at SIS. This wasn't one of them. *What could possibly be so urgent that they need me to travel into the office in the middle of the night?*

She eased back the duvet, attempting to slip out of bed without awakening Al.

A muffled slur came from the pillow next to her. "I'm awake, no need to tiptoe around."

"Sorry, Al, it's work. They want me to go in."

"Don't they have homes to go to?"

"It's Dent. His home *is* the office. You know that."

"Do you want me to drive you?"

"No, I'll take the Vespa."

"Okay." Al turned over.

"By the way, what do you think of *You and I* by George Michael?" said Emily.

"Pardon."

"To walk out to. I've been dreaming of that song all night."

"Bit cheesy."

Emily shook her head, drawing an exasperated breath. Attempts to persuade Al to fine tune the details of their upcoming wedding in two months had proved difficult. He preferred something classical such as Pachelbel's Canon in D, Emily loved pop music. She'd keep working on him.

She dressed, brushed her teeth on the move, at the same time popping a bottle of mineral water into her rucksack. "See you later." The front door eased shut on their Camden flat. Al grunted.

Thirty minutes later, Emily knocked before entering Dent's office. On her scooter ride through the city she had tried to anticipate what lay at the heart of her early-hours summons, concluding a code most likely required attention. Maybe involving the ongoing skirmishes in Yemen. Or communications traffic between Moscow and China. Or perhaps data required assessing after North Korea's latest ballistic missile launch. These were her normal spheres of operation. Dent's grave expression told a different story.

Another man and a woman sat around the glass-topped conference desk. Emily knew neither of them but Dent signalled her to sit, his introductions confirming the meeting's gravity.

"This is Roger Williams from the Ministry of Defence."

Emily's features dissolved into a puzzled cloud, but she nodded politely.

"And this is Jane Miller. Jane's an expert in Russian history, separatist groups, guns for hire, that sort of thing. She's also an expert in tracking terrorists."

Intrigued, Emily again nodded, the furrows in her brow growing ever deeper.

Dent reached for his laptop, fiddled with the keys, motioning towards the wall. A selection of pictures trawled across the big screen. Emily watched in studious silence. Close-ups of an old man's crumpled body beside a mahogany desk, mouth drooling, face contorted in a grimace of concentration, handgun clutched in his right hand. A woman, pretty, well dressed, eyes wide, surprised, lying beside him, a gaping hole in her chest, blood splatters having chased down the white wall behind her. The last photograph was a wide shot of the complete scene, a naval painting dominating the background.

When the reel ended, Dent fixed Emily. "I expect you're wondering what this is all about?"

Emily nodded.

"History is laden with men who made wrong judgement calls where women are concerned. Profumo, Clinton, David and Bathsheba."

"Bathsheba?" Emily had heard that name, but failed to bring its relevance to mind.

"Bible reference." A wave of Dent's hand dismissed the reference as unimportant, although his passion for history compelled him to explain. "Pretty girl, mother of King Solomon, David saw her bathing, lusted after her and merry hell let loose. But never mind that. It looks like we can add to the list of powerful men who misjudged the intentions of a pretty, intelligent woman … Sir Robert Bellingham. Not the first, won't be the last."

Dent pointed to the bloody scene on the screen. "This is what happens when powerful men and the people around them drop their guard. Think they are untouchable. Sir Robert was head of the Royal Navy. A brilliant strategist. An astute leader of men. The Nelson of our era. Look at him now." Their eyes were drawn to the photo once more.

Williams cast a disparaging glance in Dent's direction. The admiral may have made an error of judgement but he had paid a heavy price. The MOD man saw no worth in labouring the point, especially as the incident was not yet fully investigated. "Surely this woman was security checked, quite possibly by members of your department."

Dent bristled. "I can assure you that's not the case. Not our responsibility."

For a moment, tetchiness on both sides of the table threatened to derail the meeting, until Dent bit his lip, raising his hands in a conciliatory gesture. "You're right, someone, somewhere, has messed up. That's for later. I didn't mean to blame the admiral, simply to point out that even the most powerful are vulnerable."

Dent turned to Emily. "We may have got lucky. Sir Robert's protection detail alerted Roger here. He phoned us. Thus far the Metropolitan police have not been informed. That allowed me to send a team to the property. The early signs point to a classic Russian sting."

Emily did not appear convinced. "How do you know that? The photo shows Sir Robert pointing a gun and a dead woman with a hole in her chest. That's all. Maybe someone else was involved?"

"That would be possible if his two bodyguards were not on the premises at the time," said Dent. "Or if we hadn't found an empty vial hidden in the woman's bag. It will be sent for analysis, as will the cup of tea on the admiral's desk. My bet is that it contains dregs of a poison that when administered leaves no obvious trace unless one's looking for it."

"Such as?"

"Arsenic, cyanide, thallium, novichok, I don't know, I'm not a chemist."

Emily was still struggling to comprehend why Dent's phone call had dragged her out of bed at such an hour. She was a senior analyst with Section X, a department charged with unravelling information collected by foreign agents of extra value to the UK and its allies. Despite a quirky personality and unconventional ways, she had been fast-tracked from day one because of her uncanny ability to detect connections and decipher complex codes. Her rapid rise was further enhanced when her photographic memory and sharp instinct proved instrumental in unmasking Andrei Reblov, a Russian assassin, foiling a plot to kill the Prime Minister and other European leaders at the Palace of Versailles. During the search for Reblov, Emily was dragged into the espionage field, where she was held at gunpoint.

Rather than putting her off, those events convinced her she belonged at the sharp end of the Intelligence Service. Her security clearance was raised to that of colleagues dealing with the most sensitive secret data. She passed all the training courses for covert operatives, yearning, to her amazement, for a mission to prove herself. Murder stings involving high-ranking sailors, however, did not routinely cross her desk.

"What has this got to do with me?" said Emily.

Dent motioned to Jane Miller, who stood, fished inside a thick file, pinning half a dozen pictures on a whiteboard. She pointed to the central picture. A petite woman with cascading hair whose warm smile was instantly attractive. Unmistakeably, it was the same woman lying on the admiral's floor.

"This is Nina Volkov. She's shrewd and intelligent."

"Was," corrected Dent.

"Of course. Was. She trained as a journalist, becoming a respected commentator on defence matters for some years. But it seems it was all a cover. In reality, she was a terrorist of some infamy who went under various names and aliases. She is thought to have been involved as a teenager in bombings in Chechnya, responsible for assassinating a string of powerful men. Somehow, she managed to stay under the intelligence radar, which is a tribute to her elusiveness. Some say she was a secret mistress of Vladimir Putin, although no pictorial evidence exists. What's certain is that she's well connected, based in Moscow, with a passion for English and the UK, probably derived from the three years she studied at Oxford University."

"How come. Does she have English connections?" Emily was intrigued.

"She's the daughter of an English woman who married a minor Russian oligarch. As such, she held both British and Russian passports in her own name, almost certainly along with several more with assumed identities."

"Money and education. A potent combination," said Emily.

"Precisely." Miller pointed to the other photos. Nina at work and play in various countries. One of them posing in the wind in a gondola in Venice, hair flying wild as if the star of a shampoo commercial, another in what resembled a desert jeep, wearing military fatigues, carrying a Kalashnikov rifle.

"But who's payroll is she on? Who's she working for? Why kill a British navy chief? I don't see the point." The photos had stirred Emily's inquisitive juices.

Miller returned to her seat. "Good questions. I think we know the answer to one of them."

"Which one."

"The first one, and maybe part of the second."

"Go on."

Miller glanced at Dent, a mere twitch of an eyebrow providing assent. "Have you heard of the Ivan Group?"

Emily paused, delving through her sketchy research into terrorist organisations until a memory dawned. "Aren't they a secret, mostly female, band of mercenaries, prepared to work for anybody but mainly affiliated to the Brics – as in Brazil, Russia, India, China and South Africa?"

"That's right, Emily. They were formed at about the same time as the Wagner Group but instead of fighting on the battlefield in places such as Ukraine and Africa, they specialise in money laundering, bank heists, searching for secrets, obtaining classified information and codes from influential and unsuspecting people. If necessary, killing them."

"Such as Sir Robert Bellingham."

"As well as the empty vial, we found files of sensitive information stuffed into Volkov's bag, apparently lifted from the admiral's desk."

"I'm still struggling to see how I can help."

Miller glanced across at Dent who fiddled with his tie, first tightening, then relaxing the knot. Emily recognised the sign. Dent always did that when bad or momentous news was required, as if stretching and loosening provided an essential prelude to action.

"We've detected an Ivan cell operating in London. Been keeping tabs on it for several weeks, but it has probably been around much longer. A small band working out of an upmarket nail parlour in Chelsea," said Dent. "Normally that type of surveillance would be the preserve of MI5. But the characters are well known to some of our agents. There's a feeling, nothing tangible yet, just a feeling, that something major is about to go down. Actually, it's a bit more than a feeling. The chatter is that they have found something. Something big. The Russian word, Shelkunchik, keeps being repeated."

"As in Nutcracker?" Emily translated.

"That's right. No idea why. Perhaps to do with Tchaikovsky's opera, but it sounds more ominous. Like a codename. And the death of the admiral makes me nervous."

Dent had gained Emily's undivided attention. "Was this Volkov woman involved?"

"We know she flew into Heathrow today, or yesterday to be precise." He checked his watch. "She headed directly to Bellingham's house in Kent. No contact with a handler. We've fast-checked miles of CCTV, accounting for her every movement."

"And?" Emily was becoming impatient.

"We've no reason to believe Volkov was known personally to anyone operating from the nail parlour, although we found the parlour's address among her belongings. It provides us with an opportunity."

Miller interjected. "Look at the photo again, Emily. Take your time."

She stared at the image of Nina Volkov. Pretty face. Coy expression. Long honey-blonde hair. Eyes betraying a slight reticence. Almost like looking in a mirror. The realisation struck home. She jabbed a forefinger at her chest.

"Oh God, you don't mean me?"

Dent laid his palms flat on the desk. "That's exactly what we're thinking."

3

Katya eased the stolen four-wheel drive around the corner. She was cold, as well as uncomfortable. Should have worn thermals as Olga suggested. In the passenger seat, Olga pulled a black pistol from its holster, checking it for at least the tenth time.

They had parked up overlooking the common two hours before, dressed in all-black boiler suits, waiting for Zofia to call them in. Gone midnight, Zofia was on the main drag, in Wimbledon Village, lurking in the shadows of an alleyway, watching for action across the road.

A few drunks from the town's homeless fraternity had wandered into the alley, casting lascivious looks. Zofia's Polish version of Anglo Saxon had sent them on their way. Twice, she had ducked back several yards as police cars trawled past on routine business, although the chances of being seen from the road were slim.

When she spotted the blue G80 Cash in Transit van approaching, the road was virtually deserted, a busy night having settled into its inevitable slumber. The two-man crew stuck to company protocol. They drove past the bank to ensure all was secure before turning around, easing into the premium parking spot opposite the bank's main door.

To Zofia's relief, a minute later they pulled up.

"In position. Come on down, Katya." Zofia's tone was measured but tinged with excitement as she whispered into her mobile phone. The two guards, wearing hard helmets, visors, bulky uniforms masking stab vests, exited the van. Casting inquisitive glances along the street as the bank door eased open, they strode inside.

Events were proceeding exactly as the lady wanting two-tone lacquered nails had described earlier that week.

Katya had lived and worked at The Salon off the King's Road in Chelsea for around a year. Most conversations were mundane. What customers were cooking for dinner, what box-sets they binged on, where they were travelling on holiday.

Sometimes, it was akin to a confessional, one customer recently admitting to not having told the real father her twins were his, while letting another man bring them up. But it was a lady from Wimbledon who had piqued Katya's interest most.

The woman's husband was the local bank manager, or at least he would be until the end of the week. After that, he would be out of a job and the town's residents out of a bank as bosses were closing down the branch, along with 10 others in neighbouring localities. All part of cost-cutting and centralisation. No appeal. No consultation. The plan was to empty the branches of cash and valuables late on Friday evening. In Wimbledon's case, because it was last on the run, it may even stretch into the early hours of Saturday after the pubs had shut and late-night revellers dispersed. In time, the properties would be boarded and sold to the highest bidder.

"He's worked there thirty years but it's all over, just like that." The woman clicked her fingers, her tone sour.

"Why are they in such a hurry?" A glint in Katya's eye. In true Ivan fashion, she'd spotted an opportunity.

"No idea. All I know is that the workers have been offered peanuts in redundancy. I told my husband he should keep one of the cash bags on Friday. No one would miss it."

Katya agreed. The days of robbers routinely targeting security vans for mountains of cash were almost over. No one used cash anymore. Not on the High Street. Everyone flashed contactless cards or paid for big items with plastic. Queues for ATMs were from a bygone age. The coronavirus pandemic had accelerated the flight from cash. There was no returning.

Yet sometime on Friday night or Saturday morning a van packed with used notes, untraceable and readily available, would be trundling through Wimbledon.

"What branch does your husband work at?" Katya assumed her kindest voice, wearing a concerned expression.

"The one on the main road, by the coffee shop, not far from the Prince of Wales pub."

From her vantage point, Zofia could see all three. She also spotted the black 4x4 turn the corner, idling in the shadows. Game on. The guards emerged from the bank a few minutes later, both carrying two large bags. Easy does it, thought Zofia. Wait until the van doors open. Don't be impatient. She pulled down her black balaclava, stooping to scoop up the baseball bat hidden in the alley. As the guards turned to face the van's rear door, she stalked across the street, at first slowly but as the door opened, at a sprint.

One of the guards, a wide-shouldered hulk of a man, detected the scrape of scurrying feet. He swivelled, instinctively ducking as the flailing bat swung towards his head. It struck a glancing blow, deflecting off the top of his helmet, sending him spinning to the tarmac. His bags went flying. The other guard dropped his bags, too, reaching to slam the van door.

Katya screamed, stomping her foot on the 4x4's accelerator. If the van door slammed, they would never prise it open again in time. In line with most G80 security vehicles a sensor would detect the impact, an automatic locking system sealing the van. Even the guards would be incapable of overriding the mechanism. The 4x4 roared forward, ploughing into the back of the van, the impact resembling a mini-explosion. Metal tore against metal. Katya's bumper sheared off while the van door swung back violently, striking the second guard full in the face. He collapsed, unconscious, teeth shattered, blood pouring from his nose and mouth.

The other guard sprang up, his lightness of foot surprising Zofia. He made to flee but Zofia was ready for him. She took two loping strides, this time swinging the bat at knee level. The crack of splintering bone mixed with the guard's scream of agony echoed in the chill night air. Zofia, oblivious to his injuries, rolled him over, spitting her command. "The code. Now. What's the code?" She raised the bat. The guard thrust his hands in front of his face to deflect the anticipated blow, at the same time whimpering, "Eighty, ninety-nine." The women had done their homework. They knew the self-sealing doors were the van's outer defence. Cash and valuables could only be accessed by inputting the code to open the van's inner steel cage.

Katya punched in the number, pushing open the cage to reveal sacks crammed with cash piled high like sandbags. She grabbed two at a time, swinging them out to Olga, while Zofia dragged the moaning guard out of the road, behind the van, away from prying eyes.

It took four minutes to load the vehicle, the women working in a line, swinging bags into the spacious boot. "Right, let's go," said Katya.

"But there are thousands left in here. Just a few more." Zofia shouted from the rear of the line.

"Whoever's in the bank will have alerted the police. Probably on their way already. What are you going to do, kneecap the lot of them?"

The women jumped aboard, Katya reversing wildly away from the van before gunning forward.

"Shit!" Katya screamed. Blue flashing lights speeding towards them. "Hang on."

4

Miles Dent had built a reputation for attention to detail and correctness in his 18 months in charge of Section X. Things rarely went wrong on his watch. If they did, he protected his staff.

Sure, they felt the lash of his tongue. His gravelly Yorkshire boom was already the stuff of legend, *Wazzock!* being a familiar refrain accompanying any miscreants skulking from his office.

But mistakes were never escalated. Dent accepted responsibility, shouldering it without complaint. In return, staff invariably supplied loyalty. Which was why, by the time the meeting concluded, the office bustled with operatives prepared to ditch their beauty sleep to put the varied details of Dent's plan into operation, even though none of them were privy to the overall picture.

That loyalty was also why Emily couldn't say no. Dent had taken her aside following the meeting with the defence chief, offering her a way out. He had explained with typical Yorkshire bluntness what was at stake.

"This is the best opportunity we have of getting inside Ivan, learning what they are up to in the capital. It could be big. Threaten national security. We simply have no idea what this Shelkunchik business is all about. There could be lives at stake, you could help save them. But, Emily, if you were discovered, you know the score?"

Emily nodded, expression grave. Despite her assent, Dent spelled out the consequences.

"There would be no compromises. No trade-offs. They won't hesitate to put a bullet in your head. That's the way they operate. It's only fair I make that clear. But we'll be with you all the way. Not holding your hand, but we'll have your back. Still on board?"

Emily shook. Literally. Her hands and legs trembled. A few years ago she might have succumbed to her panic. But since meeting Al and training with the Service, the lack of confidence that had affected her as a child had steadily reversed. She still had an obsession for algebra and all things numeric, still baulked at criticism, but had learned to manage her insecurities. Her quirky nature no longer seemed an oddity, as in her childhood. Al had also instilled the power of trust and belonging. Tears were rare, but Emily cared. Sometimes, too much. In fact, she still felt partly responsible for the death of her one-time boss and friend Luke Scafell. Two years ago he had been found dead at the foot of a multi-storey car park at Heathrow on his way out of a life as a double agent. It was a complex story but, simply put, Scafell had placed his life in danger, shooting his own partner, Leanne, a Russian agent, when she was about to kill Emily. Revenge from unseen forces was always the fear. When it came, it was swift and decisive.

Those thoughts went through Emily's mind. She could smell once more the rain in the Epping Forest killing ground, sense the danger, see blood dripping on the leaves where Leanne met her fate. Relief at surviving that ordeal had always been tempered by a need to make amends for her role in it. She had yearned for a worthwhile mission ever since, learning the disciplines of the covert world. Speaking to former agents. Imagining the stress, anticipating the euphoria of a job well done. Perhaps this was her time.

She looked up at Dent, breathed deep, forcing limbs to stop shaking, even managed a smile.

"To paraphrase a trite old quote, evil flourishes when good women do nothing."

"Does that mean yes?"

"Yes, but I can't suddenly turn into Nina Volkov the respected reporter, in a few hours. I'm not confident and sexy like her. I'm about as sexy as … well, as …" She paused for a moment, her hands beseeching someone less sexy to come to mind. "Actually, I can't think of anybody less sexy."

Dent laughed. "You do yourself a disservice, Emily. You are kind, good looking, with the sharpest brain of anyone I know. You know, some men find brainy women really sexy. In fact, I'll tell you what's sexy. A sense of adventure. A passion for life. Someone who never gives up and believes she's worthy."

Emily gave Dent an admiring glance. She had to admit, he was good. She had wondered about him when he took over as section chief from the previous incumbent, a straight-talking Scotsman who commanded respect bordering on fear. No-one feared Dent, but everyone respected the composure and maturity of his decision-making, even if he did have a tendency to be a tad corny.

"All right, knock it off. You sound like you're writing a bio on Tinder."

"Seriously, Emily, you can do this. Seduction will not be necessary."

After that, Jane Miller accompanied her to the operations room on the third floor where over the next few hours she was briefed in all aspects of the mission ahead.

They sifted through the overnight bag discovered in Volkov's car, Emily familiarising herself with the terrorist's clothes and make-up. She tried on the four outfits for size, three fashionable skirts with matching tops. They were almost a perfect fit. There was also a pair of jeans, together with a pair of high-end silky cotton trousers which proved a tad tight around the waist. They were swiftly dispatched for altering. Luckily, the three pairs of shoes fitted, although Emily did not expect to require the highest heels. Next came the make-up. An operative with expertise had scrutinised the photos in Bellingham's office, discovering Volkov wore minimal make-up. A touch of eye-liner, a spot of blusher, a smear of lipstick to give her face vitality, but nothing more. Emily was relieved. Life was too short to spend hours in front of a make-up mirror. In any event, she lacked the skills to do so.

While Emily worked with Miller, Dent arranged for the picture on Volkov's passport to be switched for Emily's.

There was one more requirement, so essential that Dent delivered the news himself. When Emily heard it, her shocked expression betrayed second thoughts.

"A tattoo? Why the hell is that essential?"

Dent slipped his mobile phone from his pocket, scrolled down, handing it to Emily. "These are the latest pictures, taken by the clean-up team."

The first picture showed the naked corpse of Nina Volkov in the mortuary, a circle drawn around a marking on her right hip. The magnified image revealed the head of a fighting dog, teeth bared, mouth frothing, as if ready to attack.

"Not exactly love conquers all, is it?" She handed the phone back to Dent.

For the next hour, Emily underwent what she described as a protracted series of bee stings. She had never wanted a tattoo, nor did she know where Dent had found a tattoo artist at such an unearthly hour. But she agreed he was talented, the detail exquisite even if the content was dark and aggressive.

Next came the briefing on Volkov. Miller had done her homework, supplying details of Volkov's tutors, friends and associates from her time at Oxford where she gained a first class degree in physics. She had gone on to train at the Financial Times while being groomed for the FSB (Russia's intelligence service), where she deciphered codes in much the same field as Emily. Her time at the Washington Post was thought to have been a cover. More recently, she had become disillusioned with Russia's slow progress in the Ukraine war.

"This is when she became violent again, pursuing the sort of missions under many aliases that saw her murder and maim in Chechnya years before," said Miller. "We're still trying to pull the pieces together but it looks like Moscow recruited her for what they describe as *wet affairs*, anything that involved the spilling of blood."

"Sounds pretty hard-line." Emily was surprised at the tone of respect in her voice.

"You could say that. The Ivan Group could definitely be described as hard-line."

"Why Ivan?"

"Their founder is Ivan Petrovich, an oil magnate who owed his wealth and status to Putin, but now makes millions selling secrets to the Kremlin, or anyone else prepared to deal in blood money. It was an obvious move for Volkov. She gets paid ten times the salary of an FSB agent for doing much the same thing."

More personal details completed the briefing. Volkov was an only child, her mother, Marion, having married her father, Yuri, after meeting during a gap year at Moscow University. Marion hailed from St Albans, not more than a short train ride from Emily's parents in Highgate. As Emily absorbed the information she began to feel a surreal connection with Volkov, although she worried her own Russian, cobbled together over four years with the Service, could never fool a native speaker.

Miller sensed her apprehension. "Don't worry, according to our watchers they're a rag-tag of nationalities, speaking mostly fluent English. In it for the roubles. No true Russians. Most of them probably can't count past ten in Russian."

Emily was dubious, but she smiled. Miller went on to remind Emily of the tradecraft she had learned since joining the Service. Surveillance techniques, spotting and losing stalkers, firing all manner of handguns, remaining calm under interrogation. Until the episode with Scafell, Emily had never expected to need any of them, glued as she was to her desk-bound cryptography. But that incident had changed everything. Be prepared for anything and everything. That was her new considered philosophy. Few people were more committed to being prepared than Emily.

Finally, fewer than 24 hours after Sir Robert Bellingham had met his fate, much of which had been spent memorising her cover story, Emily was fully briefed.

Along with Miller, she returned to Dent's office. He signalled for them to sit. "All set?"

Before Emily could reply, Dent reached for the television remote, ramping up the volume. A breaking news prompt flashed at the bottom of the screen. The woman presenter's voice was grave.

"We are receiving reports that Sir Robert Bellingham, First Sea Lord and head of the Royal Navy, has died suddenly at the age of fifty-eight. It is thought he suffered a massive heart attack at his country house in Kent. Sir Robert was instrumental in persuading the government to invest in the new series of Dreadnought nuclear submarines due to come into service in two thousand and thirty. We will bring you more details when we receive them."

Dent rocked back in his chair. A satisfied expression, verging on smug, lit his face. No mention of Volkov. No sense that this had been an assassination.

"Perfect," he said. "As far as the Russians are concerned, Nina performed the textbook hit. In and out. Didn't leave a trace. Gives you a free run, Emily."

"I don't mind admitting, I'm scared."

"That's natural. I'd be surprised, worried even, if you weren't. But, remember, it will only be a few days. Enough to give us a steer to their immediate plans. We need to get to the bottom of this latest chatter. We need to know the relevance of Shelkunchik. You can walk away at any time. Just wander back into the office and it's all over."

"Won't the Russians, or this Ivan Group, be suspicious Nina hasn't checked in with them already?"

"No, they'll think she's gone dark for a few days for any number of reasons. That's normal after such a mission. Sometimes we don't hear from our own agents for weeks on end."

"Why don't we leave it a few days then, let me do more preparation?"

"That's a thought, Emily, but turning up at the nail parlour today will have impact. You'll derive more respect with the story all over the news. It will be seen as ingenuity, precluding any questions about where you've been since the hit. And, frankly, if this Shelkunchik stuff is as significant as we think it might be, we need to know the details as soon as possible."

Emily closed her eyes briefly, then nodded. She accepted the logic.

Dent reached in his desk drawer, grabbing a phone. He handed it to Emily. "This is one of three burner phones we found in Volkov's bag. It's clean, fully charged, hasn't been used. You can use it, but only in an emergency. Otherwise, for any messages, use the café drop you've discussed with Jane and the codename Nelson."

Emily nodded, fixing Dent with a look of defiance he hadn't anticipated.

"What is it?" he said.

"I have one condition. If I'm to be part of Operation Nelson, first I need to see Al. That's not negotiable."

5

Yanking the handbrake, Katya spun the vehicle around, tyres squealing, cash bags shifting, forcing the rear end to fishtail.

She hit the accelerator, screeching up Church Road, past the famous Wimbledon tennis stadium, towards Southfields Tube station, turning left, heading for the A3. The blue lights remained in her rear view mirror. Yelping sirens filled the air.

"Bleen, bleen, bleen." Katya cursed in Russian, beating the steering wheel with her fists. Tempted by the presence of easy cash, they had lingered too long. More than double the time anticipated. The plan had allowed a maximum two minutes. Enough to swipe a million or two, but not long enough for the police to react. The bank manager must have had a direct line to the Metropolitan police's fast response team. Those extra two minutes had sealed their fate.

Zofia fingered her pistol in the back seat. "We can take care of cops. The ones following us are unlikely to be armed."

"Maybe not, but back-up will be on its way when they see the state you've left those guards in. They'll all have guns." Katya was the brains of the Ivan cell. A former librarian from Belarus she had joined up after becoming disillusioned with Putin's attempts to brainwash the Russian population and its satellite countries. Katya didn't watch Russian television. She was steeped in books, loved reading history, taking her news at an early age from the BBC World Service. Not that her sympathies lay with the West. Far from it. Undercover British agents had killed her father in a shoot-out in Berlin after he was unveiled as a spy during the Soviet era. She was neither pro-East, nor West. Ivan filled the centre ground nicely.

"Meet force with force is what my daddy always told me." Zofia was direct, stubborn, didn't do emotion, her world uncomplicated. A scary mix of ruthless and carefree. She also seemed to enjoy hurting people.

"What do you reckon, Olga?" Katya spat the question, her eyes darting between the road and the car's mirrors. In contrast to Zofia, Olga was steady, dependable, calm in a crisis.

"I reckon we're done for if we don't do something fast. The car behind can track us down the dual carriageway. They'll have a helicopter up soon. Once that spots us, we're looking at the inside of a prison cell."

"You're right. We can't let that happen. As the English say, we have bigger fish to fry." Katya was regretting having listened to the bank manager's wife. It had seemed a simple job, too good to miss, easy pickings to swell Ivan's coffers for more complex and expensive projects. But Katya lived by the simple rule of a successful gambler. Quit while you're ahead.

She spun the car onto the A3 travelling west, in the outside lane, speedometer brushing 130mph, the road quiet but wet owing to fine drizzle.

"Zofia, get the petrol can from the boot." Urgency and authority in Katya's voice that even Zofia could not disobey.

"What do you want me to do with it?" The can was almost full of petrol.

"Sprinkle it everywhere."

"Even over the sacks?"

"Especially over the sacks."

"But …"

"No buts, do it now Zofia, that's an order."

For a moment, Zofia's eyes burned with malice. Katya caught a glimpse of her reaction in the rear mirror.

"Now, Zofia." The tone even sterner.

Zofia muttered something inaudible about Joan of Arc under her breath, but she unscrewed the cap, the liquid swishing, a sweet, pungent, stench of petrol immediately filling the cabin.

Olga, spluttering, wound down her window. "One spark and we'll burn alive." The panic in her voice was obvious.

"Stay calm, no-one's going to get burned." Without warning, Katya spun the steering wheel, throwing the car off the A3, across a lay-by, mounting a kerb, onto a dirt track via a farm gate. The track gave way to fields either side, wet, squidgy, but the four-wheel drive dug in, supplying traction, a vapour trail of mud flying in all directions.

Twenty seconds later the blue lights behind them turned into the farm gate. "Faster, faster," screamed Zofia in the back. Katya ignored her, realising the ground was uneven, rocky in places, swampy in others, the odd sheep wandering into the beam of the headlights. The last thing they needed was to hit anything unexpected. As she anticipated, the police saloon car struggled to make headway. It fell behind, the women disappearing over the brow of a hill.

Below them, at the foot of a steep incline, the car's headlights picked out the black form of a dense forest. Katya swept the perimeter for a dirt track, a clearing, anything they could attempt to negotiate. Nothing. For any vehicle, apart from a tank, it was a dead end.

"Right, get ready to bail," shouted Katya, braking hard, the vehicle halting on an incline at the top of the grassy slope in a field bordered by thick hedgerows.

"Everybody out."

The three women scrambled clear, the rain heavier, slicing down on a stiff breeze. For a few seconds they stood by the open hatchback boot, gazing at the mound of sacks, the smell of petrol overpowering.

Katya put a cigarette to her lips, cupping her hands to shield the wind, a throwaway lighter providing a flame. She sucked in the deepest of drags, savouring the calming effect as the nicotine enveloped her lungs. Blue flashing lights, closing swiftly, created an eerie reflection off the cloud cover. Katya turned to Olga, standing by the open passenger door. "At my command, release the hand brake."

When Olga was in position, Katya stole another swift drag.

"Now!"

The car wheels shifted a few inches, stuck at first in the impression its weight had fashioned in the soft ground. Katya's heart thumped. Then the wheels turned more easily as gravity worked with the car's weight to provide momentum. Katya calmly flicked the lit cigarette into the open tailgate. The whoosh was instantaneous, flames licking from the back, leaping through the windows as it trundled down the slope.

Crashing into a clump of trees at the bottom, the chassis exploded in a mushroom-shaped inferno, setting fire to parts of the forest.

"There goes ten million quid up in smoke." A hint of reproach in Zofia's tone.

"The cost of freedom," said Katya. "Cheap at the price. Now let's get out of here while the police think we're brown bread."

"What does that mean?"

"No idea, but according to one of our clients, that's what they say in these parts when someone dies."

6

Emily parked the Vespa in its usual spot down the alley giving access to the side of the apartment she shared with Al.

The street was alive with activity. Schoolboys swung rucksacks over their shoulders, discussing football on the way to the bus stop. A supermarket van struggled to squeeze into one of the remaining parking spots, its reversing beeps providing the urban setting with an annoying soundtrack.

"You're back then, what was all the rush about?" Al shouted from the kitchen after hearing the key turn in the front door.

"Oh, you know, usual stuff."

"You mean you can't tell me about it. And if you did ... well we know the rest of that sentence." Al's tone was jaunty. He had slept on after Emily left, rising a few hours later to prepare for a lecture that afternoon to his tutorial class at University College London. Al was a mathematician. A brilliant one. A mutual love of all things numeric was the reason he and Emily had hit it off when they first met five years ago, although Al never failed to tease her about that first meeting. He was working in a sandwich shop when Emily brought a tuna baguette to the counter. Al asked her if she fancied a drink. Emily thought he was asking her out when in fact he was merely explaining the sandwich deal included a soft drink from the same counter.

The misunderstanding had sparked an embryonic attraction, although the relationship required deft handling on Al's part. Emily could recite most academic theorems, but when it came to the formula for social interaction and friendship she was clueless. Over time, however, she had learned, until they made a formidable team.

"You're right, I'm afraid it's not for general consumption. Unfortunately, I have to go away for a few days."

Al looked concerned. He detected strain in Emily's eyes. Her right eyelid always twitched when under stress. Most people wouldn't have noticed but Al was adept at reading every sign. He knew better than to ask where or why she was going. For a wife, husband or partner, life in SIS was a litany of excuses and let-downs. You either rolled with it or ran away from it. Al was good at rolling.

"Sure you're okay?"

"Yeah, sure. I won't have access to my mobile phone, Al. I'm afraid I won't be allowed to speak to you while I'm away. Should be only a few days, a week tops. I'll use the usual code."

It was Al's idea. Whenever Emily had reason to take a trip, especially since the Scafell episode, he insisted she ring each evening. If she couldn't speak, she simply let the phone ring three times before hanging up. Code for *I'm okay*.

"I'll listen out for you," said Al. "As near to eight o'clock as you can." Emily ran up the stairs, grabbed her toothbrush and a couple of items of underwear, stuffing them into her bag on the way down.

"New bag?" Al missed nothing, Volkov's designer hold-all appearing a touch expensive for Emily's taste. She usually made do with a ruck sack.

"Yeah, thought I'd treat myself."

Al swallowed the lie. He knew she must have good reason. They embraced, Emily kissing him hard on the lips, so hard that he forced himself to stifle a sudden wave of concern.

"See you when I see you," she said.

"Yeah, and while you're gone I'll give George Michael some thought."

7

The King's Road is one of London's most prominent thoroughfares.

Built by King Charles II in the 17th Century as a private road to smooth travel from his palaces to his gardens at Kew, it was the site of a barracks housing Oswald Mosley's Blackshirts in the 1930s. More recently, it was associated with the 1960s and fashion figures such as Mary Quant and Vivienne Westwood.

It is also the area where the fictional James Bond lived.

The latter fact did not escape Emily as she walked down the famous road. Emily didn't feel like a spy. This didn't feel like a scene in a Bond movie. Spies were confident, composed, unflappable characters, suave and charming, always in control. Not with stomachs churning like a tumble dryer on full speed. At least, that's what she'd always thought.

A myriad of notions invaded her mind, many questioning why she had agreed to a mission in the field at such short notice. Doubts competed with fears, both leading to fleeting spasms of terror. *Concentrate. Remember the cover story. Act the part.*

She turned into a cosy side street off the main drag. There it was, The Salon, simply named, next door to an estate agent with a little café on the corner a few doors down. A mundane enclave of life in the capital.

Pausing for a few seconds, she trawled through her cover story one more time before drawing a deep breath, swinging the door open and stepping into an uncertain world. A couple of clients were receiving treatment in discreet alcoves. Everywhere clean and clinical. Emily made her way to the reception desk where a woman, with a pleasant, sing-song tone, was finishing a phone conversation. Emily clocked the name badge pinned to her light blue blouse. Olga.

After a few seconds, Olga replaced the receiver, scribbled a note in the desk diary, before fixing Emily with a welcoming expression. "Sorry about that, how can I help?"

Emily remembered her briefing. Don't indulge in needless conversation. Answer only direct questions. Don't give away too much information.

"Ivan sent me."

"Ivan?"

"Yes."

Olga's eyes narrowed. The name obviously meant something. Emily could sense her processing the information.

"Who's Ivan?" said Olga.

"If I have to tell you, then I have come to the wrong salon." It was a good response, Emily thought. Keep them guessing. Make them think she's in control, although the sweat dripping down her back told a different story.

"What's your name?"

"Nina."

"Could you take a seat for a moment, Nina. I'll be right back."

Olga disappeared through a doorway leading to the back of the building. Emily sat on a hard, upright chair, gripping her thighs as if smoothing her skirt, but in reality stopping her legs from shaking.

A few minutes later Olga returned, beckoning Emily to follow her down a narrow corridor with heavy doors leading off one side. The premises stretched further back than Emily anticipated. There was a musty smell, in contrast to the sweetness of the lotions and perfumes permeating the working salon, but the building had a solid, well-built feel, characteristic of many Victorian properties. A set of stairs boasted a polished, dark wood bannister. Olga led the way up the steps.

At the top they entered a large, airy room with a high ceiling and big sash windows, set out like a working office with computers dotted around, too many for a simple nail parlour. A printer whirred in one corner while a row of clocks displayed the time in several world capitals. A pretty, fine-boned woman with thick blonde hair complementing her taut physique sat at a large desk. Emily estimated mid to late thirties, around the same age as herself.

"Katya, this is the woman who says she was sent by Ivan." Olga crossed to stand behind the desk.

Katya sat back, saying nothing for 30 seconds, maybe more, studying Emily, letting her ponder her situation. A considered move, designed to unsettle. Emily fought the urge to fill the silence, although the void confirmed this was no nail parlour manager. In Emily's estimation, she was in the presence of an Ivan operative of some standing. The SIS watchers were not wrong.

Eventually, Katya spoke. In Russian. The harsh Slavic edge chipping away at Emily's nerves. "Your name is Nina. Do you have a surname?"

"Volkov. Nina Volkov," said Emily, adding in Russian, "I think we work in the same business."

"The nail business?"

"You know that is not what I meant."

Katya switched to English as Olga was Romanian and understood only rudimentary Russian. "Do you have ID?"

Emily reached inside her handbag, fishing out the passport Dent had given to her.

Katya studied it for some minutes, paying particular attention to the stamps denoting the countries visited. Among them, China, Israel, South Africa, Brazil. The most recent, *Immigration Officer Heathrow (3),* was dated the day before.

"What's the purpose of your visit?" Katya's tone had softened. Not much, but enough to afford Emily encouragement.

"Does Sir Robert Bellingham mean anything to you?"

"He's the guy all over the news, isn't he? The guy who just died. An admiral or something."

"He was the purpose of my visit."

"You mean …?"

"Yes, that's exactly what I mean."

Katya's eyes widened. Emily sensed a tad more respect in her demeanour. Before Katya could say more, another female wandered into the office, a woman in black leather trousers whose walk was as chippy as her mouth. Zofia. At once, Emily felt vulnerable.

"Who's this?" Zofia sat on the front edge of the desk, arms folded, a sullen pout challenging Emily.

"That's what we're in the process of discovering," said Katya. "It seems that Nina here is one of our star operators. She's about to tell us all about her relationship with Britain's top naval commander."

"I wouldn't call it a relationship. I interviewed him, didn't much care for his answers. At the end of our chat I decided it would be better if we went our separate ways. Simple as that."

For the next 10 minutes, Emily answered questions on Nina Volkov's mission. She would have preferred to skirt around the details, but Katya and Zofia were exacting interrogators. They wanted to know timings, the admiral's address, details of the interview, how Nina smuggled in the poison, how long it took for him to die, whether he suffered pain, if bodyguards had challenged her on departure. They even demanded the name of the poison, although Emily admitted ignorance of the technical details. Which was true. What she didn't tell them was that the vial containing the poison and the admiral's cup of tea had been sent to Porton Down, the Ministry of Defence's Science and Technology Laboratory in Wiltshire for analysis that would take several days.

Emily's photographic memory coped with every challenge. She was afraid, several of her responses sounding hesitant and halting, but it seemed Katya was convinced. Not Zofia.

"How do we know we can trust you? How do we know all this is true? If it happened as you say and the admiral's bodyguards frisked you, then you'd be the most wanted woman in London right now. The Met police would be crawling all over searching for you, wanting a statement."

"Why do you think I'm here? I need to hide out for a while. The authorities obviously think it was a heart attack. They have probably presumed it happened after I left. But, you're right. I was the last person to see him alive. I'm sure they'll want to question me."

"So, tell them the truth. He must have been so excited, or bored, at your probing questions, that his heart gave out." Zofia's eyes ran up and down Emily's body as she spoke, goading a reaction.

"What happens if the autopsy discovers he was poisoned?" Emily's retort fast and confident. "He was a big man. He required a substantial dose. Maybe traces will remain. What are my chances of getting home to Moscow then?"

Zofia shrugged.

"You could always phone Ivan." Emily spat out the words. She knew it was a gamble. Katya, Zofia and the others at The Salon comprised an important Ivan Group cell in the UK, but they were a small cog in a global network. She banked on them being in awe of the founder and money man, a character renowned for an uncompromising temperament.

"Don't think that will be necessary," said Katya. "But we will need more proof besides your passport."

"Like what?"

"How about the reason you targeted the admiral?"

Emily reached down, unzipped her bag, grabbing a bunch of papers. "Is this not proof?" She threw them down on the desk, Katya immediately flicking through them. When Dent had handed the papers found in Nina's possession to Emily, he had described them as insurance. Most had Sir Robert Bellingham's name in the top right corner along with the Ministry of Defence crest emblazoned in indelible print. At first glance they appeared to reveal weapon specifications plus locations of new ships and submarines, although in reality they were all outdated or redundant. Katya didn't know that. She seemed impressed.

After a minute or so, she glanced up at Emily. "Okay. It took balls to take care of Bellingham, we'd all concede that. You can lie low here. But we're not a hotel. There's a tiny room on the top floor with a mattress. Not exactly luxurious, especially in this part of London, but the spiders seem to like it."

Emily smiled her gratitude.

Zofia remained unconvinced. She took a step towards Emily, close enough to invade her personal space. Emily felt the hairs on her nape rise, a tingle of fear mixed with anger crawling up her spine. With eyes fixed on Emily, Zofia unbuckled the belt around her tight leather trousers. She pulled the right side down to the panty line, revealing pale flesh. Below the hip nestled a small tattoo. A fighting dog.

"Show us yours." Zofia's jaw jutted in defiance.

Emily breathed deep. She realised Nina had the same tattoo, but no-one at SIS had informed her it was an emblem of Ivan, acting as a physical and permanent password identifying members of the group. Perhaps they didn't know. She could still feel the sting as her tattoo was administered only hours before. The artist had informed her most tattoos took weeks to heal completely, but the use of his lightest technique would reduce inflammation and counter the chances of reddening and infection. It was more a surface transfer than a permanent tattoo.

Thank goodness I agreed to have it done, thought Emily. She pulled up her blouse, folded back the top of her skirt, surprising herself at how natural, yet vibrant, the artwork appeared.

"That do you?"

Zofia gave a grudging nod before flouncing across the office, turning as she reached the door.

"Enjoy the spiders, but beware, some of them bite."

8

The attic room was exactly as Katya described. Tiny. Emily had to lower her head to avoid the beam running along the middle of the vaulted ceiling. Cobwebs clung to each corner. A mattress, lying on bare floorboards, was pushed up against one of the walls. At least it was unstained. By the feel of the responsive springs, it was also comparatively new.

A small wooden desk and chair filled another wall while the single sash window was crusted in dust and lichen, although it afforded a handy bird's eye view of the road and buildings across the way.

First things first. Where to hide the tiny burner phone. Emily's training had impressed upon her the importance of securing communications. She calculated someone would search her belongings at an opportune moment when she was absent, making a hidey-hole essential. Her gaze studied the smooth rendered walls, painted white, although they had turned a grubby shade of cream. No vantage point there, but a thin crack in the ceiling by the wooden beam proved a spot where rainwater had seeped in over the years. Whoever had repaired the damage had replaced a segment of the beam, but left the job incomplete. It wasn't sealed, allowing Emily to slip her fingers into the gap between beam and ceiling. She carefully worked the hole wider until her phone slid in.

Unpacking came next, Emily draping Nina's clothes over the back of the chair, smoothing out creases. There was no wardrobe, or hangers, but Emily's world required neatness, order, and, if possible, an expensive steam iron. From what she had learned of Nina, she was also a tidy woman who treasured her appearance, but for entirely different reasons.

When she finished unpacking, she sat on the chair, gazing out of the window, studying the topography, a snapshot of the immediate vicinity settling in her memory. The room was stuffy. Someone had screwed the window shut, perhaps as a security measure, although that seemed unlikely four storeys above London's streets.

As she absorbed the London skyline, the reality of her first solo mission descended. Staring at the roofs, the jagged point of The Shard puncturing an ominous sky, in the lair of a terrorist group, she had rarely felt more alone and vulnerable. A trickle tracked down her spine, a sudden cold sweat accompanied by a feeling of foreboding.

She adopted her coping mechanism. An unusual one, enacted under her breath. It involved reciting the 118 elements in the periodic table, from hydrogen, the element with the lowest atomic number, through countless unpronounceables, to oganesson, the one with the highest. She rarely ever reached oganesson, long before then the rhythm and concentration involved in the process promoting alpha brain waves, synchronising left and right sides of the brain. Inducing calm. Like Tibetan monks chanting *Om*.

This time, as zirconium, the 40th element, tripped off her tongue, two soft knocks diverted her attention. She swung the door open. Olga stood there, offering a sweet smile and a pile of towels.

"Thought you might need these, Nina."

"Thank you. That's very thoughtful."

"The bathroom is on the floor below, down the corridor on the right. I'm afraid this place doesn't run to en-suites."

"Do you all live here?"

"Me, Katya and Zofia all have rooms on the floor below."

"I don't think Zofia likes me very much."

Olga chuckled. "Zofia doesn't like anybody very much. She's only been with us a few months. She's okay when you get to know her. Just don't cross her. She's Polish, she's a doer, not a talker."

"I'll remember that. But what about the other girls in the salon?" Emily was careful to keep the tone light, the questions general. It was too soon for detailed inquisition.

"There are only two others. Not part of our group. You probably saw them earlier. They don't live here but they run the place. Both very young, both nail experts. Neither of them have a clue who we really are. We just help out to make the place look busy."

"It's a good cover."

"It is these days when there's a nail parlour on every high street, most side streets as well, many of them run by a variety of nationalities."

"Hiding in plain sight."

"Exactly."

The conversation was natural and warm. Emily sensed a connection between them, perhaps because out of the three Ivan Group operatives she had met, Olga appeared the most vulnerable.

It was Olga's turn to ask a question. "What made you join Ivan?"

Emily assumed a hurt expression, as if the trauma of a past wrong still lingered. "In a word, Putin. I was tired of his lies. Tired of the way he manipulated and repressed his own people as if they had no minds. Tired of the young lives he was prepared to sacrifice in senseless wars to cover up his skewed vision of Russia's future and his own incompetence. Putin never cared for anyone but himself and his legacy. A vain man with a huge ego. He let me down and ... never mind." Emily's voice had risen half an octave. The passion as her words tumbled out with apparent spontaneity was obvious. So was the distaste and distrust. Which was exactly according to Jane Miller's plan, hastily hatched back at SIS. Emily had recited verbatim the soliloquy concocted by Miller.

Olga looked taken aback. She detected a complex combination of anger and fragility in Emily. Intrigued, she was drawn in.

"Did you know him personally, Nina?"

"I'd rather not say. At least Ivan Petrovich does not rewrite history. He does not claim false visions. His group works for the highest bidder, but only if it's in Russia's interests."

"Was disposing of Sir Robert Bellingham in Russia's interests?"

"Of course." Emily was surprised at how easily the dispassionate response tripped from her tongue. "He was a NATO commander who wanted every western warhead pointed at Moscow. Is there anyone more hard-line that that?"

Olga pressed her lips with a forefinger, as if in deep thought. "Let me think. Zofia maybe?"

Emily found herself chuckling as Olga bounded down the stairs. Foreboding banished. For a while, at least.

9

Fatigued from her early start and the tension of the last few hours, Emily lay on the mattress, fully clothed, pulling the single woollen blanket over her, grateful for the warmth and sense of security. She needed five minutes shut-eye to assimilate what she had learned, to ponder the way forward.

Awaking with a start, she turned her watch to the fading light. Six o'clock. She'd slept for three hours. She felt terrible, foggy brain conjuring all manner of desperate scenarios. Taking a swig of water, she fought to clear her head, aware of voices. Angry voices.

The attic was festooned with pipework, some ancient, no longer in use, although lazy workmen had left it in situ after upgrading the central heating system. A metal flue from a gas fire or wood burning stove also passed through the attic to release via a chimney on the roof.

Emily swung her legs off the bed, heaving herself onto her feet, stepping across to the flue where the voices magnified. They were speaking in Russian. A man, and a woman Emily swiftly identified as Katya.

Emily strained to hear, the sound echoing faint and tinny from two storeys below. The Russian was colloquial, difficult to understand, but one word, spat out several times with increasing emphasis by the man, was unmistakeable. *Durak*. Fool, stupid, idiot. Emily knew she could take her pick.

She pieced together more snippets of the conversation, the words for *bank* and *police* easy to identify. Emily also thought she heard *ogrableniye*, the word for *robbery* in Russian.

This sounded like a reprimand, in which case she needed eyes on whoever was dishing it out. She straightened her skirt, slipped on shoes and smoothed her hair, using her fingers as a makeshift comb. Tiptoeing down the stairway, the whispers became more indistinct, but no less vehement.

The door to Katya's office was shut, requiring a decision. Stand outside, ear to the door, attempting to decipher the strangled conversation, risking being caught by one of the other women. Or knock, swing the door open, allowing innocence to act as protection. She chose the latter. Instantly, it was as if someone had hit the mute button on the television remote. The conversation ceased.

Katya, sitting at her desk, swung around, her smile forced. The man, standing, back bent, knuckles resting on the front of the desk, also turned, glowering over wire-rimmed spectacles.

"Come in, Nina. This is the woman I told you about, Roman." Katya's warm introduction contained a respect Emily appreciated.

The man approached Emily, deference in his demeanour, in sharp contrast to the conversation she had eavesdropped. He offered his hand. Emily shook it, the man raising the back of her hand to his lips, planting a kiss. "Roman Smirnov at your service. I have heard many things about you, Nina. All of them good, I am pleased to say. Especially your work these past few days. You have struck a mortal blow at the heart of our enemy. We will capitalise on your achievement in the days to come." He wore a dark suit, together with a crisp white shirt and dotted tie. He could have been an accountant or a hedge fund manager working in the City, his manner charming and confident, yet coldness in his eyes suggesting his chivalry was fake. This was a man accustomed to giving orders and having them obeyed, Emily determined.

"I'm pleased to hear that, I wouldn't like my work to be in vain," she said.

"Katya informs me you wish to stay with us for a time, while the heat cools."

"A few days will be sufficient."

"Of course, as long as it takes. I'm sure you wouldn't mind working for your bed and board. We may have use for your special talents, isn't that right, Katya?"

Katya nodded, although Emily couldn't imagine what they had in mind. As far as she knew, SIS had identified that Nina Volkov possessed two special talents. One was cryptography, which fell neatly inside Emily's orbit. The other comprised seduction as a prelude to assassination, a combination light years outside Emily's universe. A chill settled between her shoulder blades but she knew her decision to barge in on Katya and Smirnov's conversation had paid off. Now, she had a name and a face to put to one of the Ivan

Group's chief handlers in the UK. *That is what Smirnov must surely be. He sounds like a man who calls the shots. Probably a bridge between Ivan Petrovich's henchmen in Moscow and operatives like Katya who actually process the dirty work in the field.*

Confirmation that Emily's intuition was correct arrived when Smirnov left. Immediately, Katya seemed more at ease, eager to share information, as if seeking an ally from someone who clearly had Smirnov's approval.

She gestured for Emily to sit in a soft winged leather chair by an ornate fireplace which would have been the focal point of a rich man's lounge at the turn of the 20th Century, but now competed with the panoply of office furniture dominating the room. After grabbing a half-full bottle of malt whisky and two glasses from a cabinet, Katya sat opposite Emily. She didn't ask whether Emily drank whisky, instead pouring generous measures before offering a toast.

"To women with the strength to triumph in a man's world."

"I'll drink to that."

They raised their glasses. Katya slung down a two-finger measure while Emily made do with a modest sip. Pink gin was Emily's preferred spirit with a long and fragrant mixer. The fire in whisky had never appealed, but she deemed this an occasion requiring feminine solidarity.

"I think you're one of them," said Katya.

"One of what?"

"One of those strong women who men should beware of."

"Only if they kick cats and don't put the bins out."

Katya chuckled. "In other words, only if they deserve it."

"Exactly."

Emily swirled the amber fluid around her glass. Care was required. She'd not eaten since breakfast, amounting to a slice of toast grabbed at the Camden flat. Her cover had to remain secure, but Smirnov's appearance was an opportunity.

"What did Roman mean?"

"Pardon"

"When he said, working for my bed and board, did he have something in mind?"

"Maybe."

"Such as."

"These are historic times, Nina. There is something big in the offing, something that could tilt the balance between East and West, so big it could change the face of the planet. I know that sounds fanciful, but I've never worked for an organisation with more imagination than Ivan. The Wagner Group are always looking for excuses, always blaming others for not getting the job done. We don't have the right weapons, they say. We don't have enough money. The Ivan Group thinks big, earns big, and in my experience always delivers. The guys in Moscow are keeping the details secret but we'll find out soon enough, although I'm surprised you don't know what they have in mind. I'm sure Sir Robert Bellingham must have been a small part of the plan."

Emily's brain raced to compute what Katya could mean. *If the assassination of the UK's top naval commander is a mere side-show, then what's the main event? An attack on the House of Commons, the Ministry of Defence, Downing Street itself? Dent's right. Something extravagant is planned.* She needed to keep calm, lock into the drip-feed of information that Katya could supply. Search for Shelkunchik.

"You know how things work," said Emily. "Plans and events are kept separate to preserve secrecy. No use everyone knowing what's going on. The more people know a secret, the more chance that secret will be discovered."

It was generic, simplistic, reasoning, but the reply seemed to satisfy Katya, whose attention was drawn to the door creaking open. Zofia strode into the room, her eyes fixing on the whisky glasses, a jut of the jaw telling Emily that strong alcohol in the afternoon was not an everyday occurrence. Or perhaps her displeasure was aimed at the obvious connection Katya seemed to have formed with the new girl.

"All right for some. The rest of us have work to do." Zofia fired up the computer. Her tone was sour. "What did Smirnov want? Did you tell him about last night?"

"He already knew." Katya said. "Don't ask me how, but he wasn't happy. Ranted on about putting the real job, the big stuff, in jeopardy. I told him we wore masks, all evidence was incinerated, but he didn't seem impressed. Think we'll have to play it safe for a while."

Zofia shook her head. Emily was intrigued. "Sounds like it wasn't only me who was busy last night. What did you get up to?"

Katya glanced at Zofia before answering. "Nothing as important as you. We had the chance to drop ten million quid in used notes, which would have come in useful, but we got greedy. Had to torch the lot."

Emily whistled through her teeth. "Ten million in cash. You don't come across that sort of money every day. What happened?"

Katya eyed up Zofia again. "Never mind. It's gone and forgotten now. No point crying over burnt milk."

"Spilt milk." Emily corrected the saying by instinct. Immediately, she wanted to snatch the words back. Katya did not seem to clock the relevance of the correction, but Zofia's eyes smouldered a tad more fiercely. Emily knew only a true native speaker would correct such an English idiom. She'd let down her guard. Only a fraction, but under cover fractions mattered. As a mathematician, Emily knew that more than most. *Don't become too comfortable. It's the small details that trip you up. Don't talk too much. Don't drink whisky in the afternoon.*

Fortunately, Zofia buried her nose in her computer. Katya drained her glass. Emily, not wanting to show weakness, followed suit, throwing back a last big slug, the long burn as the whisky scorched the back of her throat making her eyes water.

She spluttered, a malty rasp in her voice. "Not used to drinking so early. Do most of my work the other side of midnight."

Katya chuckled. "I'll let you know if you can be of assistance. In the meantime, make yourself at home."

Emily nodded, making her way to the doorway, heading for the stairs, one phrase from the impromptu drinks meeting, resounding in her mind.

Something so big it could change the face of the planet.

10

The smell emanating from Mario's café was enticing. The scent of Italy, thought Emily. Full of olives, tomatoes, basil and hot cheese.

She didn't fancy the delicacy of the day, a pumpkin pancake, but her mouth salivated at the thought of one of Mario's sourdough pizzas.

Olga had recommended the café a few doors away from the nail salon. It was simple, no frills, unusual for this high-end enclave. Most of the tables, sporting a single lighted candle in the middle of checked plastic tablecloths, were occupied. A good sign, the open oven proving one of the main attractions. The pizzas looked delicious. Many of the female customers appeared to think much the same about the dark-haired young man attending the oven, white bandana around his head, biceps rippling, sweat glistening as he twirled the long-handled pizza spinner, turning the dough deep inside the oven with an expertise borne of much practice.

Emily had found a small side table. Her trip was not solely to do with food, although her stomach growled, toast and whisky the only things having passed its way for some time. She also wanted to check out her code drop venue and whether anyone from the Ivan Group would be detailed to follow her.

A couple of laps around the block to check her bearings, grabbing a copy of the *Evening Standard* outside a kiosk, were sufficient to convince her there were no obvious stalkers, although she realised that did not rule out ultra-precise professionals, more experienced than her.

After ordering a vegetarian pizza and a glass of water, she sat back reading the *Standard's* crossword page. An old trick. A handsome woman sat alone in a public place tends to stand out, appear vulnerable. One grappling with a crossword assumes command and respect. Appears independent. Emily filled in the odd clue with a biro, perusing the room. The customers were mainly young couples, the hum of conversation mixed with rings of laughter providing a warming ambience. Emily had learned the art of watching without seeming to watch at tradecraft school. It involved the use of peripheral vision. Clearing forward sight without moving the head, directing concentration sideways or up and down. It took practice, but having struggled to make eye contact with anyone, including her parents, as a teenager and beyond, she was a natural.

The table she had chosen, against a wall, allowed her to scan the entire room without turning her head. A middle-aged couple in a far alcove proved fascinating, their conversation animated to the point of confrontational. Another couple sat with two children, a boy and a girl, a birthday treat judging by the number nine badge and smiley face on the boy's jumper.

The waitress approached with Emily's pizza and a salad side dish. "Enjoy." Emily flashed a grateful smile. As she did so, a couple entered the restaurant. An ordinary couple. Few notable characteristics. Not young. Not old. The woman wearing a drab brown dress, the man with thinning grey hair, sallow complexion, an odd, expressionless face. He carried a book low by his side, rather as a schoolteacher might. Emily noted them, but her eyes returned to her pizza. A few moments later a fizz of adrenalin sent a flush of heat through Emily's body.

As the teacher man sat down two tables away, he laid his book on the tablecloth, front cover facing upwards.

Nelson: Britannia's God of War.

The cover title was written in swirly handwriting font with a picture of Admiral Horatio Nelson in the foreground amid a colourful backdrop of a naval battle.

Emily felt an immediate surge of relief and renewed confidence. She no longer felt completely alone. This, she was certain, was an SIS contact from Operation Nelson. Jane Miller had insisted there would be certainty when Emily enquired how she might recognise her contact. The book left no doubt.

She chewed a mouthful of pizza, returning to her crossword. To anyone observing, it appeared she was doodling with the clues. In fact, she was writing a string of numbers, random, incomprehensible to anyone, apart from those with the key to the code. Miller had hatched the plan with Emily during their briefing after Dent had ruled out phones. Too easy to hack or track, even using end to end encryption, susceptible to listening devices, with a recorded history which could prove revealing and embarrassing if it fell into enemy hands. Emily did not disagree.

This was a mission requiring old school methods. Emily, the expert cryptographer, had devised the detail. It involved the periodic table, her coping mechanism, something she could recite in her sleep and had done many times down the years. The table's 118 elements contain 24 of the 26 letters of the English alphabet, the only missing ones being J and Q. After Z, the letters Q and J also happen to be the least used in the English language. Therefore, any word code using the periodic table as a key gained access to forming virtually every English sentence.

The additional benefit, as opposed to a normal book code, was that it required nothing physical in Emily's possession that an enemy could discover. No book. No letter grids. Back in the SIS office she had demonstrated how it worked by writing her name in code, adding two random central numbers to the fixed and crucial first and last digits. The additional numbers allowed the periodic table idea to mimic a book code, throwing off attempts to decipher by any third persons.

Thus 04-17-11-02 indicated the fourth element in the table, Beryllium, and its second letter: **E**. 19-26-06-09 indicated the 19th element Potassium and its ninth letter: **M**. 28-15-09-02 was Nickel; **I**. 52-18-03-04 was Tellurium: **L**. Finally, Dysprosium was chosen as in 66-12-05-02 to provide **Y**.

Emily's conclusion was persuasive. "It's simple, reliable, looks like a book code and works like one, apart from the random central numbers, although as long as they are kept under thirty-six and ten it would appear consistent with most paperback volumes. At first glance many cryptographers would think the first number represented page four, line seventeen, eleventh word, second letter of the key book. All they would need to gain access to the message was to find the right book, copies of which invariably would need to be in the possession of the persons writing and receiving the code. True, it's probably unsuitable for very long messages, or if lots of messages are required. A good cryptographer would also pick up on the repetition eventually, especially the necessary low final number. But it's a solid, working code."

Miller agreed. A numeric list of the chemical elements in the periodic table was immediately posted on a whiteboard in the SIS operations room.

Emily scrawled as she chewed, wearing a studious expression, as if toiling over a complex crossword clue. By the time she had finished her pizza, discarding the crispy outer crust, a row of numbers adorned the blank margin down the side of her crossword. They represented seven words.

Three agents. One handler. Big news imminent.

Draining her glass, Emily motioned to the waitress. She paid the bill in cash, leaving a small tip, slipped on her jacket and sidled to the exit. As she passed the teacher man, she heard him address his companion. "Need to visit the little boy's room, darling. Won't be a moment."

As the café door swung behind her, Emily turned, in time to see the teacher man slide the folded newspaper deftly into his hand as he passed her table on the way to the toilets.

It was almost eight o'clock, but Emily had another task before returning to The Salon. She walked to King's Road, generating a lively pace in the direction of Sloane Square. It was a dark, dank, evening, light rain falling, the twinkling lights of the capital providing a magical contrast to the inclement weather. She pulled her jacket collar close. Several times she stopped abruptly, turning to check for stalkers, before hanging a left, heading for Brompton Road.

As a London native she knew the area well. Even so, she appreciated the warm glow of familiarity when the illuminated façade of Harrods came into view. She had visited the luxury department store often, not to buy, mostly to browse. This time there were two reasons. First, she knew the shop was packed with CCTV. If anything went askew, the SIS technicians would identify anyone following her. Second, Harrods was invariably crowded right up until its normal nine o'clock closing time, cashing in on the capital's ceaseless bustle. Cruising through the departments, each oozing opulence, she made for the winter wear and picked out a smart suit.

"Do you need any help?" The young assistant was beautifully attired in matching skirt and jacket, polished nails, a fresh face retaining a pleasing demeanour even at this late hour.

"That would be nice. I'd value your opinion."

Together, they disappeared behind the discreet screen leading to the fitting rooms. Away from any watchers. Emily swiftly changed, emerging less than a minute later. She posed opposite a long mirror, the assistant immediately making encouraging noises.

"Remind me, how much is it?" said Emily.

"One thousand, eight hundred and sixty pounds." The girl's nonchalant delivery suggested she sold suits that expensive every day, which she did.

"I'm not sure. That's a bit more than I was expecting. I'll have to phone my husband. Oh damn, I've just remembered, I've forgotten to bring my mobile. I couldn't borrow yours, could I?"

"Of course, madam."

The girl dug in her jacket pocket, handing over her phone. Emily punched in the number, letting it ring three times before clicking the end call button. She left the phone to her ear for another 10 seconds, before returning it to the assistant.

"I'm sorry, he mustn't be able to take it for some reason. I'll call in with him another time. Thank you for your help."

"No problem, hope he likes the suit."

In Camden, Al's shoulders relaxed. Emily was safe.

11

When Emily returned to The Salon, a lone light burned on the first floor where the office was situated. She pressed the buzzer once, waited three seconds, pressing twice more. Olga had provided the protocol earlier. It was how the group distinguished between a friendly face and the surprising amount of customers who failed to decipher, or flatly ignored, the opening times posted on the front door.

Olga eventually appeared. “Had a good meal?”

“Yes, thanks, you were right, Mario’s pizzas are to die for.”

“Glad you enjoyed. You’ve been a while. Did you go on somewhere?”

Olga’s tone was even. Emily couldn’t determine if the question emanated from genuine interest or whether this was a test. Maybe someone had followed her, after all.

“Took a walk. Cleared my head. London’s such a wonderful city at night, don’t you think? I’d forgotten how magical the lights look in the West End.”

“Anywhere in particular?” This time the question stabbed home, lacking nuance or imagination.

Emily saw no reason to fabricate. “Harrods, actually. When I studied in Oxford, I’d come to London every so often. I always made a point of visiting the store, especially around Christmas time. It’s such a beautiful building outside, while inside it always seemed anything might be possible.”

“If you have money to burn.”

“You mean, like last night.”

“Very good, Nina. You have a sense of humour, although be careful of Zofia hearing you talk like that.”

Emily shrugged.

Olga led the way upstairs, crossing the landing to the office, a reading light illuminating the computer at her desk.

“Working late?” It was Emily’s turn to ask questions.

“Yeah. Using the peace and quiet to clear some admin.”

“Nail stuff?”

"Not exactly." Olga's eyes narrowed. Emily sensed that with Katya and Zofia absent, Olga was uncertain of what she could divulge.

"Just that Roman Smirnov suggested you had a lot on and may need some help."

Olga's shoulders relaxed. A smile returned. Emily's use of Smirnov's name in a respectful, yet familiar manner, seeming to engender trust.

"We're always busy, you know that. Working on the next big thing."

"Shelkunchik?" Emily realised it was a gamble. But Dent had impressed upon her the urgency of discovering the subject matter of the latest chatter, while Katya had confirmed something big was afoot.

Olga's mouth fell open, her brow knitted, little pools of puzzlement forming in the corners of her eyes. "You know about that?"

"Not the details, but back in Moscow there are rumours. Something big. Apparently, something that eluded even the KGB at its most powerful."

The bang of a door followed by footsteps on the stairs curtailed the conversation. Olga hurried to her desk. A few moments later Katya appeared on the landing. "Nina, everything all right. Have you settled in?"

"Yes, thanks. I was telling Olga I took a stroll to see the London lights."

"Is that wise? The Met will be on your case. Your picture's probably in every incident room in London by now."

"Don't worry, I was careful."

"From my experience, stay away from the homeless or anyone begging on the streets. Some of them are undercover cops. Especially in the West End. No-one makes eye contact with beggars, do they? But they see everything. The perfect cover when you think about it."

"I'll remember that."

Katya proceeded to talk to Olga while Emily walked down the corridor to grab a jug of water and a glass from the communal kitchen before trudging upstairs to the attic room.

Before opening the door, she checked the thin strand of dark cotton she'd cut from a blouse earlier, left dangling loosely from the knob. An age-old device, but still a staple tool of undercover operatives. For good reason. It was effective. The strand was lying on the wooden floor. Proof that someone had searched her room. Rather than unsettling Emily, she regarded the discovery as a reassuring sign that the protocols of the espionage world she had embraced were being played out in predictable fashion. *It's all a game, like chess or bridge*, she remembered her former double agent friend, Luke Scafell, telling her. *As long as you follow the rules and stay one move ahead of your opponent, you'll be fine.*

She dozed until around two-thirty listening to the creaks and scratchings that, once darkness falls, lend most rambling Victorian buildings a sense of intrigue. The front door banged around midnight, Zofia returning from wherever she had spent the evening. Murmurings emanated from the office for another hour, prompting Emily to strain towards the chimney flue. The muted conversation was indistinct. She wasn't even sure of the language, apart from it wasn't English.

Three sets of footsteps eventually climbed the flight of stairs. Emily settled down for another hour. Satisfied that the house had fallen into its night-time slumber, she heaved herself off the mattress, threw her jacket over her nightshirt and picked up the jug and glass. Her bare feet made no sound on the floorboards, the heavy door opening with the minimum of creak.

She waited several seconds on the landing to allow her night vision to kick in, the only light a borrowed ray from glass inset in one of the doors of the front-facing rooms on the floor below. Jug and glass balanced in one hand, the other sliding along the polished bannister to steady herself, she tiptoed down the first flight of stairs. No light emitted from under the doorways of the three bedrooms, although a gentle, rhythmic snore emanated from the nearest. Half-way down the next flight of stairs a chime rang. An antique grandmother clock striking three o'clock. In the stillness it resembled the rolling bong of a church bell. Emily's heart pounded. Breathing deep, she waited until the thumping subsided before completing her descent.

Crossing the first-floor landing, she entered the office. Her photographic memory meant she already possessed a precise mental picture of the lay-out, although the blinds at the window were not pulled totally shut, allowing a sliver of streetlight to stream in. She edged to the desk where Olga had been working. The computer was plugged in but it was too much to hope that Olga had left it switched on. Emily checked anyway. Nothing. Any meaningful search required more light from the table lamp. She leaned over to flick the switch, at the last moment deciding against it. Anyone stirring upstairs may sense the glow, and investigate.

Instead, she slid open the top drawer of the desk, searching by feel, her fingers alighting on all manner of stationery items, including pens, scissors, a stapler. Reaching deeper, she located a thin folder. She fished it out, moving over to the blinds to benefit from the streetlight. There were three pieces of A4 paper inside, the first two containing paragraphs written in Russian. As far as she could tell they were of little consequence. The third appeared to be a series of written notes, containing dates and times, scrawled untidily, in a language she didn't understand but recognised as Romanian, mainly because of the variety of curved, arrowed accents over the letter *A*. Two underlined words jumped off the page. *Nina Volkov*. Two more, *Mario's* and *Harrods*, left her in no doubt. They were watching her. Olga was tracking, or at least detailing, her every move. Not unexpected, but even so the realisation came as a jolt.

Emily returned the file, sliding the drawer shut, moving over to the main desk. She was about to investigate the filing cupboard when she heard a noise. The merest creak. She spun around, a cool draught signifying the door swinging open. A figure stood in the doorway, illuminated by the ray of a streetlight. Long blonde hair, flimsy white nightdress forming an almost ghostly apparition. Katya. In her right hand, in stark contrast to her attire, she clutched a stubby black pistol. The lights flicked on.

"What the hell are you doing in here?" Katya's Slavic tone rang out, cold and sinister.

Emily fought to stay calm, knowing the entire mission, perhaps even her life, rested on her attitude and response in the next few moments. She'd practised similar scenarios in training, but no amount of practice could recreate the fear coursing through her veins or the thunder rumbling in her ears. She raised the water jug, striving to keep her manner jaunty, matter-of-fact, as if facing down the barrel of a gun was as commonplace as pulling on a pair of socks. Even so, she feared her response too gabbled. "Sorry, still half asleep. Must have taken a wrong turn in the dark. Not quite got my bearings yet. It's such a big old place. Didn't want to put a light on and wake anyone up. Just looking for the kitchen for a jug of water. All that garlic in the pizza I ate earlier."

Katya said nothing for a couple of seconds, assessing the situation. Scanning the room to evaluate whether anything was out of place. Concluding that no meaningful search could be enacted in the dark with a jug in one hand and a glass in the other. Eventually, she lowered the gun. "Okay, Nina. The kitchen's down the corridor. But it's not a good idea to skulk around in the dark right now. Others might be more, how should I put it, trigger-happy, than me."

"No more skulking for water. Promise. I'm obviously not very good at it."

Katya smiled, seemingly convinced.

12

A camel is a horse designed by committee. That old saying pretty much summed up Miles Dent's opinion of group meetings. In his estimation, anything worthwhile, requiring ideas, vision and courage, came from the passion of an enquiring, individual mind.

He didn't inform the chairman, Sir Ralph Short, of those sentiments as he sat down at the weekly Joint Intelligence Committee meeting in a characterless room in Whitehall. But he thought them as he stared across the conference table, inhaling the stuffiness of men who in his opinion had climbed the ladder but too often couldn't see past their own noses.

It was a rare occurrence for Dent to find himself at the weekly committee meeting, sipping muddy coffee, mixing with the national security adviser, officials from the Foreign, Commonwealth and Development Office, the Ministry of Defence, the Home Office and the Armed Forces.

But his boss, C, for that is how the commander of SIS, Giles Somers, is traditionally known, had ordered his presence. The real circumstances surrounding Sir Robert Bellingham's death so far eluded the wider intelligence community. Dent was the only man in possession of all the facts.

C immediately pre-empted any preamble from the chairman, cutting across the usual courtesies. "We have a situation, gentlemen. It concerns the death of the First Sea Lord." C's voice was grave. He had the face for such a tone. Lined and lived in with eyes and jowls showing the first signs of drooping. A jutting jaw that had deflected a lifetime of flak completed the slightly Neanderthal look. If he had not been in charge of the UK's Secret Intelligence Service, he would have made an acceptable undertaker.

"Sir Robert Bellingham. Poor chap. He died of a heart attack, didn't he?" The chairman's voice contained surprise.

"Those were the facts widely reported, but the truth is somewhat different. I am going to ask Miles Dent, the head of Section X at SIS, to explain."

Dent took a photograph from a stiff brown envelope, raising it with both hands so everyone could see, switching it from side to side as a barber might wield a mirror to show a client the back of his hair. There was a snort, a few gasps and splutters. A chink of china as tea and coffee cups were jettisoned on the table.

"Good God," said the chairman. "What's this all about?"

"If you're imagining potentially the most compromising breach of the UK's security since the Cambridge spies spilled all our secrets to Moscow and the secretary for war had an affair with a prostitute, then, yes, I think you've got it in one," said Dent. "Except that the admiral was not having an affair with this woman. She was posing as a journalist. He merely granted her an interview. We now believe that as well as a journalist, allowing her access to all manner of powerful people, she was also a hard-line terrorist."

"Who is she?" The photo, showing Sir Robert crumpled under the desk, clutching a gun, with Nina Volkov lying dead beside him, had grabbed the undivided attention of the room. Dent went on to reveal most of what SIS knew about Nina Volkov, her association with the Ivan Group, as well as the fact that an Ivan cell was operating in London.

"What's the intention? Why kill Sir Robert? How come this is the first we're hearing about it? I thought MI5, GCHQ, special forces, the Met's anti-terrorist branch, Uncle Tom Cobley and all were supposed to track these terrorist cells." The chairman voiced the thoughts of most of those present.

"We've no idea how they've slipped through the net, Sir Ralph. We became aware of a small cell some weeks ago, not with the capacity to indulge in activities such as bomb making and terror campaigns, but one with the potential to gather the most sensitive intelligence. We have monitored at a discreet distance. As far as we know the UK cell had no involvement in the admiral's murder."

"But he was killed by the same group?"

"Yes. From our most recent investigations, we believe the Ivan Group, funded by Moscow, present a real, potentially imminent, threat to our security. By imminent, I mean weeks, maybe even days."

"How do you know this? Where's the evidence? And what sort of threat?"

"All I can say is the death of Volkov, divulged to only a handful of people with the highest security clearance, allowed us an opportunity to put an agent in the field."

"You mean under cover?"

"Yes."

"A woman?"

"Yes."

"What's she discovered?"

"It's early days. Communication is necessarily scant to protect her identity, but she has confirmed something big is afoot. The chances are the threat is of the Code Red variety."

"What do you recommend?"

"Watch and wait. Give our operative time."

"That's a big call, Dent, at Code Red."

C intervened. "I don't see we have much choice. We've infiltrated a cell that is little more than a tentacle. Go in and we might capture a couple of minor terrorists. If we hold our nerve, our agent could lead us to the brain. We might discover what the group's really planning."

"Is your agent safe? Is she experienced?"

C looked at Dent, an almost imperceptible nod signalling him to answer.

"No undercover agent is ever totally safe, everyone here knows that, but she is well-trained with a good cover story. We have a back-up team close by, monitoring twenty-four seven. She's one of our sharpest operatives with lots of special qualities."

"Experience?"

"It's her first covert mission."

"Her first mission?" The chairman's mouth dropped open. He turned to his personal assistant. "Who's here from MI5?"

The assistant flicked the pages of his notepad. "MI5 has sent apologies, something about a pressing matter elsewhere."

"Ye Gods, what's more important than a murdered admiral and an imminent threat to national security?" The assistant shrugged.

"How about Jennings?" The head of the London station of the CIA was regularly invited to attend meetings of the Joint Intelligence Committee, although Matt Jennings regarded the process as akin to watching paint dry. Nothing ever seemed to be decided. As on this occasion, it was not unusual for him to vote with his feet.

"Again, apologies received, Sir."

The chairman breathed deep. He addressed C. "Very well. I shall brief the relevant government ministers, including the Prime Minister, to alert them to put the appropriate defence personnel on stand-by. Carry on, for now. I just hope this agent is as good as you claim."

Dent stood. "I hope you don't mind, Sir Ralph. I have important issues to deal with."

"Of course, thank you." He dismissed Dent with a wave.

The wind was blowing hard, spitting rain in machine-gun bursts. A line of tourists heading for Downing Street were trooping behind a guide carrying a flag of St George as Dent emerged on Whitehall. He waited for the stragglers to pass, turned up the collar of his jacket, thrusting his hands in his pockets, before arching his body into the weather and heading across Westminster Bridge. Deep in troubled thought. Big Ben chimed. The sound of London. The toll of history. Monarchs, prime ministers, intelligence chiefs, terrorists, all come and go, yet the clock strikes on. But how much time has Emily got? Dent asked himself the question. Three more days, no longer, he surmised. Safety first. If nothing materialised by then, he vowed to pull her out.

13

Zofia leaned on the wall outside Mario's café in her leather gear, lit cigarette dangling from her lips. Trying to look tough, thought Emily, like a female version of James Dean in *Rebel Without a Cause*, her dad's favourite retro film. Emily strained at the attic window to steal a better look.

A few minutes later, Katya and Olga joined Zofia, who stubbed out her cigarette on the brick wall. They disappeared inside the café.

It was a little after eight o'clock. Emily had barely slept, all manner of scary stuff churning through her mind. Had she convinced Katya she'd taken a wrong turn, conveniently straying into the room where all the sensitive stuff must be planned and stored? Didn't seem likely. The more she thought, the flimsier her explanation appeared. Were they plotting right now over coffee and toast how to dispose of Nina Volkov?

Only one way to find out. She slipped on a top and trousers, making her way downstairs, pausing on the first-floor landing to check out the office. The heavy oak door was shut. She knocked, trying the handle. Locked. Why leave the door unlocked overnight, securing it only after finding an unexpected guest wandering around in the early hours? They didn't trust the guest. That was the obvious conclusion.

A shiver of apprehension descended, but Emily shook it off, striding through The Salon, passing a forced but cheery hello with the young girls, who had recently arrived to prepare the room for the working day, setting out lotions, scissors, files, cotton buds, amid all the other paraphernalia required in a busy nail parlour. Emily headed towards the café.

Katya and the others were sat at a table overlooking the pavement, a pillar from a supporting wall separating the area from the rest of the café. A little private enclave. Emily spied them as she approached, heads down, conference in progress, Katya's demeanour earnest.

Sucking a lungful of courage, laced with London's traffic fumes, Emily bowled straight in. Her greeting warm and friendly. "Good morning." They looked up as she approached. "Room for one more?"

"Of course, Nina." Katya dragged back the fourth chair. Emily sat down. A coffee machine gasped and grumbled annoyingly in a corner.

"We've ordered breakfast baguettes, basically egg and bacon on bread with an Italian twist," said Katya.

"What's the twist?"

"Cheese on top."

Emily pulled a sour face.

"They do a vegetarian option, if you prefer."

"What's that?"

"Egg and egg on bread." Zofia's interjection was sharp, her glance surly. Emily had already decided she and Zofia were never going to be friends. In Emily's book, Zofia was a bully, someone to be avoided if possible, but stood up to, rather than appeased. She'd met many such characters, most of them at school where her odd ways, including an obsession for making lists of random car registration numbers, invariably made her a target. She regretted not standing up to those bullies, recently vowing she would never make that mistake again.

"Egg on toast's fine, without the cheese." The waitress wandered over to take her order. "So, what's on the menu for work today?" The question was obvious and reasonable.

Katya swapped glances with the others, followed by silence. The sort of uneasy void during which Emily could sense mental cogs whirring.

She looked at them in turn, only for everyone to avert their eyes. Her heart began to race, expecting at any moment for someone to accuse her of being a spy, a traitor, or worse. "What? What is it?

"Smirnov is dropping by this evening." Katya spoke in lowered tones.

"Okay, why's that an issue?"

"Not an issue, Nina, but he has requested you meet him. He has a proposition."

"What sort of proposition?"

"I don't know the details. He'll explain, but it concerns Shelkunchik."

Olga had obviously reported Emily's mention of the word the previous evening.

"What about Shelkunchik? I've heard people talking about it, but I have no idea what it's all about."

"You will do, Nina. You will. I believe your area of expertise involves cryptography."

"That's right. I studied physics and mathematics. The way numbers and words can be juggled around in cryptic fashion has always fascinated me."

Zofia shook her head. "Takes all sorts. In English, you're what's called a nerd."

"I suppose I am, Zofia, but I prefer the term MITY."

"Never heard that. What does it mean?"

"More intelligent than you."

Katya and Olga sniggered, casting glances at Zofia, whose top lip curled in an ugly snarl.

The waitress arrived with the food. They spent the next few minutes applying red and brown sauce, chomping into their breakfast, Zofia forming what resembled a crime scene on a plate.

When there was a pause, Emily ventured. "Why did you ask about cryptography, Katya?"

"Smirnov wanted to know. He needs someone with experience in deciphering codes to cast an eye over something."

"Numbers?"

"No, words, I think."

The coffee machine fired up again, the spit and rumble even more deafening. Emily waited until it fell silent. "Don't they have someone in Moscow who can do that? An old KGB operative, perhaps. The place must be full of expert cryptographers."

"I think the point is this is in English, and English is your first language, is it not?" Katya's eyes fixed on Emily, challenging her to deny it.

"My mother's English, as I'm sure you know, but my father was born in Saint Petersburg, or Leningrad, as it was called then. Like Vladimir Putin. They were good friends."

"Yes, we heard." There was a catch in Katya's voice. Emily couldn't decide whether it was respect or scorn. The coffee machine clunked into noisy action once more, rocking back and forth on the worktop. Katya pressed on. "But your English is more fluent than your Russian?"

It wasn't really a question, more an indisputable fact.

"What do you want me to say? I spent more time with my mother as a child. My father was away working. We travelled a lot as a family, too. Many different schools, ending up at Oxford. It was only natural English became my first language."

All the while, Emily's peripheral vision was aware of Zofia's eyes seeming to bore a hole deep into her soul.

What does she want? What does she know? Why is she always having a go at me? Those suspicious eyes are freaking me out.

When Emily could bear the scrutiny no longer, she turned sharply, a stinging lash in her tone. "What's your problem, Zofia? What are you thinking?"

"Just wondering how to plant a small explosive device under that coffee machine."

14

They laughed. The mood lightened. They ordered fresh coffees, the mention of family history prompting questions about Olga's upbringing in Transylvania.

"Where exactly did you live?" Emily was keen to know more about Olga. She regarded her as different from the others. There was no edge to Olga. Unlike Zofia, she didn't exist in a universe studded with confrontation. No permanent scowl of suspicion on her face. She appeared uncomplicated, at times even sweet and innocent, although Emily realised that was unlikely.

"Brasov," said Olga. "Deep inside Romania. It's known for making aircraft, tractors and machinery. An industrial city, but parts of the old town are lovely. Lots of cafes like this, colourful buildings on cobbled streets. Years ago, when communism took hold, it was renamed Stalin City, but thank God it was changed back."

Her tone of relief registered with Emily. Olga was clearly not a disciple of the old Soviet regime, disdain for Joseph Stalin, the hard-line Soviet wartime leader, resonating loud and clear.

"What was wrong with Stalin?" Zofia piped up. "He made Russia and the Soviet Union into world powers."

"He also starved and executed his own people, killing hundreds of thousands of them." Olga spat back.

"You could say the same about Ivan the Fourth almost five hundred years ago." Zofia shrugged. She took a slurp of coffee, motioning to Emily. "What's your take on Ivan the Fourth? With a name like Nina and a tattoo like that on your hip you have to support the old rascal, don't you?"

"Sorry?" Emily looked bewildered. A sudden implant of heat coursed through her body as she realised she had been blind-sided. The other three studied her, their stares tearing at her confidence. She fought to stay calm, her mind searching for the relevance of the first Russian Tsar, who ruled in the 16th Century, known as Ivan the Terrible.

What has some ancient history about Ivan the Terrible got to do with Nina Volkov's name and the tattoo of a fighting dog? From their reactions, sounds like something Nina should know. Jane Miller never mentioned anything about Ivan the Terrible, only Ivan Petrovich, the leader of the group. Think. Think. Shit. I'm in trouble.

As Katya and Zofia picked up on Emily's discomfort, the door opened. Two well-built young men entered, resembling builders in search of breakfast. They wore work trousers and leather jackets, one of them storing a hammer and chisel in the thigh pocket of his trousers. They sidled over to an empty table. As one of them passed, Emily noticed the motif on his tee shirt. *A winner is a dreamer who never gives up*. It was the name underneath in large capital letters that resonated more than the message. *NELSON MANDELA*.

Two of Dent's watchers. They must be from Operation Nelson. Of that Emily was certain. *Thank God*, she thought, her mind still racing to solve the Ivan conundrum. The mission on the edge of oblivion.

"Oprichnina," said Olga, throwing her hands up with an air of naïve triumph. "Oh, I get it." She chortled, as if she'd solved an obvious crossword clue. Zofia threw a withering glance.

Olga's revelation sparked a sudden memory, Emily's mind seeming to clatter and fizz as she processed a plethora of facts in a matter of milliseconds. She saw the face of her Uncle Sebastian, a former Cambridge University history professor who had doubled up as an SIS agent for a solo mission to Moscow to trap a Russian assassin in 1981. Following her uncle's death a few years ago, she had helped crack the intricate code discovered in his journal. It turned out to be his memoir, complete with the full daring details of his mission.

During the slow, painstaking process of transcribing each page she learned to love and admire the uncle she had never really known. It led her to read his other books, including his seminal work, *The Two Ivans*, a meaty tome drawing rave reviews from the academic world. The book compared the characters and influence of Ivan the Terrible and Ivan the Great. Giving a lecture on the subject formed part of Uncle Sebastian's cover story in Moscow in 1981.

Emily had been fascinated ever since. She found Ivan the Terrible's massacre of the city of Novgorod in 1570 barbaric. He had ordered the killing of up to 15,000 civilians in revenge for what he perceived as betrayal of the local orthodox church, many of the victims driven into the nearby river and drowned.

The brutal slayings were part of the mass repression of Russian aristocracy between 1565 and 1572, a state policy known as *oprichnina*. Emily, sickened by the cycle of violence, had pushed the facts to the back of her mind, but now she seized on the word like one of those poor Novgorod souls might have snatched a lifebelt.

"Oh, very clever, Zofia. Oprich-Nina, I get it," said Emily, stretching and exaggerating the last two syllables. "Actually, my mother came up with Nina. It was her choice. I don't think she had Ivan the Terrible's reign of terror in mind. She wasn't into killing innocent women and children. She was a teacher. And she definitely doesn't have a tattoo."

Once Emily's photographic memory, aided by Olga's timely prompt, had made the connection, the information flooded back to her. She ran with it, the lie that she always knew the relevance of the tattoo tripping off her tongue.

"It surprised me that Ivan Petrovich chose a fighting dog as his symbol for the group. I know it's how Ivan the Terrible's police force, the oprichniki, identified themselves. A severed dog's head hanging from their saddles to sniff out treachery, together with a broom to sweep the traitors away, but a snarling dog seems a little, how should I put it, unsophisticated for the work we do."

"Effective, though," said Zofia. "Putting the fear of God into people is the best way to get results. I think Ivan the Terrible was on to something."

"You're very cynical."

"Cynical and alive. Beats the alternative."

At last, Emily sensed Zofia relax, as if relating her knowledge of 16th Century savagery had proved a bonding exercise. The imminent crisis appeared to have passed.

They drained their coffees, all rising to leave. Emily sneaked the briefest glance in the direction of the *builders*. Not a flicker of interest. As it should have been. Except that the man with the Nelson Mandela tee shirt had his arms folded, his right hand clutching his left bicep, four fingers tapping gently, as if keeping beat with a generic pop song playing in the background through tinny speakers. An innocuous act, if it hadn't been one of the signs Emily and Miller had alighted upon back at SIS headquarters. Four o'clock in the café. She made a mental note.

15

He watched the wheel turn. A fraction at a time. Not smooth like the second hand of a clock, nor jerky either. Painstaking progress. Rather like working in intelligence, he thought. Fitting the pieces together. Lots of hanging around, never seeming to get anywhere fast until the high point when the big picture clicked into view.

Dent turned his gaze away from the Ferris wheel known as the London Eye, trying to shake the metaphor from his mind. He leaned against the wall of the Victoria and Albert embankment, peering into the dark, swollen waters of the Thames, sipping bitter coffee from a paper cup he'd bought from a kiosk. Tasted foul, but it was wet and warm.

He was worried. Needed fresh air. Time out of the office to clear his thoughts. He'd asked Jane Miller to meet him. Watching her as she approached from the direction of Blackfriars, he decided, not for the first time, she was an impressive woman. Tall and slim, her shoulder-length hair tossed around on a playful breeze, grey coat tied with a loose material belt. Stride determined, a woman who knew where she was destined in life.

She greeted him with a cheery grin as a brief glint of sun painted the boats on the river in dazzling reflections. "An unusual, if spectacular, venue for a committee meeting, Miles. It could catch on. All those in favour of the view, say aye." Miller raised her right hand, "Aye."

Dent responded with a weak smile. "I'm worried, Jane."

"About Emily?"

He nodded. "We're missing something."

"In what way?"

"Not sure, but what was Nina Volkov up to, interviewing Sir Robert Bellingham? What was she looking for? It was a high-stakes meeting, visiting his home with two bodyguards on the premises. That takes nerve. The chances of escaping with what you came for are not high."

"Maybe she was fishing. Hoping to pick up something useful. Maybe she was there just to kill the admiral. A simple assassination mission, as cold as that sounds. It's what the Russians do."

"I wondered that. Perhaps you're right. The admiral could have been on a high-powered hit list, but Russians aren't into suicide missions. With two bodyguards, that's what it could have been. Something doesn't fit."

Miller pulled her coat tighter around her shoulders. A sharp bite in the wind.

"Volkov's bag was full of sensitive papers. She would probably have got away with them if the admiral hadn't shot her."

"The papers were sensitive, Jane, but most of them were outdated or redundant. There was nothing there that could have made a material difference. Nothing to sell to an enemy, which is what the Ivan Group would have done."

"What are you saying?"

"Maybe Sir Robert prevented her from completing her search. Maybe Volkov never found what she was really after."

Miller's blue eyes danced in excitement. "Which means the clue to this whole business may still lie in Sir Robert's office."

"It's a theory, that's all, but I think it may be worth a look."

"I'll get the team on it right away."

Dent sipped coffee, now cold as well as bitter. He pulled a sour face. "How's Emily doing?" His tone concerned.

"As far as our watchers can tell, she's doing great. Judging by body language, the Ivan women seem to have swallowed her story, but we can't get too close. The group members know the area well. They've been in situ some time. They'd notice anything or anyone out of the ordinary. But the code drop in the café worked well. We've set up a drop for four o'clock today. We may know more then."

"Keep me informed."

"Of course."

Dent shuffled his feet and bit his lip. Miller sensed there was something else bothering him.

"What is it, Miles?"

"Oh, nothing."

"Come on, Miles. I've known you long enough to know that's not true." In what seemed another lifetime they had been students together at Birmingham University, studying politics. Gone to the same parties, drunk in the same pubs, attended the same debating society. Never been an item, although that was more a consequence of bad timing than lack of desire, Miller having endured a long, fruitless partnership with a chemistry geek who proved to be inert.

In those days, Dent's ambition was to become a politician, while Miller simply wanted a job far away from anyone who sucked the oxygen out of a relationship. By coincidence, they had each applied to SIS at the same time, not knowing where it might take them. They passed the probationary period, rising quickly through the ranks, albeit with the odd change of department.

Dent's straight-talking bluntness had served him well. SIS bosses despised baloney, fabrication, or plain simple *BS*, as they preferred to refer to it, something of an irony considering the whole ethos of the Service most of the time was to hide what it was really doing.

Dent sounded plaintiff. "Have you read Emily's personnel file?"

"No. Why, should I have done?"

"She's a brilliant operative, no doubt, but she's had issues with anxiety. I just hope this doesn't turn ugly in a hurry."

"You worry too much. She'll be fine." Miller pulled up her collar. "Can we hold all our meetings out here?"

"Why."

"Feels like a scene out of a John le Carre novel."

16

The car pulled up alongside Emily. The driver's window wound down revealing Katya's face. "Jump in."

Emily had been taking a short stroll up the King's Road with no other intention than stretching her legs. The Salon was in full swing. Olga was manning reception, Zofia nowhere to be seen. Emily had offered her services, but the salon girls had turned her down. Probably after studying her nails, which in one or two cases were bitten down to the quick. Not the best advert for their service.

She walked around the back of the car, sliding in beside Katya.

"Don't worry, Nina, we're not going far." Katya hit the accelerator, merging smoothly with the traffic.

"I wasn't worried."

"You're a cool one, Nina. I'll give you that. Half the cops in London are probably looking for you as we speak, but you seem relaxed."

Emily's stomach didn't agree. It was griping, gurgling so loudly she was sure Katya would hear. It always performed such gyrations when she was nervous.

"Where are we going?"

"Nowhere in particular. Thought we could go for a drive, get to know each other better. I wanted to give you the heads-up on Smirnov."

"Okay. I'm all ears."

"How should I put this? He can be scary."

"In what way?"

"Do you recall the slightly mad guy once in charge of the Wagner Group?"

"Prigozhin? The man who led a mutiny, started marching on Moscow, turned back, then died in a mysterious plane crash two months later?"

"That's him."

"From what I've heard, *slightly mad* doesn't do him justice."

Katya smiled. “Perhaps not. The point is Smirnov and Prigozhin have a lot in common. Brothers in madness. The English have a phrase for people like them. Bat-shit crazy.”

“But Smirnov runs the show in London, doesn’t he?”

“Not just in London, Nina. The word is Smirnov runs the entire group. Yes, Ivan Petrovich is the top man. The figurehead. The man who founded Ivan. He’s the man who pays the wages, as I’m sure you know, but Smirnov is the enforcer. The man who gets things done. More and more, he decides the direction of the group.”

Emily familiarised herself with the route as they trundled at reasonable speed considering mid-afternoon traffic in central London. They turned onto the Brompton Road, past Harrods where Emily had been the night before, onto Wellington Arch. From there they ran into busier roads as they negotiated Piccadilly, Green Park on the right, its open spaces and tall trees a welcome relief from the stone and concrete of the city. The car came to an idling halt almost directly opposite the Ritz Hotel. Emily remembered her 21st birthday. Her parents had taken her to dinner there as a special treat, even paid for an overnight stay. The breakfast next morning, when her father insisted she sample the *free* champagne, had formed a magical memory.

“That’s where Smirnov lives.” Katya nodded towards the hotel.

“Really?”

“Has a suite on the fifth floor. Must cost a fortune. Petrovich doubtless picks up the bill. You don’t spend money like that on someone unless they are getting results.”

“Why are you telling me this?

“Because Smirnov doesn’t take no for an answer. Whatever he wants you to do concerning Shelkunchik is not negotiable. He may seem charming. He’ll smile to make you feel important. He’ll promise all sorts of things. But if you say no, then he won’t hesitate to kill you, or have you killed. That goes for any of us.”

“You have to stand up to bullies, Katya. That’s a rule where I’m from.”

“Maybe make an exception for Smirnov.”

The traffic started to flow again. Katya chose the scenic route, picking her way through Piccadilly Circus, skirting around Trafalgar Square where hundreds of nurses were staging a protest in support of the NHS. The sight of Nelson's Column was not lost on Emily. Cars beeped as they passed, Katya adding an extended blast of her own.

They headed towards Westminster, veering past the Houses of Parliament, spires shimmering gold in the pale sunshine, before feeding back towards Chelsea via the embankment.

"Why did you join Ivan, Katya?" The query was warm and genuine. Emily liked Katya. She seemed straightforward, even tempered, although Dent's *they'll put a bullet in your head* warning about the Ivan group was also never far from Emily's thoughts.

"Money." Katya shrugged. "I could tell you I was here for principle. That I hated the West and wanted to wage war on democracy. But I would be lying. I'm here for the money. I'm good at what I do. Ivan pays well. Life is not easy in Belarus. My grandfather worked all his life in a factory, then died of cancer as he was about to retire. Radiation from Chernobyl. No-one will admit it, but I know it's true. One of my two sisters also suffered. She was sick as a child, dying a few years ago from a disease thought to be caused by radiation. Most parts of Belarus suffered contamination from that disaster."

"But Chernobyl's in Ukraine."

"A few hundred miles didn't stop death and destruction blowing on the wind. Thousands were affected. Somehow, I escaped. But I want a better life. Comfort. Security. I want to buy my mother a nice house of her own in a safe place. If I have to do a few ugly things to get that beautiful life, then so be it. But I'm sure you know more about that than I do, Nina."

The photo of Sir Robert Bellingham lying dead on his office carpet came to Emily's mind. She found herself uttering the first phrase in her head. "The end justifies the means."

"Pardon?"

"I guess I'm trying to say, the admiral had to die."

"That's right, Nina. You know, I think we are alike."

Emily shuddered. They drove the rest of the way in silence, Emily scanning the river, fascinated by the imposing height of a new south bank development, admiring the impressive bridges, taking comfort from the familiar sight of the old Battersea Power Station chimneys thrusting like ship's funnels into a slate-grey sky.

When they reached The Salon, Katya pulled up, but kept the engine running. For several seconds she checked the rear-view mirror, searching for any cars turning off the King's Road, making sure no one was following. Emily reached for the door handle. Katya stretched across. "I have to go on somewhere, Nina. I'll see you later, but remember what I said about Smirnov."

Emily jabbed a thumb in the air, jumped out, but before shutting the door, leaned back in. "Got it. Bat-shit crazy."

***

Emily spent the rest of the afternoon in the attic room, musing on what she had learned while compiling another coded message.

She had saved a receipt from the café, one of those long strips of flimsy till papers that roll up annoyingly by themselves. On one side the itemised bill for her eggs-on-toast breakfast, barely legible the ink was so faint. The other side blank. Laying the paper flat she started to write. It was painstaking work, but the periodic table coding was her idea for a reason. It was second nature, a language in which she was entirely fluent.

Numbers quickly filled the paper. Neat and tiny, each representing a letter, forming words for anyone with the key code. The fact that she lived in an age capable of dispatching entire dictionaries across continents in nanoseconds at the flick of a button did not escape Emily's attention. But she enjoyed that hour compiling the note. It soothed her nerves, deflected her mind from imminent danger. It also allowed her to assimilate Katya's warning. When she was finished, she read it through letter by letter to ensure no mistakes, whispering under her breath.

Meeting handler Roman Smirnov tonight. Decoding task. Something big.

She wandered downstairs a little before four o'clock. The Salon was still busy, a lively hum of conversation, women having clocked off early to fit in manicures and pedicures. No sign of Katya or Zofia, but Olga still manned the phone on reception. Emily waved as she passed, receiving a sweet smile in return.

By contrast, the café was slack. Diners at four tables, another two customers, both young city types, sitting on stools, arms leaning on a counter, drinking tea. A man in a blue boiler suit was fiddling with the coffee machine in the corner, spanner in hand, his own intermittent huffs and wheezes blending with the sucks and groans of the machine, suggesting maintenance was not proceeding according to plan.

Emily ordered a pot of tea and sat at a side table, away from the coffee machine, but providing a clear line of sight of anyone entering the café. She flicked open the free newspaper she'd grabbed from a stand on the corner. A few minutes later the two *builders* from earlier wandered up the road, chatting animatedly as if discussing the dynamics of a busy day. The one with the Mandela t-shirt twirled a long-handled screwdriver in one hand, carrying a tool bag in the other. They laughed and joked as they entered the café.

The waitress behind the counter had a lively, welcoming demeanour, a dazzling diamond nose stud lighting her face. She scrutinised them, her tone confident as well as teasing. "Back again? You can't keep away from this place, can you? What do you fancy this time?"

"Still you, darlin', still you. Only you." The one without the bag pulled a wistful face, complete with dreamy eyes.

The waitress groaned. "Do you know how many times I've heard that line? You need to brush up on the chat, mate."

It was typical builders' banter. But with the waitress distracted, *Mandela man* sidled towards the table next to Emily's, depositing his bag and screwdriver on one of the chairs. The screwdriver rolled off onto the floor, the man stooping to retrieve it. As he did, he scooped up what to any onlooker resembled an old receipt, crunching it in his hand before popping it in his pocket.

Emily sat reading the newspaper, sipping tea for 15 minutes, half-listening to the *builders* discussing football, something about England's chances in a forthcoming international against the

Netherlands. They could have been talking Dutch for all Emily understood, but the time raced by. She paid the bill, stuck the newspaper under her arm and wandered back towards The Salon, a walk of no more than 100 yards, that evening's meeting with Smirnov and the implications of her chat with Katya dominating her thoughts.

Around half-way, she sensed a black figure, scurrying feet and a swiping movement to her left. No time to react apart from an instinctive bracing of her body. Off balance, she found herself propelled violently sideways into a narrow alleyway that separated two tall buildings under renovation, but where work had temporarily halted due to danger concerns. Her head smashed against a scaffolding pole as someone pushed her deep into the passage. For a moment everything went black. Then she was on her front on the ground, rough brickwork digging into her stomach, the sound of broken glass and shale scrunching as the attacker fell onto her back, pinning her down, grinding her nose and chin into the debris. Her mind strove to compute. *A mugging? Druggies looking for easy cash? My purse? There's fifty quid. Give it to them.* She tried to mumble her purse was attached to her belt, but no words came, gasps and grunts her only language as she tried to spit gravel from her throat.

An arm around her neck yanked her head back. She tried to suck in oxygen to scream, but felt the cold harshness of a gun barrel thrust into her mouth, cracking against teeth, gouging her tongue, bile burning her throat as her gag reflex activated. For several seconds her body went rigid, her heart pounding with fear.

"Who … the … fuck … are you?" The whispered voice, so close that hot, wet, hissy breath filled Emily's ear, was grotesquely distorted, although the pitch of it sounded strangely familiar. Anyway, she couldn't answer. Not with a gun filling her mouth. As if realising that fact, the attacker withdrew the barrel slowly. "You've got three seconds to tell me who you really are, or I'll splatter your brains against that wall. And don't say Nina Volkov. One …two …"

"Okay, okay." High-pitched panic in Emily's voice. This was no mugger. If Emily had been unsure, then the mention of Nina clinched it. She was in mortal danger. Convinced these were her final moments, she tried to concoct a convincing lie. She had practised all sorts of scenarios, all manner of diversionary tactics. Untruths designed to manage risk and play for time when events were at their most desperate. In the classroom, they seemed highly plausible. Not, however, with the metallic taste of a gun barrel in her mouth, blood running out of her nose, down her chin, an unseen, unknown assailant speaking death in her ear. No lie came. So Emily told the truth.

"I'm SIS. Secret Intelligence Service. I'm on a mission. Being watched by a surveillance team."

17

A loud chuckle echoed in the alleyway. It speedily morphed into a braying laugh. Full-throated. A shade forced. Touch of mania around the edges.

Emily didn't know what to make of it, except that she was alive, relatively unharmed. Her attacker had withdrawn the gun, no longer pinning her down.

Hoisting herself on an elbow, Emily turned to see the blurry image of a black-clad figure sitting on her haunches with her back to the brick wall. Emily blinked a couple of times, the pounding in her chest beginning to subside. Her assailant slowly came into focus. Zofia. Grinning now, a Glock pistol dangling from her right hand.

Emily's brow furrowed. Disbelief oozed along with blood from her nose, her body still trembling in shock, a thousand thoughts converging like careering cars in some mental version of Spaghetti Junction. A laughing Zofia was the last person she expected to see.

"What? … Why? I don't understand."

"I don't fucking believe it."

"What don't you believe?" Emily sat up, pawing at her face, picking gravel from her nose and mouth.

"SIS. What a joke. If it wasn't so bloody serious, it would be hysterical."

"What?"

"I'm CIA. I've been under cover with Ivan for the best part of six months. I'm just getting somewhere when you come barging in to queer the pitch."

"How did you know?"

"That you weren't Volkov?

Emily nodded.

"I've got eyes in my head. That's how. The rest of them are too blinkered. Too tied up in their own little world. They're not looking for the same things as I am."

"Such as."

"I clocked the guy with the Mandela shirt and his mate in the café this morning. Never seen them before. I have breakfast in that café almost every day. I could give you most people's address, occupation, how they like their eggs, inside leg measurement if you were interested. Never seen those two guys, so I followed them and guess what?"

"What?"

"Mandela didn't walk to freedom, or even to a building site. He and his mate headed straight to the underground, across town, where they wandered into an office block. So when they turned up again this afternoon I looked for a connection, a common denominator. The only other two people there this morning and afternoon at the same time as them were Lily the waitress and you. And Lily isn't in to big, hairy builders, if you get my drift."

"Do the others know?"

"Of course not. Do you really think you'd still be breathing if they did?"

Zofia pulled a cloth handkerchief from her pocket, handing it to Emily, who was busy trying to clean her face. "You've missed a bit. Actually, you've missed a lot. Sorry about the rough stuff, but you understand it was required?"

Emily threw a withering look. Zofia ignored it.

"What's the real story?" said Zofia. "What happened to Volkov?"

It took a few minutes to recount the details SIS had pieced together about Volkov's meeting with Sir Robert Bellingham, including the theory that the admiral had shot her after being poisoned. Zofia listened without interrupting, absorbing the facts.

As Emily spoke, her mind tried to fathom what needed to happen next. When she finished her story, she put that question to Zofia, who answered immediately.

"Nothing changes, Nina. Our lives depend on that. By the way, don't tell me your real name. I don't want to know. Can't be blurting that out. There's obviously been a monumental balls-up. I thought my lot and your lot were supposed to be on the same side, sharing intelligence, fighting the same enemy. Turns out neither of us has a scooby what the other one's doing."

"A scooby? I thought you were Polish." Zofia's use of Cockney rhyming slang confused Emily.

"I'm Polish by birth. My dad's from Gdansk but my mum's from Leytonstone. We emigrated to the United States when I was young. What is this, happy families?"

Emily again tried to explain SIS involvement. "It happened so fast. When Sir Robert Bellingham and Volkov were found dead, we spotted an opportunity. And took it. How were we to know you were already on the case?"

"Don't you lot have meetings about that sort of thing, or are you too busy throwing parties? I've heard you're good at that in Whitehall."

"We've been watching The Salon for weeks."

Zofia shook her head, although she took pride from the fact that the SIS watchers, despite daily surveillance, had not rumbled her as a CIA agent. She stuffed the Glock into a holster strapped under her armpit and shuffled over to Emily.

"Look, Nina, we're stuck with each other now, but maybe that's a good thing. We can work together. I've seen Roman Smirnov once in six months. That's when you arrived. You've definitely sparked some action. We all know there's something big going down. When it does, we'll be on the case. It may even be tonight."

"How often do you report in?"

"Only when I need to. Sometimes not for weeks on end. Olga's a techie. She's all over communications. She can track any phone signal, email, even encrypted messages, coming in or out of The Salon. Don't ask me how. To be on the safe side, I use a public phone box at Clapham Junction, or message from a burner phone at a safe distance."

Emily didn't tell her she used a sales assistant at Harrods.

"Is there anything I should know?" Emily's heart rate had returned almost to normal, her head was clearing, although it throbbed, along with her swollen nose.

"Be careful. Katya and Olga may come across as friendly, but they're ruthless. I've seen them in action. They don't take prisoners. They're prepared to do anything, hurt anyone. You can't be seen to be soft or indecisive. They respect force and violence. But, most of all, they fear Smirnov."

"What about me? Do they trust me?"

"They don't trust anyone, but Katya has done her homework into Nina Volkov, as you'd expect. She was a formidable woman. Anyone close to Putin must have had influence and power. That will have impressed Katya. For now, you're safe. But too many people must know Volkov is dead. In SIS. The defence department. Bellingham's bodyguards. The mortuary. It only takes one small leak."

Emily shivered.

"Come on, let's get back to The Salon. You need to get cleaned up. You wander in first. I'll give you twenty minutes start."

Zofia offered a hand to help Emily to her feet. Emily took it, easing her way back along the alleyway, brushing down her clothes as she went. Zofia shook her head, whispering under her breath. "S.I.S. Shit Intelligence Service. What a shambles."

By the time Zofia returned, The Salon had shut for the night. Nina was the talk of the place. She had bathed, tending her bruised face, but her nose was still swollen, a raspberry red shale rash, raw and moist, discolouring one of her cheeks.

Zofia smirked when she saw her talking to Katya in the office. "What the hell has happened to you, Rudolph? Your nose looks like it's had a row with a bumble bee, and lost."

Emily threw a filthy look. "Very funny. I tripped over the kerb by that mound of rubble builders have left down the road. Head-butted the pavement. Cracked it, I shouldn't wonder."

Olga entered carrying an ice pack wrapped in a towel. She handed the pack to Emily, who pressed the ice to her injured face. "Thanks." She managed a smile, the cold compress bringing instant relief.

"Should take down the swelling a bit," said Olga.

"Okay." Katya's tone business-like. "Excitement over. Let's meet back here at eight. Smirnov should be here by then."

18

The red stain forming an almost perfect circle on the cream carpet was the only clue to the recent lethal events in the admiral's office.

Dent stepped over the stain, pointing to warn Miller to do the same.

"Was this really a good idea?" Miller stood behind the admiral's desk, her gaze sweeping the room, fascinated by the portrait of Nelson, whose eyes seemed to track any movement Mona-Lisa style.

"That remains to be seen." Dent was more interested in the other three walls, two of them packed floor to ceiling with books. Many of them naval history, others classical literature, an entire shelf dedicated to Dickens. More shelves, full of files, dominated the other wall, set around a picture window overlooking the manicured garden.

Dent and Miller had motored down to the pretty hamlet close to Faversham, a market town mentioned in the Domesday book which resides close to the Swale, a strip of sea separating mainland Kent from the Isle of Sheppey in the Thames Estuary. A fitting country home for a distinguished admiral. They had told no one of their trip apart from Roger Williams at the MOD, who arranged security access, the guards at the gate waving them through after they produced their SIS warrant cards. The fewer people who knew, the fewer questions, the less chance of a leak.

"Did the MOD not do a thorough search?" Miller's voice contained a modicum of doubt.

"They cleared the safe of confidential papers, but found nothing worth killing for."

"Wouldn't anything of that nature be in the safe?"

"Maybe." Dent sighed, pausing for a moment. "But the admiral was known as a bit of an old-school maverick with his own way of doing things. He may have reasoned that the safe was actually unsafe, being the first place anyone would search."

"If they had the combination."

"We know better than most that there are ways of gaining access to combinations."

One of Miller's eyebrows arched, but she did not contradict.

Dent continued. "Look around, the room is filled with distractions. Books, files, papers, some of it ordered, lots of it haphazard. A nightmare to search. A burglar would take one glance and move on, knowing it would take too long. Volkov's heart must have sunk when she saw the state of this place, which is why she grabbed the first things that came to hand in the desk drawers."

"We might need to get the team in to do a proper search."

"Best way's, do it thi' sen."

"Pardon."

"My mother's favourite Yorkshire saying. Means do it yourself."

"Okay, let's start with the files."

For the next three hours, they worked through each shelf, starting from different ends, meeting in the middle, sitting at either side of the desk to sort through piles of paper. Many of the documents were dismissed by glancing at the date. The admiral was clearly a hoarder. Some files went back more than 30 years when he had launched his career as a simple midshipman. He had kept everything. There were even items such as certificates in music theory, as well as correspondence relating to his patronage of half a dozen local charities.

One document caught Miller unawares. The speech he had delivered at his wife's funeral two years ago. He paid tribute to the courage with which she had battled a long illness, thanking his three children for their love and support.

"He seems such a nice guy," she said. "Military men always appear one-dimensional when you see them in their uniforms. Stiff and regimented. It's easy to forget they're ordinary folk like the rest of us with the same hopes, dreams, fears, triumphs and tragedies."

"Except the rest of us don't have to drop bombs, launch ballistic missiles, or send youngsters barely out of college to almost certain death." Dent's cynical tone surprised Miller. As chief of Section

X, never a day went by when he did not make decisions which affected the lives of agents in the field. He had worn responsibility that would crush other men with apparent ease. For the first time, Miller sensed the cost of that responsibility.

She studied him across the desk. His face as honest as a bishop, but weary too, lines forming around the eyes, the creeping years beginning to announce themselves. A section chief had a certain lifespan. Dent's predecessor had discovered exactly that, the job becoming intolerable when decisions, however agonised, led to the death of members of his staff. Dent had lost no-one, but Emily's current mission weighed heavily on his shoulders. It was part of the reason he was taking such personal responsibility and why he was at the admiral's house in Kent right now on what increasingly appeared a fool's errand.

As Miller returned to ferret through more papers, Dent sat back, arms behind head, taking a breather.

He stared into the eyes of Horatio Nelson on the wall opposite, allowing his mind to wander, musing at the audacity of one of England's greatest commanders in skirmishes such as the Battle of Cape St. Vincent, when his crew alone fought off seven enemy ships. The pounding of guns, billowing smoke, the screams of the injured. Dent's imagination conjured them all, concluding that Sir Robert Bellingham must certainly have done the same on numerous occasions.

"I wonder." Dent uttered the words almost under his breath but Miller caught them, watching him stride around the desk, approaching Nelson with a determined strut.

"What is it?"

"I had a thought. Might be nothing. Probably fanciful. Come here, I need help."

Miller detected a fresh vigour in Dent's demeanour, joining him in front of the painting.

"Okay, Jane, you take that end, I'll take this one. Be careful, it probably weighs a ton."

"Why?"

"Never mind. We'll know soon enough."

Between them they raised the painting a couple of inches each side to free it from the brackets on which it hung, before carefully sliding it down the wall until it rested on the floor.

Dent pulled the top edge towards him, balancing it so he could inspect the back. He expected to see dust and cobwebs but the thin wooden board protecting the canvas was in pristine condition. It was held in place by a series of small metal stays that swivelled to open and shut. With Miller's help, Dent laid the painting on the floor, freeing the metal stays.

They each lifted the opposite sides a fraction. "Okay, let's stick it against that wall." Dent was eager to view the back of the canvas. When he did so he found a two-inch gap between the canvas and the back of the frame. In the bottom right-hand corner, attached to the side of the frame, sat a brown A4 envelope.

Miller's eyes were wide with expectation.

Dent cautioned. "Don't get your hopes up. It might be nothing more interesting than the admiral's tax return."

He peeled the envelope free of its wooden holder, taking care not to tear it, slicing the seal with a letter opener he found on the desk. There were two documents inside. Dent read the first one out loud. It was a speech that Sir Robert intended to deliver later in the year to the Ministry of Defence and a House of Commons select committee, lamenting the fact that the Royal Navy, once a formidable force of 332 ships, was down to fewer than 30 fully fit for service. Defence cuts meant that no longer could Britain launch a campaign such as the Falklands. *It would be hard pressed to take Disneyland* was one of the emotive lines. The facts were damning, the language incendiary, the admiral's intention to embarrass government ministers obvious. He had made notes of proposed TV and radio interviews in the margin.

The title of the second document sent an instant chill up Dent's spine. *A Child Could Crack the UK's Nuclear Code.*

19

Roman Smirnov had a name designed to confuse, which was probably how he liked it.

Think of Roman, the Slavic variant of the Latin Romanus. The image conjured is of a gladiator, an expert swordsman, hand-to-hand combatant, as well as a shrewd military strategist. A powerful, ruthless individual.

Smirnov, on the other hand, as well as being one of the most popular Russian surnames after Ivanov, translates as quiet, peaceful, and gentle. A middle-aged history professor at a small university comes to mind. Deeply dull, highly respectable. A man who takes his wine with lots of water, who wouldn't dream of having a stand-up row with a traffic warden, even if he was in the right. He'd rather pay the fine.

Roman Smirnov balanced the alter ego with extraordinary aplomb. No one was quite sure who was the real Roman Smirnov.

That thought struck Emily as Smirnov appeared in the office at precisely eight o'clock. His strut was business-like. His face benign. He made straight for Emily.

"Nina, my dear. How are you? Sorry to hear you had a fall. I'll have a word with the builders. Disgraceful leaving loose materials like that on a public highway."

"I'm fine, just a few scratches. No big deal." Emily acknowledged his concern with an appreciative smile.

"It is a big deal. A scar on a pretty girl's face is like a tear on a great work of art."

"No problem there then." Zofia interrupted, a mischievous smirk tightening her lips.

Smirnov ignored the interjection, but his eyes smouldered. "Okay, let's get down to business."

He motioned to Katya, who picked up the cue, crossing the room to close the door.

Smirnov sat in Katya's winged chair at the desk. The others crowded around, Katya, Olga and Emily pulling up office chairs, Zofia perched on the edge of an adjoining desk.

"First things first." Smirnov lowered his voice, almost to a whisper. The women leaned forward. "All activity with even a suggestion of illegality must cease for the foreseeable future. No fraudulent cash cards. No bank jobs. No carrying weapons. No international calls, especially not to Moscow. Nothing that could bring attention to this nail parlour. This is Ivan's command."

It was the first time any of them, including Katya, had heard Smirnov speak of Ivan. He did so with reverence and conviction. As if with Ivan on his lips he held a weapon in his hand.

He paused, allowing his words to strike home, sensing uncertainty tinged with disappointment around the desk.

"Why?" Zofia was first to break the silence, face sullen, her tone challenging.

"I'm glad you ask. It's only natural you are curious. I can tell you it concerns Shelkunchik. But for now, for the safety of everyone concerned, most importantly the success of the mission, that's all I can say." His jaw clamped shut, thin lips forming a tight zip.

"We've been hearing rumours about Shelkunchik for weeks. That's not news. Nothing ever seems to happen. No-one seems to know what it means." The pitch of Zofia's voice rose half an octave, frustration obvious.

"What you say is true, but patience is required a little while longer."

Olga piped up. "Zofia's right. We're fed up of hanging around rich, pampered women with more money than brains."

"Do you not get paid well for what you do?"

"Yes, but …"

Katya sensed Smirnov's irritation at being questioned, intervening to ease the atmosphere. "I'm sure we'll get to know soon enough. Let's all calm down. Is that all you came to say, Roman?"

"No, there's more."

"Go on."

Smirnov swivelled his chair to look directly at Emily.

"Nina, I'm afraid the papers you retrieved from Sir Robert Bellingham did not yield what we expected. Moscow have studied them in detail. There is nothing, how should I put it, of strategic value."

"They were all I could get. There wasn't much time. It all happened so fast." Emily felt herself gabbling, heart pounding, a sudden implant of fear.

"My dear, that wasn't a criticism. We realise sensitive information is not served on a silver platter, but Ivan would like to speak to you personally." He glanced at Olga. "Could you set up a face-to-face, encrypted of course. Tomorrow afternoon, say two o'clock." He turned back to Emily. "Does that suit you, Nina?"

Emily could sense a tidal wave of freak proportions, splashing her face, sweeping her off her feet, dashing her against rocks, the sort that envelops surfers caught in an ocean phenomenon whose dangers they could never have envisaged.

She heard herself say, "Of course", but in her head the voice sounded like one of those tapes played at half-speed.

"Good." Smirnov adjusted his spectacles, turning to Katya. "Now, would you mind if I had a private word with Nina?" It was phrased as a question, but there was no doubting it was an order, although it took Katya a couple of seconds to process. Eventually, she responded.

"Okay, guys, let's grab a bite to eat at Mario's."

The women trooped out, Zofia adopting the surliest of lopes, leaving Emily and Smirnov alone.

They sat for a few moments in silence, Smirnov eventually rising, walking to the door, where he listened for several more seconds to ensure the others had descended the stairs.

When he returned, his tone was warmer than before. "Ivan is pleased you are safe, Nina. He's looking forward to hearing from you. I didn't realise you were close."

Neither did Emily, but she managed to hide her surprise, the phrase leaving little doubt that Smirnov was talking in romantic terms. She endeavoured to project a coy smile, although it felt forced and unnatural as she concentrated on where this chat was heading.

Smirnov raised his hands, palms facing her. "None of my business." He paced behind the desk, wandering over to the window. Pulling back the curtain a fraction, he observed the street for a few seconds, the night miserable and wet, raindrops pattering like soft footsteps on the pane. "You can't be too careful."

Emily didn't respond, instead remembering her training. Don't talk too much. Don't be sucked into a conversation you cannot control.

"You're not a big talker, are you Nina? Not like Zofia. She always has something to say for herself. Always an opinion. Usually off the cuff. Full of hot breath."

"I find it's better to think before I speak, and speak before I act. That way reason usually wins over misunderstanding."

"Precisely. Exactly what is required."

Smirnov sat again at the desk. He fished inside his suit jacket, dangling a white envelope in front of Emily. His voice grave. "Inside this envelope is the secret to Shelkunchik. The secret to restoring the might of the Soviet Union, taking control of Europe, making Russia great again. Only three people in the world know the contents."

"Who are they?" Emily was intrigued, the inherent fear of her situation supplanted by a desire to discover the secret.

"Ivan, me … and the British Prime Minister."

20

Emily's brow knitted. Smirnov studied her quizzical expression.

"I can see you are curious. That is good. The thing is, Nina, we need you. At the moment we have the gun." He thrust the envelope in the air again. "But we need you to supply the bullets."

"How? What's the gun?"

Smirnov fiddled inside the envelope, pulling out a white piece of paper. He laid it on the desk, beckoning her closer.

At once she recognised the letterhead: *10 Downing Street London SW1A 2AA.*

Her blood fizzed. She studied the crest, a lion and a unicorn either side of a crown with the motto written in French: *Dieu et mon droit.* As a schoolgirl, it had always intrigued her why the royal coat of arms of the Kingdom of England had a French rather than an English motto. It was one of the reasons she had studied history, learning that Norman French was the preferred language of the English royals and ruling class following the reign of William the Conqueror of Normandy and later the Plantagenets.

Dieu et mon droit. "God and my right." She translated the motto, Smirnov impressed at her accent, Emily noticing from the fold lines that the letter was a photocopy rather than an original.

Her attention turned to the heading above the handwritten text.

Letter of Last Resort: Only to be used in the event of a nuclear attack.

Her hands began to shake. Fortunately, they were hidden behind the desk. Emily knew exactly what this letter meant. She had not seen one before. No-one had, apart from the British Prime Ministers who wrote them, but such a letter had featured prominently in her SIS training.

During the Cold War, the KGB had made securing one of these letters a primary goal. Many times they had tried. They had always failed.

Emily's photographic memory zoned in on her studies. *Think. Think of the detail. The procedure. The consequences.* Everything flooded back to her. In an instant. Especially the sobering fact that the letter contained handwritten instructions by the sitting Prime Minister to each of the UK's nuclear submarine commanders, giving orders on how to respond if the nation came under nuclear attack and the PM had been killed.

For an enemy, especially one prepared to push the nuclear button, knowing your target nation's response was crucial. The stakes could not be higher. Emily recalled there were around 40 warheads on a nuclear submarine, all with the capacity to strike multiple cities at long range, killing millions of people. The fact that each warhead had an explosive capacity of 100 kilotonnes, more than six times the pay load of the bomb that destroyed Hiroshima, was also imprinted on her brain.

"Do you know what this is, Nina?" There was a suggestion of triumph in Smirnov's attitude.

"Of course, I worked for FSB. They would have killed for this." Emily did not have to manufacture the incredulity in her tone.

"They did, on several occasions."

"Yes, I suppose they did."

"How did you get this?"

"That is of no concern. The fact is we have it. Do you know what CASD stands for?"

"Of course. Continuous At-Sea Deterrence. It means the UK has at least one nuclear submarine on patrol at all times. Unlike America, and other nations, the UK gave up the capacity to drop nuclear bombs in favour of the submarine option. It means it has a constant moving target. No one knows the whereabouts of the submarine on patrol, even though the UK depends entirely on America for maintenance of its warheads."

Emily's up-to-date knowledge was detailed, the precise manner in which she answered clearly impressing Smirnov. The gripe in her stomach, however, was due to the realisation that this letter proved Britain's defence had already been severely compromised.

Her eyes flitted to the body of the prose but before she read it, she asked the question that troubled her most.

"You've got the letter. What do you want me to do?"

Smirnov sat back, eyeing her up and down. "Ivan said you were direct. I like that. Nina, we want you to crack the code."

"What code? Everyone knows the UK nuclear protocol isn't like the United States. It doesn't depend on codes."

"That's what the British media peddle, what the defence department want everyone to think. They want everyone to believe that their system relies on the discipline and goodwill of their military. Because their military is the best in the world. No need for checks and balances. Just a gentleman's code of honour. As if it were some sort of cricket match. What typically arrogant nonsense." The sneer accompanying Smirnov's explanation betrayed the depth of his hatred for Western democracy.

At this point, Emily was out of her depth. She suspected the same would have applied to Nina. The existence or absence of nuclear codes was out of their natural orbit.

"So there is a code?" Emily ventured.

"Yes, Nina. We want you to crack it. Ivan says you are the best cryptographer he has come across, better than anyone in the West. Your first language happens to be English. The planets appear to have aligned with perfect timing."

"But every code requires a key?"

"Exactly. We believe this letter contains the key. It just needs someone as astute as yourself to find it." He handed over the copy of the letter for Emily to peruse.

"I think you may have overestimated my ability."

Smirnov shook his head.

"I don't think so. Let me explain how the system works. Every time a new Prime Minister is elected, he or she is required to write the Letter of Last Resort by hand. The previous Letter of Last Resort is destroyed without ever being opened so no one ever discovers the intention. The new letter is put in a safe within a safe, with the outer safe including another letter carrying instructions on the final steps required to open the inner one."

"So how do you have a copy of the letter?"

"Let's just say Ivan has agents of outstanding military calibre who have worked for many years in pursuit of the cause."

"Agents within the British military?"

"Put it this way. Our understanding is that two submarine officers are required to arm a warhead on the Vanguard class, neither of them can be the captain of the vessel, to guard against a rogue individual leader. Two-person integrity, I think, is the correct phrase. Both have to be in possession of a precise but different code of numbers. They have to be inputted in the correct sequence at the same time. We don't believe we can turn two officers or extract the necessary information from them. But, as a failsafe, we believe the letter itself contains the clues to the coding. Crack the code and one person, a Russian agent who happens to have the most exemplary record in the Royal Navy, can take control. That's where you come in."

"I know now why you called it Shelkunchik. It's quite a nut to crack."

"Do so, and Ivan shall forever be in your debt."

"It could take days, weeks, months even."

"It will have to be days at most, I'm afraid. Our agent on board will be useless to us after that."

"And what happens if I crack the code?"

"That is for Ivan to answer. You can ask him yourself tomorrow when I will supply you with a copy of the letter. But think of the bargaining power of Russia if it could take control of another nation's nuclear arsenal. Even being able to tamper with an enemy's nuclear missiles would have value. Think of the embarrassment that would cause. Think of the protesters. They'd be marching from Downing Street to Faslane."

Emily perused the letter once more. As she read, the enormity and absurdity tugged at her gut, a plug of bile rising in her throat.

This letter has been the hardest I have ever undertaken. I must level with you. If you are reading it, it means I and many of my colleagues are dead and our nation is under threat of extinction. In these circumstances and in the knowledge that I will never forgive myself for allowing these events to occur on my watch, I direct you to my final instructions. My civic duty. Meet force with force. retaliating with every means at your disposal. Further to that, forwards or backwards, you should sail to an ally closest to your location and put yourself and your boat under their command.

It was signed, *Your dutiful Prime Minister.*

For several seconds, Emily could barely comprehend what she was reading. Her fingers trembled as she imagined her beloved London reduced to rubble, buildings burning, iconic landmarks destroyed, people incinerated. A nuclear wasteland. Uninhabitable for a century or more.

She had to warn Dent at SIS. If Smirnov's information was accurate, a British nuclear submarine patrolling the oceans right now could have an enemy on board, an enemy within days of taking control of the nation's nuclear capability. SIS needed to identify that enemy. Identify the leaders, find evidence that Russia was bankrolling the operation. She needed to play along, to pretend to crack the code to protect the code. Yet Emily had even more pressing matters on her mind.

Tomorrow afternoon she had to convince the man who apparently was her lover that she was Nina.

21

For the next hour, Emily sat at the desk in her room formulating a coded message, again on a spare receipt she had lifted from Mario's. She contemplated using the burner phone but decided against it. There were still too many imponderables.

The message included the timing of the proposed face-to-face with Ivan Petrovich the next day, the fact the Ivan Group was in possession of the Letter of Last Resort and, most important, a foreign agent was potentially aboard a nuclear sub at sea.

She folded the message tight, stuffing it inside a secret pocket fabricated by unstitching part of the lining in her cash purse. When she reached Mario's, the café was packed, a wave of heat and the smell of Italy greeting her as she entered. Spotting Katya and the others at their usual table, she wandered over.

"What did he want, or are we not important enough to know?" Zofia spat out the question.

"Hello to you too." Emily slid onto the one spare chair.

"Well then?"

"Smirnov just wanted to check I was on board and prepared to speak to Ivan tomorrow."

Olga chipped in. "What does he want you to do?"

"Help with a code. That's what I was trained for. I guess I'll learn more tomorrow."

It was a semblance of the truth, minus the detail. Lily the waitress came over, Emily ordering a pizza. The others had finished eating. Lily stacked their plates, side bowls and cutlery, ferrying them back to the kitchen with expert technique.

Katya got up to leave, surprising Emily as she thought there would be more interrogation. "Sorry Nina, we need to go. You'll have to eat alone. Some business to attend to."

"No problem." Emily managed a warm smile.

"I'll stay. I could do with another coffee. I don't mind watching the golden girl eat." Zofia's comment contained a dollop of sarcasm. Katya frowned, showing a hint of surprise, before departing with Olga.

Emily watched them walk towards The Salon.

"What's occurring?" said Zofia in a soft voice.

"Lots, but let's not talk here. Later." As she spoke in a whisper, her eyes returned to the café's customers, searching for sign of *teacher* man or *Mandela man.*

Neither was present. She scanned each table. Nothing. No reference, pictorial or prose, with relevance to Nelson. An empty feeling griped at the pit of her stomach, not helped when she remembered she had forgotten to call Al at eight with their private code. She knew he would worry. It couldn't be helped. He would understand. She would make sure she called tomorrow instead.

Emily's pizza arrived, Zofia attempting fractured conversation as she ate.

"What made you take up what you do?" Zofia was careful to speak in generics.

"Don't laugh, but I wanted to help. Do something useful with my life. Use the few talents God gave me."

"How's that panned out?"

"It's still a work in progress. I used to be scared of my own shadow, lacked confidence, couldn't look anyone in the eye. But I met this guy. I don't know why, but we just clicked. He brought out the best in me. Showed me that you can be different. Actually, more than that, he showed me you should be proud of being different. It's what makes people special. I'm not saying I'm special, but I stopped feeling that being different was some sort of handicap. Do you get what I'm saying?"

"Can't say I do, Nina. But then I'm a cynic from McLean." Their eyes met, the mention of Emily's assumed name jolting them back to the business in hand.

Zofia sipped coffee while Emily chewed, having all but given up hope of passing on her message tonight. As she laid down her knife and fork, she spied a man approaching the café. He was alone, but Emily scrutinised him for several seconds before concluding this was *teacher man*. The shuffle in his gait gave a clue, but the book he carried was the clincher. *Nelson: Britannia's God of War*. Same as before.

The café was thinning out, the evening rush dissipating. The man checked with staff at the entrance before sauntering over to a side table. He ordered a cup of coffee, a pasta dish, and opened his book. Emily and Zofia talked for a few more minutes. When the small-talk ceased, Emily opened her purse, withdrawing a couple of notes. In the same movement she plucked the message from the lining, placing it behind the condiment set in the middle of the table.

Her peripheral vision focused on *teacher man*, who appeared engrossed in his book, but in reality was studying Emily's every move. A few moments later his pasta arrived. He rose from his chair, sidling over to Emily's table to enquire in a soft voice if they were finished with the salt and pepper.

"Help yourself," said Zofia.

As he leaned over, he scooped up the condiments. When he turned, the message had disappeared. Emily breathed easier. At least Dent would know the score soon enough.

Emily and Zofia left together. Behind the counter, Lily the waitress, tapping to the music beat in her headphones, gave them a cheery wave. "Have a good night. Don't do anything I wouldn't do."

"That doesn't leave much," Zofia always had to have the last word.

Instead of returning to The Salon, they headed down Smith Street, past the Enterprise Car Club, in the direction of the embankment. There was a chill in the air, but they set a brisk pace, Zofia fishing for news.

Emily was reticent. She wanted to believe Zofia was a CIA agent. Everything pointed to that being the case, but Emily had not yet independently verified her identity. Nothing could be assumed or taken for granted. Few professions were as duplicitous or as murky as the world of intelligence. She couldn't run the risk of sensitive information about the UK's defence falling into American hands, or worse, before SIS had acted to neutralise the danger.

Besides that, her chipped teeth were sensitive, the roof of her mouth still painful from the wound inflicted by Zofia's gun.

She told Zofia the bare bones of her chat with Smirnov. About being pressed to decipher a code that could endanger the UK's defence systems, as well as her understanding that Ivan was Nina's lover.

"How in God's name are you going to pull off a face-to-face chat?" Zofia, as usual, laid it bare. "You might look a bit like Nina Volkov, but I've got news for you. You're not exactly sex on legs. The chances are you sound nothing like her. It'll take Ivan five seconds to work out you're an imposter."

"Thanks."

"Nina, you know it's true. Harsh maybe, but true."

Emily did not disagree. Her stomach churned at the thought of meeting Ivan. Since speaking to Smirnov, she had thought of little other than how to delay or postpone the next day's video chat. Nothing had come to mind.

They reached the embankment, crossed the road, turning towards Chelsea Bridge. A sniping wind stung their faces, but still Emily admired the illuminated stanchions and archways of the metal road bridge, the suspended strings of lights shimmering in the dark waters of the River Thames.

"A thing of beauty, isn't it?" she said.

"If you like that sort of thing. I've always been wary of objects that look better in the dark." Zofia could always be relied upon to put the alternative view.

They trudged as far as the bridge. It struck Emily that if she carried on walking another mile and a half she could amble into SIS HQ, spill everything she knew, leaving it to men like C, paid 20 times what she earned, to decide what to do. *Just walk into the office whenever you like and it's all over.* That's what Dent had said. But if she did, the Ivan cell would plead innocence, Smirnov would go to ground, evil individuals at the heart of state terrorism would remain at large. So they turned left, picking their way back to the King's Road, walking mostly in silence.

When they reached the street leading to The Salon, they became aware of police sirens in the distance, 500 yards away at least. The reflection of blue strobing lights bounced off several buildings.

Not an unusual sight in many areas of London, but not commonplace in Chelsea.

"Something's kicking off." There was a glint in Zofia's eyes. "Fancy taking a look?"

"Not me. I need some peace and quiet. Need to think about tomorrow."

Zofia shrugged. "Think I'll take a wander to see what's going on."

They parted ways. A few minutes later Zofia approached the incident by Markham Square. Four police cars and two ambulances in attendance. Officers had closed the road to traffic. A small crowd had gathered, craning necks behind a police cordon. Zofia squirmed her way to the front. Paramedics were using a defibrillator to try to save the life of a man slumped on the pavement by a set of railings, although the action was too far away to make out much detail, apart from a stream of blood snaking six feet or more to the kerb.

"What's happened?" Zofia asked one of the onlookers.

"Stabbing. Poor chap's in a bad way."

Zofia watched for 10 minutes until it was obvious the paramedics had ceased heroic measures. London's knife culture had claimed another victim. Police started to disperse the growing throng, an officer with a firm voice and sergeant stripes repeating, "Let's go home everyone. Nothing more to see."

As Zofia turned to leave, she caught sight of two paramedics returning to their ambulance, one carrying what appeared to be the victim's belongings. In one hand, he carried a jacket and some clothing, in the other he held a book. As the paramedic passed a streetlight, Zofia caught a glimpse of the colourful cover. *Nelson: Britannia's God of War.*

The book looked familiar but Zofia couldn't think why. He must have been a historian or an academic. She wandered back to The Salon.

22

Miles Dent rented his apartment. It was easier that way. He lived on his own now after divorce from Sandra. Nothing fancy. A two-bedroom flat in Hampstead, handy for the heath and the underground, as well as an array of restaurants. He'd tried to make a go of the marriage. He really had. However hard he tried, the job always came between them.

Long days, overnight stays, the fact that he checked his car for bugs and worse every time they travelled. And the secrets. The secrets were the killer. Whenever Sandra asked about his day, or enquired what was bothering him when he adopted his tell-tale vacant stare, he always answered in generics.

"Everything's fine, Darling." Except everything was rarely fine. Dent would make predictable noises and Sandra would nod in the certain knowledge that she could no longer hold a meaningful conversation with the husband she'd married in Harrogate registry office 15 years ago. Not because he didn't love her, but because the Official Secrets Act forbade him from discussing any element of his work. It seemed their interaction was reduced to nothing more exciting than what he wanted to eat for dinner or whether he would have time to creosote the fence.

There were no children to consider. A blessing in some ways, not that Dent looked at it like that. He had always wanted a son. He and Sandra simply drifted apart. Which was why Dent consumed himself with work and why he had taken a copy of the letters concealed in the dead admiral's painting home with him.

On the surface, the first one read like a timely warning to the defence department not to let its guard fall in the fight against hostile forces in an uncertain world. After delving deeper, the more Dent perceived a deliberate attempt to unveil the incompetence of the Ministry of Defence, thereby undermining the support and confidence of military personnel in the respective services. Dent didn't like to leap to conclusions. His job required forensic analysis, considered judgements, but if he hadn't known Sir Robert Bellingham as a man of honour and substance he would have been forced to conclude the letter bore the hallmarks of an enemy within.

Each glance at the second letter discovered something more worrying. He phoned Jane Miller.

"Jane, what are you doing?"

"Why?"

"I need your expert opinion."

"Okay, fire away."

"Not on the phone. My place."

"Now?" There was an irritating undercurrent in Miller's tone. She was in the middle of baking cakes. A new recipe that seemed to have spread all manner of collateral damage around her kitchen. Burnt pans, butter smears, eggs and flour debris, assorted cake-top dressings, many of which appeared to be scattered all over the floor.

"If you don't mind."

"I'm in the middle of …"

"If it's not convenient."

"No, of course, I'll be there in fifteen minutes."

It was more like half an hour later that Miller pressed Dent's intercom. He buzzed her up to the fifth floor.

"What's so urgent, Miles?" Miller made straight for the panoramic window. She loved the view. To the right, a crane, all gangly metal with a bucket device scooping for scraps like some prehistoric wading bird, scarred the grey skyline. To the left, in the distance, she glimpsed the cross on the top of the dome defining St Paul's Cathedral. All around, a forest of buildings, old, modern, small and humungous, jostled for light. Every square foot of London's concrete jungle accounted for.

They sat opposite each other on two soft swivel chairs. Dent got straight down to business. "I've been looking through the letters we discovered. I'm struggling to make up my mind."

"You're a man, Miles."

"Meaning?"

"Nothing. What's bothering you."

"It's the second letter we found. The one entitled, *A Child Could Crack the UK's Nuclear Code.*"

"Just a guy sounding off, in my opinion. A guy whose budget has been slashed, who has to make cuts all round to make ends meet."

Dent scratched his head, mulling Miller's opinion for a few moments.

"I'm not sure, Jane. Remind me of the protocol on the UK's nuclear codes."

Miller laughed. "There aren't any. That's the whole point. The US have codes. The French have codes. In the UK it's down to the line of command. The UK's military is trusted to obey orders unswervingly."

"How does that work?"

"The commander of the nuclear submarine at sea would take orders passed down from the Prime Minister to the Minister of Defence to the First Sea Lord and Commodore. If the PM and his deputy had been incapacitated or killed then two officers on the sub, not the commander, would have access to the safe containing a letter giving orders in the event of a nuclear attack. It's called the Letter of Last Resort."

Dent glanced again at Sir Robert's letter.

"I'm sure you're right. The admiral mentions all that. But he also talks about a code, a rotator code, embedded in that Letter of Last Resort. A code crucial to the firing of the warheads."

"That's way above my pay grade. With respect, above yours as well, Miles. Why would Sir Robert commit that to record?"

"No idea. The admiral's note contains no details that I can fathom, but you can see why a foreign agent might have been attracted to it. The mere confirmation of a code would be worth the risk Nina Volkov took. I'll flag it up to C, to put it to this week's meeting of the JIC."

Dent slipped the copy of the letter inside a brown envelope.

"Is that it? Can I get back to important stuff?" Miller's tone carried a sarcastic edge.

"Such as?"

"Lemon drizzle, cupcakes, banana bread."

Dent chuckled, but a furrow to his brow suggested he was still cogitating.

"Who advises the PM?"

"On what?"

"On how to write the Letter of Last Resort. If it's a letter written as soon as the PM takes office there must be a briefing, an explanation of the detail, a conversation on the current loyalty of allies. At least an exploration of the potential consequences of various actions. The PM needs some damn clue about how to make the most momentous decision of his or her entire life. I mean, some PMs are only in the job months, even weeks, these days."

There was angst and animation in Dent's reasoning, his voice rising in pitch. He had made enough life-or-death decisions in his short time in charge of SIS to appreciate the turmoil they caused.

Miller nodded. "Of course, you're right. The PM's first task is to meet the defence chiefs from all the armed services. Army, RAF, the Navy, including the Royal Navy Submarine Service."

"Would Sir Robert have been present?"

"Almost certainly."

"Thanks Jane, that's what I thought."

Miller left. Dent poured himself a whisky from his favourite bottle, a Macallan 25, an expensive indulgence but one he regarded as essential. The amber fluid warmed his throat as he mused, watching the crane dip for another heavy load, running his fingers down the smooth leather upholstery. If Sir Robert advised the PM, almost certainly he would have known the gist, if not the precise detail, of the Letter of Last Resort. If there was a secret embedded code, denied to everyone other than a select few, did Sir Robert know that too? If so, then surely that was the prize Volkov was seeking.

Dent shivered. If he was right, then the stakes for Emily were even greater than he could have imagined.

23

Images of herself peering into a mirror, Nina Volkov's corpse leering back at her, dominated Emily's sleep. She awoke agitated, an unsettling sense of foreboding clouding her thoughts.

Heaving herself off the mattress, she stumbled to the desk, observing the creeping light of dawn until her mind began to clear. Elbows on desk, she cradled her face in her hands, allowing the mental picture of the letter Smirnov had shown her the evening before to form.

Emily's photographic memory had proved useful during school and university exams, formulae and theorems conjured on demand. It had helped in her first job as an analyst at SIS, plotting useful connections, enabling her to retain masses of information.

One scan was usually enough to store simple images. Smirnov's letter had taken several reads, but it was now fixed, readily available as a memory stick in her computer-like brain.

She ran through it several times, looking for connections, sifting words, filtering letters, investigating potential patterns. Codes, especially those representing numbers, were always logical. If there was a key, Emily usually struck gold on the first or second read. Yet nothing transpired. No obvious connections. No anagrams jumped out at her. Not simple ones at any rate. Perhaps no secret key existed, or maybe the stress of her current predicament had fogged her brain.

A soft tap at the door snapped her concentration. Emily turned the handle gently, opening the door a few inches. Zofia, with a finger to her lips.

She pushed her way in, beckoning Emily to the furthest corner, away from the metal chimney flue.

"What is it?" Emily's whisper laced with puzzlement.

"I had an idea."

"Go on."

"Katya is out all morning. Olga goes for lunch at twelve o'clock. The office will be empty for the best part of an hour."

"But since I arrived, Olga locks up every time she leaves, even if she's manning reception."

Zofia rustled in her trouser pocket, holding up a key. "A spare. Kept in Katya's drawer. I lifted it last night. She won't miss it. Olga's in charge of security."

"What are you planning?"

"The computer, Nina. Come on, keep up. Olga's computer is the one used for communication. It's the only device trusted to send encrypted messages. Katya's paranoid about the cyber geeks at GCHQ listening in. Phones are easy to track. She's probably right. This cell has been here too long."

Emily didn't mention the eyes SIS had on the place. "But you can't knock out the computer. It'll look too suspicious."

"I'm not an idiot. I'm not going to take a hammer to it. But at The Farm I learned how to disable all manner of computers."

"The Farm?"

"Holy crap, Nina. Camp Peary. Virginia. Where agents learn how to do all sorts of useless things. We call it The Farm. It's a military reservation with a training facility for intelligence officers. In York County, near …. I've not got time for a geography lesson. Do you Brits know nothing?"

Zofia's exasperation spilled all over the attic floor. Emily ignored the criticism, imploring Zofia to lower her whisper.

"What do you have in mind?"

"If I can get in there when Olga's out, I can tamper with the screen. It's been playing up for months. It's a simple job to disable it. There will still be sound, but no vision. With time, perhaps half an hour, Olga would discover the fix, but the chances are she'll go on line minutes before the meeting with Ivan."

"I'd still have to talk to Ivan."

"True, but remember, you're pretty beat up at the moment, Nina. Nose and mouth bloody and bruised. Hardly surprising if you sound different. See, I did you a favour roughing you up in that alleyway, after all."

Emily rolled her eyes. She was not convinced, but conceded it was a better plan than anything she had come up with.

"Okay, let's do it, but as soon as the meeting's over, as soon as we know what Ivan's planning, I'm out of here."

Emily's tone was strident, brooking no discussion. Zofia asked anyway. "Why?"

"Smirnov showed me a letter yesterday that suggests an enemy has breached Britain's defences. From what I can tell, the Ivan Group is close to taking control of the nuclear arsenal. Probably got an agent aboard a nuclear sub right now, just waiting for the word. It's too scary to contemplate. Once we know what Ivan has in mind, our job is done. Leave the rest to special forces."

"Shit, Nina, I thought something big was going down, but this is huge. I should let Langley know. You know what Langley is?"

"No. I mean, yes, of course I know what Langley is, but no, don't say anything until we're both out of here."

Zofia pondered what they'd discussed for a few seconds, before nodding. "Okay. Sounds like a plan. See you at two."

***

Emily spent the rest of the morning mulling over the letter. She popped into Mario's for a coffee and poached egg on toast, but it was quiet. No sign of Katya or Olga, the café manned by two young lads wearing dark blue pinafores and pleasant demeanours, one cooking, the other serving.

As she waited for breakfast she concentrated on the positives. Last night's message to *teacher man* had contained the most crucial information. Dent was probably sitting in C's office right now relating the news that Ivan was in possession of a copy of the Letter of Last Resort, having smuggled an agent aboard one of the UK's nuclear submarines. If she had gauged Dent right, he would now be advocating for the deployment of a special forces team. Already, she imagined, snipers were sweeping the immediate vicinity, probably on the roofs of adjacent buildings. Doubtless, steps were also being taken at ministerial level to recall the submarine on patrol. *Thank goodness for teacher man.*

Another encouraging sign for Emily was that her nose and mouth, if anything, were even more swollen than the night before, the waiter having struggled to understand her order. She still didn't relish speaking to Ivan Petrovich, but she felt confident of doing so, especially if the conversation revealed the full story.

She ate her eggs slowly, deliberately, the roof of her mouth raw and painful from its meeting with the barrel of Zofia's pistol. When she returned to The Salon it was mid-morning. The two nail girls were in the process of packing up for the day. They didn't look or sound pleased.

"What's going on?" said Emily.

"No idea. Olga told us to go home, cancel the rest of today's clients," said one of them.

"Just like that."

"Yup. Said it was an order from Katya. She isn't even here. Must have her reasons, but it beats me. Still, we get paid, so why complain?" A disconcerting tremor affected one of Emily's forefingers as she watched them tidy up, pack their implements away, turning the sign to *Closed* as they left. She recognised the affliction. In days past, it would have become a full-blown shake, but now was hardly noticeable. Represented success in her lifetime battle against anxiety.

She climbed the stairs, noticing the office door was shut, even though the sound of clacking computer keys emanated from inside. Must be Olga. No sign of Zofia. She wanted to knock on her door to reinforce their plan, but decided it wasn't a good idea. Zofia had made it plain to the others that she and Nina were not like minds. Seeking her company would not be wise.

Instead, Emily sat at her desk, revising all she knew about the Ivan Group. Revisiting her briefing with Jane Miller, not 48 hours ago, although it felt like weeks.

At precisely five minutes to two there was a knock at the door. Katya. Something odd about her. Emily couldn't put her finger on it. Not brusque, or unfriendly. A smile even played on her lips. Maybe it was the fact that she had knocked, when normally she would have sent Olga or Zofia. "All set for Ivan?"

She nodded, following Katya downstairs into the office.

Olga sat bashing keys at the computer. Smirnov lounged in Katya's chair, fiddling with his tie, a cold glint in his eyes. Zofia, as usual, perched on the edge of the desk.

"Come in Nina, my dear, we have been waiting to see you. How are you feeling today?" There was an edge to Smirnov's voice. He was calm, measured, but everything he said sounded fake and rehearsed.

"I'm fine. Bruises always look worse a day or so after. My mouth's the most painful. I'm not sure Ivan will be able to understand me."

"Oh, he understands, all right. But I'm afraid he will not be joining us this afternoon." Smirnov appeared to be enjoying himself.

"Why not?" Emily's eyes jagged around the room, a sharp surge of panic rising. She fought for control, breathing growing heavier.

"Sure you're all right, Nina? Or would you like to tell me who you really are?"

The words landed like darts in Emily's chest, complete with stabbing pains. Heart pounding. Still, she endeavoured to roll with it. She smiled, trying to work out whether this was a fishing expedition, or if she had been rumbled. *I've been careful. Not spoken to anyone, apart from Zofia. They can't know. How could they know? Oh God, I hope Dent has mobilised that special forces squad.*

"I'm Nina Volkov. You checked my passport. Made me strip. Clocked my tattoo. Quizzed me about Ivan the Terrible and the Oprichnina. What more proof do you want? Let me talk to Ivan." She sounded convincing. But as Smirnov listened to her earnest tone, the door opened and a woman walked in. A young woman with a cheery face and a diamond stud in her nose dazzling under the artificial light. Lily, the waitress from the café. In that moment, all hope extinguished.

To underline Emily's predicament, Smirnov drew a black pistol from underneath the desk, a dull thud sounding as he laid it on the top. The gun was fitted with a silencer. Katya walked over to the door, twisting the lock. When she turned, she too held a pistol.

"What in God's name's going on?" Zofia was no longer perched on the edge of the desk. She had manoeuvred into a position where she stood between Emily and Katya.

"I think we should let Lily explain, from what I hear she's been doing all the work around here. It's a tribute to her efficiency that most of you may not realise she's one of Ivan's most crucial covert operatives." Smirnov's tone was respectful.

Lily strolled to within a few feet of Emily, a quiet daintiness to her movement that was appealing, yet sinister, her voice having ditched the welcoming trill at the café.

"You must think we are stupid."

"Pardon." Emily's right forefinger trembled.

"The builders, the man with the book. They were convincing, I'll give you that. But I had filled the condiments that evening myself. There was no way the book man needed to use yours. While he was eating, I took a look at the CCTV. Not many people spot the camera in the café. It's tiny. I did a good job there, if I say so myself."

Emily squirmed, trying but failing to manufacture a credible riposte.

Lily continued. "Obviously, you know what I saw. Along with the salt and pepper, the book man lifted a small rolled-up piece of paper. A paper you had left. When I met up with him later he didn't seem to want to part with it. But we came to an arrangement. The numbers written on it looked suspiciously like code to me."

In her peripheral vision, Emily caught a glimpse of Zofia. She detected her mouth dropping a fraction, her eyes conveying the merest glint of horror. Emily remembered the blue lights and sirens from the night before. In that moment she realised she was on her own. No special forces. No Dent. No back-up. Not even the satisfaction of having relayed the crucial message about the Letter of Last Resort and the potentially sabotaged submarine.

"Who are you?" Zofia snarled, striding towards Emily, striking her across the face. Not a limp slap, but a hard, punchy blow, opening the scabs on her lips and nose. Blood spurted. "I knew you were bad news. Had a feeling the first time I saw you. That tattoo looked too red and new." Zofia struck her again, this time a blow to the stomach. Emily sank to her knees, for a fleeting moment wondering if Zofia was an Ivan soldier after all. Yet, even in the midst of her panic, Emily forced herself to think clearly. *Of course, she's trying to help. Playing for time. Staying in character. Acting out the role of the hard-nosed terrorist. Hit me again, Zofia. Hit me again.*

Smirnov held up a hand. "No need to be uncivilised. It doesn't matter exactly who you are, Nina, my dear, or who you are working for. MI5, counter-terrorism, I don't expect you will tell us in the time available. I'm afraid there is only one course of action."

"Maybe she could help us." Zofia swivelled to face Smirnov. "She says she's a cryptographer. She was passing codes in the café. That could come in useful."

"Hmm, a smart thought, Zofia, but I don't think so."

"She's right. I can help." Emily found her voice, although the plaintiff tremor betrayed her fear. "I'm trained in all manner of codes. I can crack almost anything." She was in survival mode, needing space to think, time to formulate an escape plan. *Say or do anything. Keep them talking. Make yourself useful. Give them a reason to change their minds. Don't give up. Remember what I learned in training. Remember, remember. For God's sake, remember.*

"No, I think this can only end one way. Zofia, could you do the honours, please?" Smirnov's tone was cold, callous even. He picked up the gun from the desk and stretched out to hand it to Zofia. A momentary pause. "Come on, Zofia, you're good at this. The best we've got. Katya tells me you enjoy hurting people."

Zofia took the gun. She turned towards Emily. Their gazes met. Pointing the gun at Emily's head, her finger squeezed softly, playing with the trigger. Emily could see doubt in Zofia's eyes. She wondered what she would do in the same circumstances. *Sacrifice a fellow agent to protect her cover and potentially save more lives down the road? That was the only smart move. Try to fight her way out, even though the odds were against her? Try to negotiate to save them both?*

In the surreal suspension of time that accompanies such moments, Emily alighted on the second option, but now the gun was no more than three feet from her head. Zofia mouthed something. Emily thought it was "sorry". Closing her eyes, accepting her fate, she didn't see Zofia's sudden swivel.

The gun was now pointing at Smirnov's smirking face. Zofia fired.

24

No shot. No click. Nothing. The pistol did not contain a revolving chamber or a cocked hammer. Or a bullet.

Instead, silence. Emily opened her eyes to see Zofia pulling the trigger a second and third time, her wrist jerking, a frantic, confused, expression on her face as nothing happened. Smirnov smiled. Zofia's mouth opened. She appeared ready to scream. The only sound that came was the crumping thud of a gunshot, Lily's silencer suppressing the crack of her 9mm Glock pistol.

Zofia collapsed, blood and brain fragments splattering like raindrops on the hard wooden floor, a tidy precise hole in her forehead, mouth open, her face contorted in surprise, her left leg twitching three times. Emily stared transfixed for several seconds. This was not supposed to happen. Zofia was strong, feisty, decisive. Indestructible. The Ivan women respected her. Some even feared her.

"Why?" said Emily. "Why shoot her?"

"You tell us." Smirnov's face set concrete hard. Emily's body shook with shock and fear. Lily slid the gun back inside her jacket. Not a hint of emotion, the routine movement of someone who had killed many times before.

"A spy knows the score, whatever the side," said Smirnov. "Most sane spies assess the ruthlessness of their targets and their capability for counter-intelligence. It's a risky business. Only the bravest, most committed, can survive undetected as long as Zofia. I salute her. The CIA will be poorer for her passing."

He sounded like a vicar giving a eulogy at a local dignitary's funeral.

"How did you know?"

"That she was CIA?"

Lily interjected before Smirnov could explain, a smirk on her lips. "As well as CCTV at the café, I also have a very useful listening device. About this big." She held up forefinger and thumb to signify something the size of a matchstick.

"You bugged the café?"

"Of course. So many hiding places. Under a table. Inside a pepper pot. In a vase. I listen in through my headphones. Everyone thinks I'm listening to my favourite music, when in fact I'm eavesdropping their most intimate conversations. Think of me as an all-seeing, all-hearing guard. Not part of the group, but protecting the group from a short distance. The bug was under your table when you came in with Zofia. It would have been unprofessional not to have taken the opportunity. Katya had told me you and Zofia didn't get on, so why did you eat together? We needed to know."

"But Zofia didn't say anything. Neither did I."

"A cynic from McLean."

"Pardon?"

"That's what Zofia said. I couldn't hear you, Nina, your whispers were too soft. You were obviously being careful. But I heard Zofia loud and clear. A cynic from McLean. A meaningless phrase. Except, I looked it up. McLean is in Fairfax County, Virginia, which happens to be the home of the George Bush Center for Intelligence."

"Oh." Emily couldn't recall the conversation, but she knew it was the spy's nightmare. The unguarded moment. One chance remark that betrays years of meticulous preparation.

Emily wiped blood from her nose with her sleeve. Her heart no longer pounded in her chest, even though the expanding pool of blood beneath her feet was a grotesque and constant reminder of the execution that had taken place.

She felt awful about Zofia, who she realised was a brave and selfless colleague. She had even started to like her. But Emily was also exhausted, wearied by the stress of two nerve-shredding days, rendered numb and uncaring by the events of the last few minutes.

"What happens now?" It was all she could think to say, knowing there was no prospect of escape, but also reasoning that if they intended to kill her she would already be lying alongside Zofia on the blood-stained floor.

Smirnov rose from his seat, placing an arm around Emily's shoulder. He handed her a tissue for her dripping nose. She could smell his musky deodorant, mixed with a whiff of tobacco. He led her away from the killing zone, sitting her down in the leather armchair.

His voice was soft and measured. "Would you like a drink? You've had a shock. It might soothe your nerves."

Emily shook her head. Smirnov took a soft seat opposite.

"I wasn't being quite truthful earlier when I said we don't know who you are … Emily Stearn."

The mention of her full name stung her into combat mode. In an instant her mind refocused, fighting to piece together how she might survive her predicament.

"How do you know my name?"

"So many questions. You ask as if we are some sort of amateur outfit, planning to rob the corner shop. Don't you know who you are dealing with? We are the Ivan Group. We have access to technology even SIS could only dream of."

Emily's mind fizzed. Her name. Her organisation. How did he know? SIS had underestimated the Ivan Group. That was the obvious conclusion. The group was regarded as an irritant, a minor bunch of mercenaries, on the payroll, if not always under the control of the Kremlin. This proved Ivan, by association Smirnov too, was more powerful than SIS could have imagined.

Smirnov warmed to his theme, a swagger in his delivery. "Like you, Emily, we have facial recognition technology. On Lily's recommendation we sent your passport photograph to Moscow. Guess what, the FSB machine lit up like the lights in Nikolskaya Street. You're quite a celebrity in Moscow. The woman who tracked down Andrei Reblov."

Emily shuddered at the mention of Reblov's name. He was the Russian hitman, codenamed Tinman, a master of disguise, responsible for killing countless defence chiefs across Europe in revenge for the deaths of Russian generals at the start of the Ukraine war. Emily's forensic analysis at SIS had uncovered his plan to kill several European leaders, including the British prime minister, at the Palace of Versailles. A special forces squad eventually caught up with him in Paris, but Leanne, the Russian double agent who met her fate in Epping Forest, had reported Emily's role in the affair to Moscow.

No one at SIS knew for sure how much Moscow knew. Until now.

"You know who I am. What do you want from me?"

"You have already helped us enormously."

"How?"

Smirnov motioned to the lifeless body of Zofia. "We had to be sure about her, despite Lily's suspicions. If she had shot you, then she would have lived. But she chose to shoot me. I admit I wasn't convinced she was a spy. It could have gone either way. So we played our little version of Russian roulette. Without bullets, of course."

A wave of nausea gripped Emily, the responsibility for Zofia's death weighing heavy on her shoulders.

Smirnov continued. "Now we'd like you to help us again. In fact, we want you to do exactly what Zofia suggested."

Emily understood what he was saying, but she asked anyway. "What do you mean?"

"The Letter of Last Resort. We need to crack the code. As you told us only minutes ago, you can crack almost anything."

Emily's jaw set firm, eyes glinting fire, a drop of blood ran down her chin. When her response came, it screamed from the edge of her sanity. "I won't … I couldn't … there's no way I would betray my country. Never. I'd rather die. Nothing you can say would change my mind."

Smirnov nodded slowly as if applauding the sentiment. When he spoke his lip curled, face contorting into an evil scowl.

"Oh, I think we have ways of changing your mind."

25

Dent brushed specks of dandruff from the shoulders of his dark jacket. He had become accustomed to the lifetime ritual, like cleaning his teeth or tying his shoelaces. He'd tried every shampoo. Nothing worked. Head and Shoulders was merely a reminder of where to brush. In the end he'd embraced his minor affliction, looking upon the four in every five men who didn't have it as odd.

He knocked on the door of C's office. He'd received a summons a few minutes before from the chief's secretary, demanding his presence.

"Come in." It was the briefest clue but there was a steely ring to C's tone. Immediately, Dent's feeling that this was not a routine meeting was confirmed. Opposite C sat the chief constable of the Metropolitan police, Mark Anderson, appointed within the last month, tasked with the job of improving the police's reputation in the capital. A reputation that had hit tawdry depths in recent times, the Force accused of a culture of racism, misogyny and corruption.

"Thank you for coming, Miles, you know Mark, don't you?"

"I know who you are, of course, but I don't think we've met," said Dent. They shook hands across the table.

C motioned to the chief constable to address the meeting.

"I'm afraid I have some bad news." He fixed Dent with a grave expression, his jaw dropping a fraction at the end of the sentence, like a door with a loose hinge.

"Go on."

"Several of my officers attended a stabbing incident at around ten o'clock last evening. A particularly brutal and senseless stabbing that left a middle-aged man dying on the pavement. Despite the efforts of the paramedics, the gentleman died at the scene."

"That's sad, of course, but not that unusual in London. What does it have to do with us?"

"It happened in Markham Square."

"Chelsea?"

"Yes."

Dent's antennae twitched. Markham Square was no more than a quarter of a mile from The Salon. Dent's years in SIS had nurtured a sharp nose for bad news. If the chief constable was required, then this was several notches past bad.

"Do you know the man's identity?"

"It took us a little while. There is no formal identification as yet, but from a credit card we have established the gentleman is a Mr Brian Baker."

Dent closed his eyes for a moment. This was what he dreaded. He knew immediately that Baker, known to his team as *BB,* was part of the surveillance squad monitoring The Salon, tasked with providing back-up for Emily.

What he couldn't understand was why no one had alerted him to Baker's absence.

"You say he was identified from a credit card," said Dent.

"That's correct. His wallet was in his coat pocket. It contained two hundred pounds in notes."

"Not your average capital mugging then."

"No, that's why I'm here in person. Was Mr Baker working on anything so sensitive that people would have wanted him dead? I know you don't routinely divulge matters of national security, but there is Mr Baker's family to consider. This was a particularly nasty crime."

C twitched an eyebrow. Dent wasn't sure what it meant, but took it as a signal to lead the response.

"Baker was one of our senior operatives. A fine agent, an even finer man. He will be sadly missed. But nothing comes immediately to mind as to the motive for his stabbing. Like many of our officers, he would have been working several cases, some of them undercover. We don't tend to mix with too many upstanding members of the community, as I'm sure you appreciate. Leave it with me, Chief Constable. I'll endeavour to discover exactly what he was doing in Chelsea last night."

"Very well." The chief constable rose, shaking hands in turn with C and Dent.

When he left, C peered over the top of his spectacles. "What the hell is going on?"

Dent explained Baker was one of Emily's contacts, charged with picking up clandestine communications. He also told C about the letters he and Miller had found in Sir Robert Bellingham's office, suggesting Volkov knew what she was looking for, implying that it involved the possible compromising of Britain's nuclear capability.

"My God. What are you saying?"

"The mission in Chelsea is bigger than we thought. It could well be a matter of national security. If Baker was rumbled, then the chances are that Emily is in real and present danger."

"What are the options?" C's jaw jutted Eiger-like in Dent's face.

"As I see it, only two. One, hope that Emily is safe. I've heard nothing to the contrary from our surveillance crew. We could watch, wait, carry on with the mission, hoping Baker's death was unrelated, or hadn't compromised Emily."

"The other option?"

"We go in with special forces, pick up as many Ivan Group operatives as we can, then let the *persuaders* have a crack at them." The *persuaders* were an ultra-secretive special team inside SIS, officially known as the interrogation section, expert at persuading foreign agents to divulge information. No one quite knew how they worked. They rejected comparison with debriefing teams used by the United States at the infamous Guantanamo Bay detention centre, but Dent knew they were good at their jobs. They got results. They saved lives.

"In light of what appears to have happened to Baker, I favour the second option."

"Me too." Dent breathed easier. He realised there was little chance Baker's murder was coincidental. He also knew they had not heard from Emily for 24 hours. Not concerning in the normal course of events. But this didn't feel normal. It was time to go in. Fast and hard.

26

Dent and Miller sat in the back seat of the blacked-out 4x4 at the end of the street.

"All quiet. Almost too quiet." Dusk had fallen. Dent swept the buildings through powerful binoculars.

Mario's café was busy, the brisk end-of-day trade in full swing, but the rest of the road was empty. He trained the lens on The Salon. No sign of life. The *Closed* sign hung in the doorway, although the roof watchers across the way had reported lights and activity in the living quarters that afternoon.

Dent was taking no chances. He had called in G Force, the special forces arm allied to SIS that normally backed up intelligence reports requiring armed intervention on foreign shores. It meant the Met's chief constable had to be informed, which was vaguely embarrassing considering their earlier chat at HQ. The chief constable would have known they had withheld information at that meeting, but that's what SIS did, wasn't it? Part of the description. The very first word. Secret Intelligence Service. Anyway, C would have to deal with the fall-out.

A couple of snipers had taken positions on surrounding roofs. A squad of 12, split into two groups of six were in vans at either end of the street. All wore special forces regalia, complete with bullet proof vests, black visors and MP5 machine guns. At the chief constable's insistence, half a dozen police officers in an unmarked van observed from a discreet distance.

In the front passenger seat of the 4x4 sat the commander of G Force, Jack Easton, a man SIS had worked with on many occasions, most notably when tracking down Russian assassin Andrei Reblov in Paris.

Easton knew Emily. They had formed a bond, borne of respect and admiration for each other's talents. When Easton discovered Emily was involved, he had insisted on being present. He left Dent in no doubt who was in charge.

"Okay, this is my shit-show now. Don't move until I give the all-clear. Do you understand."

Easton was an experienced forty-something, although his gait and expression were full of youthful vigour, the symmetry of his boyish face marred by a mole on his right cheek. He fixed Dent and Miller with a stare not to be ignored until they both nodded.

"As far as we can tell from the plans, these buildings are back-to-back properties. They have no rear escapes so everything should be straightforward."

Dent leaned forward, placing a hand on Easton's right shoulder.

"We need everyone alive if possible, Jack. We need to know what this cell is up to."

"That's the aim. But my first concern is for the safety of my officers. If you're right and these terrorists are armed to the teeth, then we'll be shooting first and interrogating later."

Dent slumped in his seat. He knew the drill. Realised Easton would meet force with overpowering force. The next few minutes could go one of two ways. The scenario pulsing through Dent's mind was not pretty.

Easton lifted his Clansman radio. "All set Jonesy?"

"Roger that."

"Spike?"

"Roger."

"Go … go … go."

A rev of engines. A squeal of tyres. Dent witnessed the next 30 seconds through his binoculars, although it was little more than a blur. The officers piled out of the vans, guns at the ready. A boom sounded as the first officer fired a pump action shotgun, the explosive round designed for the exact purpose of blowing the front door off its hinges. Then the officers were inside and Dent and Miller anticipated more gunshots. None came.

Ninety seconds later Easton's radio crackled. "All clear, Sir."

Dent glanced at Miller, perplexed frowns lining their faces. Easton gunned the accelerator. The Salon looked unremarkable. The front-of-house nail parlour appeared as one would expect. Clinical. Dent and Miller climbed the stairs, pausing twice to turn sideways to allow officers carrying heavy equipment to pass on their way down. They entered the office. Again, nothing of note, apart from lots of electrical points but an absence of computers. The window blinds were also closed. Miller's nose twitched.

"Bleach." She sniffed.

"Pardon."

"Definitely bleach. Or some similar cleaning fluid. The sort you might expect downstairs, rather than up here."

"A professional cleaner?"

"Possibly."

That meant one thing in SIS parlance. An active attempt at concealment.

Miller plugged in one of the desk lamps with a long trailing lead. She swept the room, the bright beam searching for any obvious signs of spillage on the walls and furniture. There were none. She turned her attention to the wooden floor, rolling back a Turkish rug in front of the largest desk. Tracking back and forth with an easy swing, her practiced eye spotted a blemish. Not easy to determine. The stain was a foot or so in length, nestled not on the surface of the wood but in the groove where one of the floorboards had expanded.

She took a nail file from her bag. Dropping to her knees, she slid it an inch or so along the groove, scooping up the reddish dirt, showing it to Dent before depositing in a plastic bag.

"What do you think, blood?"

Miller nodded. "Judging by the consistency, fresh blood, a few hours old at most."

A shout, urgent and authoritative, came from downstairs. One of the officers informing Easton they had found something.

Easton clattered down the stairs, Dent and Miller in his wake. They turned left at the bottom, proceeding to the back of the building where several officers had dragged a panel away from the wall to reveal a door. A heavy metal door, held by four solid hinges.

The officer with the pump-action shotgun glanced at Easton.

"Go ahead."

The round resonated in the confined space, bruising Dent's ears even though he'd clamped his palms tight against them. The door, lock destroyed, swung open to reveal a passageway into the building behind, whose front entrance led to the next street along.

"The escape route." Miller said what everyone was thinking. "Explains why our watchers didn't alert us."

They tramped back upstairs, investigating each space, including the attic room where Emily had stayed. There were signs of recent life, including depressed pillows, creased bedding, bottles of water. A discarded sandwich alongside a pan of half-boiled rice in the kitchen suggested whoever lived there had left in a hurry. But there was nothing incriminating, no computers, no files, no weapons, the entire place appeared to have been stripped of evidence.

"We've been played, Jane." Dent's voice was flat, dark thoughts swirling.

In the last few hours one of his officers had been murdered, another was missing, the blood stain on the office floor suggested recent violence had occurred, while a dangerous group of terrorists had trooped out of their hideout under the noses of his department.

Dent had experienced better days.

"Actually, there is a positive way to look at it." Miller didn't sound convinced but Dent needed something to hold on to.

"What's that?"

"They know they've been rumbled. We're on to them. They've broken cover. The Ivan Group is on the run. We've disrupted whatever they had in mind. We know their starting point. We must be able to track them via CCTV. They can't get far."

Dent fished his phone out of an inside pocket, punching in the office number. It connected almost immediately with his deputy.

"George. Need everyone on the cameras. Start at the intersection between Anderson Street and Coulson Street, off the King's Road. Concentrate on the property to the rear of The Salon. Look for vehicles loading up. Track them. We need to know where they went. And George …"

"Yes?"

"Let me know if you spot Emily."

27

Total darkness. The black hood tied tightly around Emily's head let in no light. A small filter at the back supplied air, but with a gag restricting her breathing it was not enough to prevent the sensation of impending suffocation.

Hands tied behind her back, Emily shut her eyes to block out the blackness, trying to stem the recurring image of Zofia's silent scream. She recited the periodic table, fighting to remain calm, breathing through her nose while listening for clues to her whereabouts.

She had not been harmed, although she bore bumps and bruises after being rolled in carpet-like fabric, then tossed into the back of what she suspected was a large people carrier.

The car journey was slow, the sound of revving engines, beeping horns mixed with the odd shouts of pedestrians, attracting her attention. She sensed she was still in the city. At one point she detected a drop in temperature, a slow windy descent, a squeal of tyres on concrete, as if the vehicle had entered an underground multi-storey car park. She felt herself lifted, thrown this time into a larger vehicle, tinny echoes and metallic floor suggesting a van.

All the while, she could hear Katya, Olga and Lily whispering, fast, furtive conversation. Not an argument, but agitated nevertheless, as if the debate to what happened next was taking place. She picked out a few words, but nothing to lend form or sense to their destination.

The van started rolling. This time there was no talk, no hint that anyone was present other than Emily and the driver.

Emily felt certain they were bound for an Ivan Group safe house. It was the obvious deduction from Smirnov's demeanour. He was being reasonable, as if he realised his plans would take several days. He had even allowed her to pack a small bag before they left The Salon. With Olga's attention distracted from her guard duties by a call from downstairs, Emily had taken the opportunity to smuggle the burner phone hidden in the attic beam into a concealed pocket in her toiletry bag. No chance to use it, but in the knowledge it may come in useful.

As she lay on the hard floor, thrown around by the pitching vehicle negotiating corners, Emily's mind wandered.

She wondered how they had disposed of Zofia's body. She had heard dragging, rubbing noises, suspecting a clean-up operation was under way.

She also thought of Al. He'd probably be preparing dinner in their apartment right now, throwing spices and herbs into a vegetarian stew, checking for taste via a wooden spatula. Probably had a glass of Shiraz on the go, only one, but a good one to make the cooking as pleasurable as the eating. She realised he would be worried by her silence, but he was the most logical, level-headed, composed, human being she knew. If she'd gone dark, he would deduce it was for good reason.

Emily's thoughts returned to Smirnov. He had revealed his hand. He needed Emily to break the code to the Letter of Last Resort. She had no intention of doing so, but she was not stupid. Zofia's murder had alerted her to the group's brutality. They would stop at nothing to complete their mission. Emily didn't know whether she was strong or brave enough to resist what would surely follow. She shivered at the thought.

A retired colleague, an old-school section chief in charge of managing foreign agents, had spelled out the perils of the spy world to her some years before when she was young and naïve, albeit the office golden girl because of her ability to connect and detect what others couldn't.

"Miss Stearn, you are an evaluator, not an operative," he had told her. "Evaluators are bright-eyed, full of optimism. Sharp brains. Few cares. Operators have dead eyes. They act hard, a dullness about their demeanour, never knowing whether they are right or wrong, but always with the notion that one day almost certainly they will be discovered. There is an inevitability about their fate. Knowing that makes for a harsh existence."

That avuncular advice had not deterred Emily, but she tried to put the fate he had predicted out of her mind. The van stopped once, briefly, then again for a much longer period, perhaps half an hour. Too long to be stuck in traffic. Emily heard scuffling outside, but with no clue to what was happening. When the van restarted she anticipated a long journey, putting distance between the group members and The Salon. Yet less than an hour after leaving what she was sure was an underground car park, and no more than 15 minutes after the extended stop, the engine cut again.

The back doors opened with a clunk, several pairs of strong hands dragging Emily out of the van. To her surprise, someone ripped off the hood, prising the gag from her mouth at the same time. Gratefully, she guzzled life-giving oxygen, sweet and calming. She could smell wet leaves. When her eyes adjusted to the fading light announcing dusk, the silhouette of a vast building filled her vision. More like a palace than a house, complete with portico formed of eight cream pillars, ornate and ostentatious, framing an enormous wooden door that looked too heavy to move.

Olga shoved her in the back, a signal to trudge to a much smaller side entrance 20 yards away. As she walked, Lily cut the rope tying her hands. Blood coursed into her fingers, burning and stinging. Emily ignored the pain, searching for her bearings. The grounds were extensive, the garden manicured, a huge lawn of lush, green grass fronting the property, a high wall together with thick metal gates providing protection from public scrutiny.

The house looked vaguely familiar, reminding Emily of car trips with her parents as a child. They would drive around wealthy parts of London, Phillimore Gardens, Kensington, Grosvenor Square, Holland Park and areas of Hampstead, marvelling at the houses on what were regarded as some of the world's wealthiest streets. Emily would pretend the houses were occupied by emperors and princes, or famous rock stars. Many of them were, although in recent times most had been snapped up by oil sheikhs from Saudi Arabia or Russian oligarchs, parking their wealth in London's finest real estate.

Maybe this was such a property. It would make sense. Ivan Petrovich had money to burn, thought Emily.

Olga guided Emily inside to a hallway, resplendent with crystal chandeliers, a sweeping staircase adorned with gilt-edged friezes. Smirnov stood on the bottom step.

"Miss Stearn, welcome to the jewel of the Ivan Group in the UK. I hope you will be comfortable and your stay beneficial for both of us."

This was the safe house. The one Emily had anticipated, although she hadn't expected anything as plush.

"Olga will show you to your room."

"I won't do it. Whatever you say." Emily fixed Smirnov with a defiant glare. He ignored the remark, motioning to Olga, who pulled Emily away from the opulent staircase, towards a much more rudimentary passage heading downwards.

Two flights later they reached what Emily imagined were servants' quarters in another century. Olga, pistol in hand, guided her along a corridor with doors off either side. No natural light. At the end, Olga ordered her to push open a heavy wooden door, giving access to a small basic space, more like a prison cell than a bedroom.

A small camp bed and mattress with a single white sheet filled one wall. A tiny desk, chair, and a small basic sink with a dirty sign stating *Not drinking water* completed the furniture. The stone floor was cold, crumbling plaster from floor to ceiling betraying damp patches. No window, a single light bulb dangled on a cord from the ceiling. A metal bucket served as an en-suite.

As Olga pushed her further into the room, a sudden panic attack caught Emily by surprise, her breathing fast and shallow, head dizzy, overwhelmed by helplessness.

"You all right, your face is the colour of that sheet? There's a paper cup and water over there if you need it." Olga pointed to the sink. Despite the warning sign, it was the first hint of tenderness Emily had witnessed since her identity was revealed.

"Thanks Olga, I'm okay. I'll be all right in a minute. I'm not good with tight spaces, or men like Smirnov. Never have been."

"If you know what's good for you, do what he says. You've seen what he can do."

Emily gasped before adopting her calming routine, rapid short breaths for half a minute followed by several deep inhales until her heart stopped racing. She risked filling the cup, taking several small sips of water. "Why are you here, Olga? You're not like the rest. You're not a killer."

"You don't know me. I don't pretend to be anything that I'm not. I can't say the same about you."

Olga tossed a bag containing a few of Emily's clothes onto the bed, slamming the door. Emily heard a heavy key turn in the lock, Olga's parting remark, coupled with the disappointment it contained, troubling her more than she anticipated.

When Olga's footsteps had receded, Emily dived on the bag, toiletries spilling as she plucked the tiny burner phone from the inner pocket. A giddy rush of adrenalin surged through her veins. She fumbled with the start button, the screen immediately activating.

Olga was away from her computer. It would take time to set up her monitoring system at this new venue. There was no better opportunity to call in the SIS cavalry.

She punched in the number, fingers trembling with excitement, holding the receiver to her ear. *We couldn't connect your call. Please try again later.*

"Shit!" The crushing reality of the announcer's monotone message landed like a heavyweight punch to the gut. She tried again and again, ten times at least, before realising no signal could penetrate the depths of this basement and its two-foot thick stone walls. Emily's mind swirled with a kaleidoscope of emotions. She felt foolish for indulging her premature excitement, as well as nauseous and utterly helpless. Collapsing face-down on the bed, she pounded the mattress with her fists, screaming into the pillow, releasing hours of pent-up frustration.

28

"Any luck, George?" Dent ripped off his jacket as he strode into the operations room at such a brisk pace Miller almost raised a jog in his wake.

"Yes, and no."

"What does that mean?"

Dent's deputy stood in front of the big screen, arms folded, studying the fuzzy image of a large green people carrier. A multitude of smaller screens piped recorded video from a targeted area in central London. Almost 20 staff were busy analysing. Computer keys clacked, pens scribbled, phones rang. Urgency permeated the office.

George wore a concerned expression. He stroked his straggly beard with one hand, pointing at the big screen with the other.

"Yes, Miles, we think this green vehicle is the one the gang loaded up from the back of The Salon. It was parked outside the back-to-back property. We have footage of three figures, all wearing caps or hoodies. None easily identifiable, but the gait and dimensions of at least two of them correspond to Ivan personnel."

"Good work. What were they loading?"

"All sorts, big and small. Computers, filing cabinet, boxes, office stuff in the main."

"Okay, where did the vehicle go?" Dent was anxious to cut to the end game.

"I'm afraid that's where the no comes in."

"Don't say you lost them."

"Yes, and no."

Dent smashed his fist into the nearest desk, the resounding thud causing necks to turn. "For Christ sake, George, just give me a straight answer."

"Okay, we lost them."

Dent's flat vowels screeched to a higher octave. "How is that even possible? There are nigh on one million CCTV cameras in London, more than fifteen hundred for every square mile. There's nowhere to hide. You couldn't lose a one pence coin. How can you have lost them?"

George shuffled uneasily for a few moments before recovering his poise.

"We didn't just lose them. We followed the vehicle into central London via several of the main thoroughfare cameras. It couldn't have been easier. The green vehicle stuck out like a sore thumb. There were at least two passengers as well as the driver. It got as far as Marble Arch, turned into Mayfair, then disappeared into a car park."

"And?"

"It never came out."

"It's still in there?"

George nodded, but the hangdog expression told Dent that was not the end of the story.

Miller spared George more embarrassment. "They swapped vehicles, didn't they?"

"Yes, but it's more complicated than that, I'm afraid. We've studied footage from the next hour. The only vehicle exiting the car park capable of carrying anything like the same load is a white van."

"So, let's follow the van."

"There are six of them, all white, none of them with signage or distinguishing characteristics, apart from big black bumpers. Chances are at least three of them, perhaps four, maybe all six, belong to Ivan. It's like trying to find a zebra in a herd of zebras."

Dent clenched fists and bit his lip. He had been out-manoeuvred. The Ivan Group clearly had an exfiltration plan in place. Secret doors. An escape route. Spare getaway vans in long-stay car parks. He blamed himself for underestimating them. Even more for allowing Emily to become involved in a mission rapidly spiralling out of control.

"Okay, George. It'll take time, but it's still worth a shot. Keep tabs on all the white vans. I want to know where all of them go, even if they end up in John o' Groats. Circulate the registration plates to the Met. I'll have a word with the chief constable. We need as many eyes on those white vans as possible. Let's get a team down to that car park."

"Already done. They've found the green vehicle. It's empty, but they're giving it a fine tooth comb search anyway."

Dent hadn't mentioned Emily, but George realised she was the reason for his tetchy mood.

"I'm sure Emily will be okay, Miles. If anything had happened, I think we would have discovered by now."

It was the sort of platitude Dent detested, but he let it go. Dent and Miller stared at the screens for a few more minutes, assimilating the scale of their task, desperate to compute where the Ivan cell may be headed. One of the analysts approached George, passing him a sheet of paper. As he absorbed the message, the colour drained from his face.

"What is it?" Miller missed nothing.

"One of our operatives has found a burnt-out white van on waste ground close to the road to Brighton."

"And?"

"There's a dead woman in the back."

29

The Lockside bar was teeming. Al Andrews and his mates had taken up residence outside, camped around a picnic table on hard bench seats.

Light drizzle had dampened the wooden furniture but the shimmering lights reflecting on the Camden canal and the brightly-coloured stalls, bars and restaurants gave the spot a holiday feel. At a hefty push, with a shaft of sunshine, it could have been a popular corner of Spain or Venice.

One of Al's pals was moving on from his university department. It would have been rude not to mark his farewell with good wishes and craft beers. As the night wore on the mood became increasingly convivial. A chorus of *Sweet Caroline* emanated from the bar. The bunch of tutors and lecturers joined in, arms swaying above their heads, a couple of them even in tune. A discussion on Neil Diamond followed.

"Great song writer."

"Yeah."

"He wrote *I'm a Believer*."

"No, that was The Monkees."

"It was Neil Diamond."

"Never. Al, who wrote …?"

Al jumped in, playing his version of Solomon, mainly because he was most sober, as well as being the guru his friends and colleagues deferred to on all things musical. "You're both right in a way. Neil Diamond wrote the song. The Monkees had a number one hit with it."

Al had not wanted to drink tonight. If the date had not been in his diary for months he would have stayed in, waiting for Emily's eight o'clock call. He was worried, the early-hours summons playing on his mind. The urgency of Emily's phone chat with Dent, followed by her rapid departure, bothered him, triggering all sorts of scenarios, none of them with positive outcomes. Which was why he had limited his drinking to two pints, determined to retain a clear head.

He stood up. "Look guys, I have to leave. Early morning tomorrow."

A predictable round of boos greeted his decision. A couple of the group begged him to stay. One of his fellow lecturers, a woman who had sampled more than a few gins, pulled at his arm. "Come on, Al, ten more minutes. We've not sung *He's a jolly good fellow* yet."

"There's a good reason for that."

Al sat back down. "Okay, ten minutes."

He used the time to canvass the group's opinion on George Michael's cover version of *You and I*, revealing it was Emily's choice for their wedding.

"That's lovely, beautiful lyrics, Al. Perfect choice," said the gin lady, raising her glass in a gesture of affirmation.

"Not too cheesy?"

"No."

"I thought you'd say that."

Twenty minutes later, after listening to a couple of slurry speeches, Al rose again. This time he was adamant, zipping up his leather jacket, pulling the collar tight. "I'm off."

He toyed with ordering an Uber, but decided to walk. The flat was no more than a mile and a half away. It would take 20 minutes at a brisk pace. Rain was falling heavier, but it was not yet unpleasant. Crossing the Lock Bridge at Camden Market, he set off for the flat, following the contour of the canal. *Red Red Wine* by UB40, another number one hit written by Neil Diamond, came to mind. He hummed a few bars, wishing he'd remembered it earlier.

Rounding a corner, the music from the bar faded, swiftly drowned out altogether by a siren wailing in the distance. Al crossed the road, entering an unlit area, streetlights temporarily out of order. A few parked cars but no moving traffic. A report of recent stabbings at Camden Lock in the *Evening Standard* came to mind, prompting his pace to quicken.

A few moments later he heard a vehicle approaching from behind, splashing through puddles, a tell-tale fizz on the wet tarmac. Out of the corner of his eye he detected the front grill of a black van, the passenger door opening before the vehicle had stopped. Despite the evening's beers, his senses were sharp and alert, courtesy of a stiff infusion of adrenalin.

For an instant, the sweep of a car's headlamps travelling in the opposite direction lit up the scene. It was all Al needed. Two figures were exiting the van, both wearing balaclavas, neither bulky of frame but moving with a lithe physicality that suggested fitness and strength. They each carried a black pistol.

Al bolted. He had stared down the barrel of a gun once before in the garden of a previous apartment. The gunman had turned out to be a protection officer from Emily's section, but Al didn't know that. The experience had left a scar. This time he could only imagine he was the potential victim of thieves on the prowl for an isolated target, or maybe a victim of mistaken identity in gang warfare. Either way, he had no intention of hanging around to find out.

As he sprinted along the pavement, no houses, only lock-up garages either side, he could hear scuffling feet chasing him. At any moment he expected a gunshot, or the searing impact of a bullet in his back. But reason cut through fear. His pursuers could not shoot while they ran. A simple calculation. Not in the dark. Not with any accuracy. He sensed he was stretching away. Al played football every Sunday morning. It wasn't the Premier League, but a decent local amateur standard. He ran three times a week to bolster his fitness levels, as well as visiting the gym on a regular basis. His mid-thirties were in the rear-view mirror, but he prided himself on retaining a semblance of youthful vigour.

Still, his lungs burned, muscles straining as he raced towards the corner at the end of the street. The fact that the masked duo continued the chase troubled him. This was not an ordinary mugging. In, out, and away, in a matter of seconds. The further he ran, the more he sensed his pursuers were on a hunt, and he was the prey. They must be mistaken. He'd heard of it before, victims shot or knifed for no apparent reason, only for loved ones to discover they had simply been the wrong person in the wrong place at the wrong time. Or could it be more sinister? Could it have something to do with Emily's rushed mission? The thought raced through his mind amid a thousand others, with no time for consideration or resolution. Survival was his prime focus.

Al knew the area well. Four possible directions would present themselves when he rounded the street corner approaching. He judged himself far enough ahead to lose the chasers in the maze of concrete estates disfiguring parts of Camden. His spirits lifted, stride lengthening, the prospect of escape flooding him with a sense of relief.

Then, suddenly, nothing. No warning. Total blackness.

Amid the dark shadows and heart-pounding panic of the chase, Al never saw the swing of the baseball bat, nor felt its crushing force. As he rounded the corner, the blow connected with his nose, jaw and cheekbone, fracturing all three, as well as displacing his right-eye socket. Mercifully, unconsciousness was instant, too fast to register pain.

***

"You've killed him. We needed him alive. You were supposed to go for the legs." A catch of alarm, verging on dread, in Katya's voice as she gazed at Al's mangled features, blood spurting from mouth, nose and ears, his flattened nose skewed at a grotesque angle.

Lily dangled the baseball bat by her side, at the same time dragging a balaclava from her head. She shook her thick golden tresses. "I've not killed him. I've just put him to sleep for a while. I doubt he'll win any beauty contests in the future, but he's still breathing. Better than putting a bullet in his back." Her tone matter-of-fact.

Katya checked Al's neck for a pulse. After a few moments, she gasped with relief, nodding at Olga, who ripped off her balaclava and stowed her gun in her jacket. The women had watched Al at the bar, setting a trap. It hinged on him taking the obvious walking route home by the canal, rather than a taxi. But once he had, and Katya and Olga had set him running towards Lily, his fate was sealed.

"I'll get the van." Olga turned, jogging back the way they had come.

Lily and Katya dragged Al's limp body, propping it against a brick wall, his head lolling as if sleeping off an alcoholic haze, like one of the area's homeless fraternity. The rain was now pelting down. Even if someone passed, clocking something untoward, they would be unlikely to stop to investigate.

A few minutes later Olga arrived with the van. It took the strength of all three women to lift Al's prone body, tossing him in the back.

"Mission accomplished. The eagle has landed." Lily chuckled, chucking in the baseball bat, the metallic clunk as it hit the side of the van echoing.

"This is all a game to you, Lily, isn't it?" A hint of reprimand in Katya's stern tone.

"Lighten up, Katya. You know what they say in England. It takes a lot more muscles to frown than to smile."

"Where I come from they say a friend's frown is better than a fool's smile."

"Stop arguing. Let's get out of here." Olga cut through the banter. The women piled into the van.

30

Every pitch of the van detonated grenades of pain in Al's head. Grievous pain, a sort he had never encountered before. Not even when he broke his leg as a schoolboy playing football, his teammates carrying him home, each jog sparking another wave of nausea. This was worse.

He slithered in and out of consciousness, one moment trying to figure why his hands were tied behind his back, why he couldn't breathe through his nose or see through his left eye, the next singing *Sweet Caroline* in his dreams, back at the pub when all seemed well with his world.

A scary image of two pursuers carrying guns pestered his brain. Nothing made sense. Maybe he'd been shot. Stabbed. Mugged. Perhaps a road accident. Maybe he was on his way to hospital. But this didn't feel like an ambulance. He drifted again, in his mind singing, trying to remember other famous songs written by Neil Diamond.

The van braked hard, the jerk dragging Al back to awareness. He heard a metal barrier creaking open, the bright timbre of women's voices. Someone said *Litvinenko,* at least that's how it sounded. The word seared through his pain, but he had no idea why, or if his memory was real or imaginary.

The engine revved, the van trundled on, but no longer at speed, stopping a few minutes later. A draught swirled as the van doors opened. Al felt himself hauled feet first, hands grabbing his arms. Soft hands, sharp nails. A woman's hands. His legs gave way. He fell to one knee, disorientated, but more hands helped pull him upright, leading him down a passage, the crunching sound of wet gravel underfoot, a narrow torch beam searching the shadows, lighting the way.

Struggling to breathe, his one good eye sticky with blood, a firm shoulder barged him towards a portico, the distinctive triangular shape of an Egyptian pediment forming the upper part. The image was blurry but somehow pleasing. Brushing against the walls he sensed stone. Slabs of stone with boxes either side, perhaps a dozen, some with ornate carvings. The space contained no homely frills, no furniture, nothing but ice-cold darkness.

They edged to the back of the room, the torch catching mist on their breath, casting eerie figures on the walls. Turning left, they stumbled through another doorway, down three steps. At the bottom, Al's last dregs of strength expired. He slumped dead-weight to the hard ground. The hands let him fall. He lay there, not knowing, nor even caring, whether he lived or died. All he wanted was sleep.

A woman's voice told him to stand but she might as well have asked him to part the Red Sea. He felt himself dragged once more, this time into a corner where the women propped him against the angle of two walls.

The torch beam dazzled his eye. He heard one of the women whisper, although the echo magnified the sound.

"We need a picture, Katya."

"No names."

"The state he's in, I don't think that matters."

The shape of a smart phone came into focus, silhouetted against the torchlight, Al leering into the lens as the flash stole his night vision.

One of the women knelt, reached behind him, cutting the tape tying his hands. Another threw a blanket over him, leaving a small plastic bottle of water.

"Okay, let's get out of here."

He heard scuffling feet, the metallic slam of both doors, sliding bolts, a heavy key in a lock, followed by comparative silence, apart from the hiss of his breathing competing with an unnerving scratching noise on the other side of the room of animal origin.

For several minutes he sat there, chin on chest, a thunderclap headache bursting his brain, still oblivious to the events that had seen him leave a convivial drinks party and end up … where? He had no idea.

He pulled the blanket around him, staring into the blackness, trying for many more minutes to piece together scraps of information.

What did *Litvinenko* mean? His instinct told him the reference must concern Alexander Litvinenko, a former officer of the Russian security services, a prominent critic of President Putin. Litvinenko defected to Britain, dying after being poisoned with polonium-210 at a London hotel. But why was Litvinenko relevant? Again, he wondered if it could have something to do with Emily. The world she inhabited was full of dark forces. The work call in the middle of the night. The unexpected trip. The fact she couldn't use her phone and would be out of contact for a few days. And she had history, a sinister history, with Russians ever since she had helped track down Andrei Reblov.

Maybe it was all an illusion, a mish-mash of unconnected thoughts and distant memories, triggered by his injuries, famous names popping into his mind for no reason. A trick of a damaged brain.

The hours passed. He strained to take a swig of water but opening his mouth even a fraction caused an explosion of pain of such magnitude that he made do with drizzling it over his lips. Even so, he was grateful, drops trickling through to his tongue, the liquid sweet against the bitter, coppery taste of blood. For the rest of the night he drifted alternately between wakeful agony and agitated oblivion, snatches of unconsciousness becoming more frequent.

After one of the longer periods of sleep, he jerked awake, the sudden clarity of his thoughts taking him by surprise. This time he knew for certain where he was imprisoned. The realisation sent shudders down his spine.

31

Dent sat with Jane Miller and C at one end of the table, Chief Constable Anderson and JIC chairman Sir Ralph Short at the other.

They indulged in awkward small-talk for five minutes before Matt Jennings popped his head around the door.

"Good, I've gotten the right room at least. Howdy. Hope I'm not late." The head of the CIA's London station had the infuriating characteristic of never seeming to take anything seriously which, added to his reputation for unpunctuality, did not endear him to C, or anybody else in charge of the UK's defence and intelligence departments.

A larger-than-life character, in both frame and personality, he relied on bluff and bluster, which probably was viewed as an asset in his home state of Texas.

"What can I do for y'all?"

"I'm afraid it's what we can do for you, Matt." C's grave tone instantly wiped the almost-permanent grin from Jennings' face. "We have reason to believe one of your undercover agents has been murdered. I'll let Dent here explain."

Dent clicked the tablet in front of him, an image appearing on the screen on the wall, a fresh-faced woman with dark spiky hair.

Jennings immediately looked perplexed, a flicker of recognition combined with trepidation, a hand going to his mouth to try to hide his obvious shock.

Dent began. "We believe this is …"

"Sophie. Sophie Austin. One of our most trusted and bravest agents." Jennings broke in. He obviously knew her well.

"The papers found on her say Zofia Kowalski."

Jennings nodded. "She's … she was Polish. Or her dad was. Her mother is American, born in England. Dual nationality. Actually, triple nationality. American, British, and Polish passports. She'd been under cover for an extended period with a Russian-based group. Making good progress, although she did have a tendency to go off-piste, if you get my drift. Had to have words with her on a few occasions. Kowalski's not her real Polish name, of course. This is dreadful. What happened to her? Any ideas?"

Dent tried to bite his lip, but the stress of the last couple of days erupted, hissing its way to the surface in a bilious outpouring. "If you'd told us what she was doing, or bothered to come to the last meeting of the JIC, you lazy, self-righteous shit, she might not be lying in a morgue right now. And one of our best agents would not be missing, probably having suffered the same fate."

Dent's cheeks burned bright red. Miller had never seen him as angry. This was Dent, rarely agitated, always composed, the man whose measured view on life acted like a soothing balm to those around him. She thought C would intervene, but he didn't. The chief sensed Dent had to let it out. Exorcise the guilt he felt over exposing Emily and Baker to the Ivan executioners.

When news had broken about the dead woman in the white van, Dent had raced out of the office, jumped in a car and sped towards Brighton. He didn't wait for Miller. He was desperate to see with his own eyes. All the way he berated himself, pounding the steering wheel with his fists.

When he arrived, police had set up a cordon around the blackened vehicle. A stench of burning rubber filled the air even though the fire brigade had hosed it down. Dent presented his SIS warrant card, police allowing him through the cordon. A forensics team in white boiler suits were on site, a photographer taking pictures from various angles. As the doors were open, the detective team allowed Dent to view the van's contents, amounting to little more than a pile of ash from incinerated carpet material and a shrivelled corpse. The body was propped in a back corner, one arm extended, torso blackened and blistered, facial features unrecognisable.

The chief crime scene investigator warned post-mortem computed tomography would be required for precise analysis, but when pressed confirmed it was a woman. A woman with a bullet in her head. At that point, Dent experienced an instinctive spasm of dread, a foreboding he could barely contain, followed almost immediately by a rush of euphoria, with associated shame, when he learned the dead woman had dark, spiky, hair. It wasn't Emily.

That's when SIS had got lucky. It could have taken days to track down Zofia's true identity. The van, stolen two days ago, contained few clues apart from one crucial discovery on moving the body. A charred passport tucked away in a slim metal cigarette case, spotted by an eagle-eyed investigator, concealed in a secret thigh pocket. It had survived the worst of the inferno, mostly due to the case's metal coating and the fact that it was pressed to the floor of the van, under the weight of the body, below the most intense heat.

The name, Zofia Kowalski, meant nothing, but one of the analysts at HQ had a hunch, running Zofia's picture through American, as well as UK, records of Polish immigrants. The facial recognition technology captured an instant match, Zofia Kowalski becoming Sophie Austin, an employee of the United States government.

Jennings had confirmed what SIS already knew. Unfortunately, he could add little more. Sophie had supplied details on Roman Smirnov, the configuration of the Ivan cell and the mystery surrounding Shelkunchik. But that's what it remained. A mystery, albeit a mystery with a ticking time clock. Under more probing, Jennings also admitted the CIA had given Sophie permission to take part in illegal activities to preserve and consolidate her cover without fear of prosecution by the United States. Such immunity was not unusual. SIS did much the same for UK agents under cover in nations across the globe. It was the pragmatic way to fight international terrorists. The fast route to getting results.

An embarrassed silence followed Dent's outburst. The chief constable dived in to exploit the gap, jabbing a forefinger on the table for emphasis.

"It's about time everyone put their cards on the table here. I don't know what games you all think you're playing, but as far as I can see two people have been murdered on my streets while you lot have been scoring points off each other. I need to know what's going on."

C coughed. "You're right, Mark. We all need to be singing the same tune."

C admitted Baker, *teacher man* from Mario's café, was part of the surveillance group monitoring the Ivan cell in Chelsea, murdered almost certainly after the group rumbled his identity. It seemed Sophie Austin, aka Zofia, had suffered the same fate. To demonstrate the cell's ingenuity and meticulous preparation, it had immediately evacuated The Salon, performing an intricate exfiltration.

"Let's not sugar-coat this. You mean the terrorists have given you the slip. You've cocked up big time. Lost not one, but two agents. And somewhere on the streets of London we have a bunch of professional killers. Armed. Dangerous. Prepared to kill anyone who gets in their way." There was a heavy hint of derision in the chief constable's tone.

C bristled. "I wouldn't quite put it like that, but yes, broadly those are the facts."

Dent jumped in. "Apart from the most important detail."

"What's that?" said the chief constable.

"We have a missing agent. An operative of the highest calibre. If the Ivan Group knew Emily's identity, why didn't they dispose of her along with Sophie? That would have been the smart, as well as the obvious, thing to do. My bet is that the blood we found in The Salon is Sophie's. She was shot in Chelsea, driven out of town, then dumped in the burnt-out white van."

"So where is your missing agent?" This time Sir Ralph provided the question.

"Three possibilities," said Dent. "One, she's already been disposed of like Sophie and we haven't found her yet. Two, they don't know her identity, she's still undercover, unable to contact us, although that scenario is highly unlikely given what happened to Baker. Three, they know exactly who she is, and she's being held captive."

Miller spoke for the first time. "We're working on the third option."

"What makes you favour that?" The chief constable looked puzzled.

"Emily is an operative with many talents, including powers of deduction rare in our murky world. If they know who she is, they may believe she could be an asset to them."

"A bargaining tool, you mean."

"Perhaps. Or maybe someone they could turn. It's happened before."

Dent shook his head. "I'm sure they couldn't turn Emily. What Jane's saying is that we believe she's still alive, remaining so until she's no longer of use to them. We have to find her before that happens."

32

The last thing Emily wanted leaving with were her thoughts. But they were all she had for company in that room with no windows, no books. Not even a pencil or a piece of paper.

All night the same sequence infected her brain. *Teacher man* dead. Zofia dead. The shot. The blood. The terror of the van ride, convinced each stop meant a bullet in the head. The letter. The code. The chilling look on Smirnov's face.

She was sure she would never sleep but she must have done. When the key turned in the lock she jolted awake, propped herself up on an elbow, head full of fog and fear.

"What time is it?"

"Seven o'clock." Olga in the doorway, gun in hand. She tossed a bottle of mineral water. Emily caught it, tore off the top, glugging for several seconds, the cooling liquid swilling away the stale taste of a tortured night.

"Smirnov wants to see you."

"Tell him I'll think about it."

"It doesn't work like that, Emily. Smirnov gets what he wants when he wants."

"I was joking, Olga. I think I've worked out exactly what sort of man Smirnov is. Remember, I was there when he ordered the murder of Zofia."

A tilt of Olga's pistol signalled Emily to stand.

"Do you really need to wave that thing around?" Emily pointed at the gun.

"Concentrates our minds on what side we're on. And it wasn't murder. This is war. We are soldiers. Zofia was going to kill Smirnov."

"Smirnov ordered Zofia to kill me. She didn't know there were no bullets in that gun. I'm not a soldier. I'm a woman who's trying to do her best to stop people like you killing for no reason. Why are you doing this, Olga? It can't just be for money. You're not like Lily and Katya, I can tell. You don't believe in Smirnov. You don't even like him."

"Who says you have to like your boss? Do you like yours?"

The image of Dent's kindly face came to mind. She wondered where he was. What he was doing to try to find her. She knew the SIS watchers would have reported the flight from The Salon. Even now she felt sure a special forces detail would be primed, ready to strike. All they required was the location. Yet, even though she sensed they were no more than ten miles from central London, she had no idea in what direction.

Emily dragged herself off the mattress, slipped feet into flat shoes, ran fingers through her hair and brushed past Olga.

Smirnov was waiting in the lounge, a huge oval room, full of ostentatious grandeur, two intricate chandeliers sparkling from the ornate ceiling. He was dressed formally in a dark three-piece suit and crisp white shirt despite the early hour. Katya and Lily were also present, admiring panoramic views of the manicured gardens, watching a soaring red kite sizing up its breakfast. Artwork adorned the walls.

"I trust you slept well, Emily." Smirnov's greeting was civil, warm even. Emily ignored the remark.

Smirnov sat in a deep red leather armchair by the inglenook. He signalled for Emily to sit opposite. A huge oil painting depicting an old man cradling a stricken younger man in his arms dominated the wall above the fireplace. Blood poured from the younger man's head wound.

"Are you familiar with this painting?" He pointed at the canvas. Emily nodded. Her Russian studies at SIS had featured iconic cultural milestones, including the music and artwork commemorating them.

"It's by Ilya Repin."

"Very impressive, Emily. Not many from the West would know that. In that case, I won't insult you by asking if you know the story behind it."

The picture depicted Russian Tsar, Ivan the Terrible, cradling his dying son, Ivan, in his arms after he had struck a fatal blow to his son's head in a fit of anger in 1581. Emily didn't tell Smirnov, but the image also featured in her Uncle Sebastian's book, *The Two Ivans*.

"I know the Tsar killed his son. It's what happens when brutal men allow pride and temper to control their actions." Emily had formed her opinion of the Russian Tsars long ago.

Smirnov's head tilted to the left. A natural affliction, as if sifting his thoughts, providing a chute from which they could slide out. "That's a fair point," he said. "But Ivan was not just a man, he was a Tsar, a leader of men. Sometimes, brutality is a legitimate tool. Sometimes, greatness can only be achieved by resorting to brutality."

He spotted Emily's sneer.

"You think I'm wrong."

"Keep telling yourself that, if you like. I think you're deluded."

"Tell me, Emily, is the killing of more than two hundred thousand men, women and children an act of brutality?"

"Of course."

"Yet the only nation to carry out such an act is the United States of America, supposedly the land of the free, the so-called protectors of justice and liberty. I wonder if that went through President Truman's mind when he cleared the Enola Gay for take-off to drop Little Boy in 1945."

The detail in Smirnov's words perplexed Emily. It was unnecessary. Not everyone knew, or wanted to remember, the name of the plane that dropped the first atomic bomb. Nor would everyone be able to recall the codename for the bomb itself, even if both were punctuation marks in the history of war.

Smirnov was drawing Emily in. She felt obliged to respond. "It's a tired argument to make out that America is the bad guy, just as it's facile to say that dropping the bomb shortened the war and saved many lives. War is more nuanced that that."

"Tell that to the people of Hiroshima and Nagasaki, some of whom are still dying today because of the fall-out. There isn't much nuance in death."

Smirnov sat back, gazing at the picture. He continued.

"Of course, Ivan was brutal, but he was also an accomplished leader, a man who transformed Russia from a medieval state into a great empire. We have him to thank for the autocratic rule that has dominated Russian government for the past five hundred years."

"There are many, most of Ukraine for a start, who would dispute that."

A derisive wave of Smirnov's hand dismissed Emily's argument.

"People can see the original of this painting in the State Tretyakov Gallery in Moscow. Not many know, but the canvas is owned these days by Ivan Petrovich. He bought it so that as many people as possible could be inspired by its dramatic beauty. He is committed to keeping it on display, such is his generosity." Smirnov cupped his hands, tilting them upwards in a praying motion.

It was probably the moment Emily truly recognised the depth of the irrational, depraved values that drove Smirnov and the Ivan Group.

This is madness. He's using a father's senseless, psychotic slaying of his son in the 16th Century as an example of how to live and rule in the 21st Century. He has to be stopped. The Ivan Group has to be stopped.

"But enough art talk, Emily. I have some different pictures to show you."

He motioned to Katya, who ambled over to a writing desk, fiddling with the keys of a laptop computer for a few seconds. The big television screen in the corner of the room nearest Emily flickered.

It took her many seconds to realise what she was looking at. At first she thought Smirnov was endeavouring to make another philosophical point. The figure on the screen resembled a bombing victim, the injuries so extensive that it was almost impossible to determine the nationality, or even the gender.

Face grotesquely swollen, teeth shattered, one eye totally shut, a lump the size of a tennis ball deforming the features, the other eye staring dull and vacant into the lens. Blood everywhere. Emily turned away.

"Take another look." Smirnov's tone cold and insistent.

This time Emily's gaze dropped to the bottom half of the picture showing the blood-stained white t-shirt the figure was wearing. She could make out writing, numbers and words, a motif perhaps, although the blood smears made it difficult to decipher. Straining her eyes, she mouthed the inscription as it came slowly into focus.

5 out of 4 people struggle with maths

"Al." Emily shrieked. Panic and horror. "You've killed Al."

33

"Let's not be dramatic. Mr Andrews still lives and breathes. For now, at least." Smirnov tried to calm Emily, but she couldn't hear anything.

Her ears filled with thunder, eyes misted with emotion, heart pounding as she recognised the t-shirt she'd bought for Al's birthday. She thought she must surely pass out. All the training in the world could not prepare her for this. The man she loved. The only man she'd ever loved beaten within an inch of his life, it seemed, as a lever to get to her. The guilt was desperate.

"Breathe." Olga put a hand on her shoulder. "Breathe, Emily. Deep breaths. He's alive."

It took many gulps for Emily to calm her panic, but when she did she threw a look of evil intent in Smirnov's direction. "You bastard. You absolute bastard."

"Now, now, Emily. You did this, not me."

"What? … Why?"

"When we spoke of my proposition in Chelsea you said nothing I could say would change your mind. I believed you. You're a determined, headstrong woman. So I had to do something. Something that would concentrate your mind on the job in hand. Now, I hope we can talk again."

Emily recalled the conversation about the Letter of Last Resort, the Ivan Group's wish to crack the code, the fact that she was probably the only person who could decipher it.

"Al has nothing to do with any of this. He's a sweet guy who teaches maths and minds his own business. Let him go. Please. Just let him go."

Even as she pleaded, she recalled her training. The fact that successful pleading with terrorists in hostage situations depended on encouraging negotiation, building rapport, defusing heated emotions through the passage of time. She remembered the statistics. Around 80 per cent of hostages escape unharmed. She also remembered that successful negotiation depended on the negotiator not judging or emotionally attacking the perpetrator.

Fighting for calm, she banished evil thoughts, concentrating on the way forward.

"What do you want me to do?"

"That's better, Emily." Smirnov eased forward in his chair, seeking to gauge from Emily's eyes whether acquiescence was real or fake. "As before, we need help with Shelkunchik. We need the code. I will supply a copy of the Letter of Last Resort, you will extract the code and the set of co-ordinates it represents."

"What will you do with it?"

"You asked this before. It's not your concern. Our aim is not to kill people. Our one objective is to demonstrate that Russia is the arbiter of justice, the nation with ultimate authority when it comes to world affairs." He almost preened, as if imagining the medal that surely would be pinned to his breast if he could relay the code to the Russian president.

"What if I can't crack the code?"

"Then I will have no way of knowing whether that is truthfully the case, or whether you are pretending. In that case, I will have no choice but to assume the latter. You have 48 hours to deliver."

Emily drew a long breath, gritting her teeth. The contents of the letter swirled around her brain, photographic memory providing every detail. Much had happened in the last two days but normally a complex code would embed in her head, her subconscious mind assimilating its complexities, working behind the scenes, before spewing out the solution. What if she genuinely couldn't master this one?

She played for time. "You can't put a figure on how long it takes to crack a code. There are many variables. It could take weeks, months."

"You have 48 hours."

"That's ridiculous. Only an idiot …" Emily tried to snatch back that dagger, laden as it was with fire and judgement, but already it had skewered its target. Smirnov bridled.

"Let me say this nicely once more, Emily. I'll make it as plain as I can, so there can be no room for doubt. Forty-eight hours, not a minute longer, or you and your fiancé take a bullet to the head."

Emily fixed his gaze with a steely stare of her own, mindful that hostage negotiation was an intricate exercise of give and take, only successful if neither side occupied entrenched positions. If she could force Smirnov to budge a little, maybe she could persuade him to shift even further later.

"Okay, forty-eight hours, but that time starts when I see Al breathing and talking with my own eyes. For all I know he could be dead already."

"I can assure you that is not the case, although without prompt medical treatment that could become a concern."

Emily shivered. She fought to stem another wave of anxiety. Al's wounds appeared serious. He must have lost much blood. Suffered a brain injury perhaps. She had no time to waste. While her domestic head screamed in terrified concern for her fiancé, her SIS training told her she needed an element of control. She reiterated her demand.

"I see Al alive and well, moving, talking, or you can whistle for your code."

Smirnov glanced at Katya and Lily.

"See to it."

34

Sheer exhaustion eventually acted as the most efficient painkiller. Al was thankful. It meant the night passed more swiftly than he could have imagined.

Not that there were any clues to dawn. No chink of light penetrated the stone walls of his dungeon. He tried to stand on several occasions, but while his legs felt strong enough, his brain swam, dizzy, confused, pitching him back, his head banging against the wall, causing searing pain, the resulting wave of nausea taking many minutes to subside.

Shouting for help, even if he could shout, would be fruitless, the stone slabs too thick. He had mused on the sheer density of those slabs in the blackness, recalling flashes of lucidity in his memory of being half-lifted and dragged into his prison.

The fleeting image of the triangular pediment over the portico refused to leave, reminding him of geometry lessons, the times he had messed around with compass and set square, studying the mathematical genius of the ancient Egyptians.

It was the pediment that convinced Al he knew where he was.

Buoyed with enthusiasm as a young lecturer, he had taken delight in introducing his university students to the pioneering work of William Kingdom Clifford, a 19th Century mathematician and philosopher, also a professor of mathematics at University College London. Al liked to think he was following in his footsteps. Explaining Clifford's concept of geometric algebra to his class, however, proved somewhat dry. Vectors spanning an n-dimensional parallelotope had limited appeal. As an antidote, Al told tales of Clifford's life. How he survived a shipwreck off the Sicilian coast, wrote a collection of children's fairy stories, died at the age of 34 on the island of Madeira after contracting tuberculosis.

Clifford became something of a hero to Al's tutorial group. Which was why Al was persuaded to lead a pilgrimage to his grave in Highgate cemetery. Al's group, having photographed Clifford's modest tombstone, had taken the opportunity to visit one of

London's more iconic architectural structures nearby, the Circle of Lebanon, a set of burial vaults full of Egyptian pediments, identical to the one at the portico of Al's dungeon.

Not that knowing his location helped. It meant he was imprisoned with the dead of three centuries, unable to stand, as incapable of escape as the bones in the caskets keeping him company. Survival logic told him not to dwell on such thoughts. Already, he had dissected the events he could remember from the night before so often, exhausting all possibilities to what was happening, that he deemed it more beneficial to think of good times.

So he waited, his fate in the hands of whoever had brought him to this place of eternal darkness. He pulled the blanket over his head, a makeshift tent capturing his body heat, shielding the mustiness, bringing a fleeting, if false, sense of security.

The memory of his mother, Lena, brought comfort. She had fled Moscow for Latvia as a child after her own mother had disappeared following the assassination of a high-ranking Kremlin officer, Igor Kalenkov, in the crumbling final throes of the Soviet Union.

By a quirk of fate, combined with a small helping of design, meeting Emily had filled some of the frustrating gaps in the family history of Alexei Andreyevich, for that was the name on Al's birth certificate. He discovered that his grandmother, Anna, and Emily's Uncle Sebastian, a history professor cum reluctant SIS agent, knew each other. Anna had acted as Sebastian's guide and handler in Moscow in 1981 during the mission to take out Kalenkov.

Could history have prompted the current episode? Would the Kremlin seek revenge on a family member who wasn't even born and had no direct involvement in events that happened the best part of half a century ago? Al dismissed the notion. Even in the paranoid world of Russian leaders such a prospect seemed far-fetched to the point of fantasy. Kidnapping Alexei Andreyevich, or Al Andrews, made no sense.

The turn of a key, harsh slide of a metal bolt, followed by the clatter of boots on the inner stone floor, interrupted Al's musing.

The iron door swung open, a light, much brighter than the torch beam of the night before, illuminated the room. Even more Spartan than he anticipated. Bare grey walls, cobwebs covering the ceiling like linen shrouds. The floor covered in building debris.

"Rise and shine." The mundane jolliness of Lily's greeting in an accent he couldn't place perplexed Al. He blinked, his one seeing eye blinded temporarily by the light.

He heard a scrape of wood and metal on the stone floor. When his eye became accustomed to the light he saw two women. One of them held a pistol. Both wore gardening clothes, waterproof jackets over green dungarees, with green wellington boots that came half-way up their calves.

"He doesn't look well." There was a tremor of concern in Olga's voice.

"He's still with us, isn't he? That's the main thing."

Olga knelt beside Al. Taking a sponge from a shoulder bag, she gently wiped crusted blood from his mouth and nose. He winced, yet found comfort in her touch, any human contact preferable to the fears and traumas of the night before. She raised the bottle of water to his lips. This time he sucked it down, even though the cold liquid set his broken teeth on edge.

"What's … that?" Al's voice no more than a weak croak, forced through tight lips, his fractured jaw unable to move. He pointed to Lily, who was busy setting up a tripod and camera on the other side of the room.

"We're going to make you a star." A callous chuckle in Lily's teasing response.

"Don't worry. We're going to put you in touch with Emily. She wants to see you. I'm sure you'd like to talk to her." Olga's voice calm, her explanation more sympathetic.

Despite his fog of confusion, Al's mind raced, his spirits lifting. He was going to see, maybe even speak to Emily. His main worry over the last few hours was that some catastrophic misfortune had befallen her. She hadn't clocked in with her usual phone code. He knew there were many reasons for an SIS officer going dark, but Al's main fear since Emily had chosen her unconventional way in life was always that she could become a target for terrorists. His elation at hearing her name was tempered by the fact that his jailers were obviously in control. The beating, the dungeon, the camera. This had the smell of a hostage situation. If he was the hostage and was going to speak to Emily, then the probability was that she was a hostage too. A simple mathematical equation. Al's forte had always been logic. Logic also told him something even more sinister. His jailers were not hooded. They were not hiding their identity. That could mean only one thing. Al pushed the thought to the back of his mind.

"The Circle of Lebanon." Al's slurry utterance was no more than a whisper, but Lily heard it. She strode from behind the tripod, kneeling beside Olga.

"What did you say?"

Al pointed at the floor, repeating the phrase. "The Circle of Lebanon."

"How do you know?" Lily shook Al's shoulders so hard that Olga intervened, shielding him with a straight arm.

"Leave him, you've done enough damage already."

"But he knows where we are. He knows this place. If he knows that, what else does he know?"

Olga's eyes darted from Lily to Al.

"Where are we, Al? What does the Circle of Lebanon mean?"

Al was drifting into unconsciousness, the puzzle of the boxes he'd spotted at the entrance, solved. Coffins. Lead-lined, ornate coffins. Probably a whole family, spanning three generations or more. The effort of memorising, concentrating and speaking was too taxing for Al's bruised brain.

"Stick with it, Al. Don't go to sleep on us." Olga poured water over his face, into his mouth. Al choked back the liquid, but his good eye opened.

"Quick, Lily, let's get him onto the chair."

They hauled him to his feet, heaving him onto the wooden chair they had brought with them. Olga held on to him, placing his hands on his thighs until she was confident he was steady. She took the front cover of that day's edition of the *Evening Standard* out of her bag, folding the top edge inside his t-shirt like a baby's bib, so the splash headline was easily visible.

Mortgage Misery For Millions.

"Okay Al, we want you to look into the camera, to say a few words to Emily. Tell her how much you love her, that sort of thing, you can't wait to see her again."

Lily bent down, whispering in Al's ear, pinning a microphone to his tee shirt, pistol pressed against his right temple. "No dodgy business. No trying to tell her where you are. No questions of any sort, or I'll shoot you here and now. Got it?"

Al nodded. Olga set the camera rolling. Lily nudged Al's shoulder with her gun, signalling him to speak.

The words were little more than a hoarse croak, Al's mouth fixed like a ventriloquist, leaning forward slightly on his hands to balance, an anxious twitch now and then, but sentiments expressed with his usual light touch.

"Hello Emily. It's Al here. I don't think I'm looking or sounding my best at the moment. But please don't worry about me. I'm in safe hands and I hope you are too. Hope to see you soon for a good catch-up. If you ..."

"That's enough." Lily yanked the microphone from his t-shirt.

They lowered Al on to the floor, took the chair away but left another blanket along with two bottles of water.

"Well done, Al. That was perfect." Olga gave him a sweet smile. Lily rolled her eyes.

***

When they had packed up the camera, bolted and locked both doors and loaded up the black van, Olga fixed Lily with a puzzled expression.

"What's the Circle of Lebanon?"

Lily laughed. "Sounds a bit more exotic than it actually is. You're standing in it."

"Pardon."

"Yeah. This is it. The Circle of Lebanon. Some say Highgate Cemetery's most spectacular feature."

"But why Lebanon?"

With a sweep of an arm, Lily invited Olga to look around. "Because all these vaults, catacombs, mausoleums, sunken tombs, whatever you want to call them, were originally built around the roots of an enormous cedar of Lebanon tree. More than one hundred and fifty years old. It was ageing and decaying so much that it was chopped down not long ago. The vault we're using is one of the bigger family ones, although it was sealed up years ago and is unlikely to have any more additions."

"How did you know about it?"

Lily explained she had worked at Highgate Cemetery for almost a year as part of the environmental renovation team, thinning out and clearing trees suffering ash die-back. The plan was to promote distant views of St Paul's Cathedral and other iconic landmarks in central London. The work was suspended because of the coronavirus pandemic.

"I enjoyed it. Didn't pay much, well, not compared to Ivan. But I nicked some gate and vault keys. Thought they might come in handy. When I heard they were shutting the place to the public for a few weeks for more extensive landscaping it seemed the perfect solution. On the doorstep. The bulk of the heavy work starts in a week's time. We'll be long gone by then."

"What about CCTV. Does no one monitor for vandals? It's one of the world's most famous cemeteries."

"The main entrance is full of cameras. That's why we came in via the temporary entrance off Swain's Lane. The contractors have had to demolish part of the wall so they can get the big cranes through next week. Couldn't be more helpful. A makeshift barrier in place. A soft spot. If anyone challenges us, we've got spades and forks in the van. We're part of the gardening team, aren't we?" Lily did a little jig, nodding to the green garb they both wore.

Olga studied the vista. It was hard to imagine seeing St Paul's, the Shard, or any of London's iconic landmarks through the dense panoply of decaying trees, overgrown ferns and organic detritus before them. The cemetery had hit hard times in recent years. It was running out of space, no longer a profit-making concern, as it had been for the private owners of old. The dead appeared to have taken over. Probably would have done for eternity if the Friends of Highgate Cemetery, a charity concern, had not rescued it in the 1970s, renovating graves, monuments and buildings, transforming it into a recreational enclave of historic importance. One that relied on entrance charges, guided tours and exorbitant burial fees to pay its way. Much work still remained. Parts resembled a jungle. Yet, somehow, it retained a magical, mystical quality.

"It will take forever to clear this. It must be costing a fortune." Olga whistled through her teeth.

Lily drawled. "The dead pay enough to get in here. It's only right they get a good view."

They jumped in the vehicle. Olga revved the engine. There was still something troubling her.

"How did Al know? How did he know where we were?"

"I wondered that too. I think I've worked it out."

"Go on."

"Your big mouth."

"Pardon."

"Litvinenko. On the way here last night you said this was where Litvinenko was buried. And Katya mentioned him too. Al must have heard. He might have a face like a squashed melon but there's nothing wrong with his ears. He's sharp. Maybe he's been here before. Or he just knows this is where Litvinenko was buried, along with all sorts of famous people."

"Like Karl Marx," said Olga.

"Now there's a revolutionary socialist for you."

"Do you think he would have approved of Ivan?"

Lily cackled, punching the air. "Up the workers. Working women of all countries unite."

35

"You look like …" Miller decided to abandon the simile.

"Go on, say it."

"Okay, Miles, you look like you could use a cup of coffee."

"That's not what you were going to say."

"Have you been home?" It was seven o'clock. A watery sun had only recently decided to get up.

Dent didn't respond. His creased white shirt flapped out of his trousers, hair hung lank and greasy, streaks of grey in two-day stubble glinted in the office light. He slumped in his chair, dragged both hands down his face, massaging his eyes, rubbing, kneading, trying to erase the tiredness induced by eight hours searching CCTV tapes.

Miller glanced at his computer screen. "For God's sake, Miles, tell me you haven't been here all night."

A prolonged yawn followed by a sheepish grin supplied Dent's answer.

"We have analysts coming out of our ears to do that sort of work. All of them with younger, keener, eyes than you."

"All right, Jane, don't rub it in. I'm not that old. I was trying to help."

"Found anything?"

Dent shrugged. "Nothing definite. The Met have ruled out three of the white vans from the Mayfair car park. Then there's the burnt-out one. That leaves two."

"Can't be long before we track them down, although they could be miles up the motorways by now."

"Hmm, maybe." Dent's gaze was distant. Something was troubling him.

"What is it, Miles?"

He sat up, motioning for Miller to watch. Pressing keys, he zeroed in on a white van negotiating the junction connecting London's Holloway Road and Archway before proceeding up the A1.

"This was one of the vans out of Mayfair. Easy to track all the way to this point. Picked up at all the major junctions." He switched screens, pressing more keys. "The next CCTV point is a few hundred yards up the road. Should take a matter of seconds. But the van never arrives."

"Must have stopped or turned off somewhere."

"Maybe. That's what I thought. The thing is, it does pass that exact camera half an hour later. What was it doing for half an hour? That doesn't feel like a getaway vehicle."

"Probably because it wasn't."

Dent sat back, scratching his nose, more in contemplation than to relieve an itch.

"I'm not sure, Jane. Why pick a plain white van?" He didn't allow her time to respond, instead supplying his own answer. "Because they are everywhere. They're like rats of the road. You're never more than about six feet away from one. Unobtrusive and unremarkable. No distinguishing characteristics. All pretty much the same. Put yourself in Ivan's shoes. They know we're on to them. Probably expect us to be tracking every road with every camera at our disposal. So what happens if the white van stops for half an hour?"

Miller set down her bag on the desk. Dent's logic suddenly clicked.

"Twenty or more white vans go by," she said. "The chances are CCTV will not catch all the registrations. Too many lorries and buses forming sightscreens. It means all those vans have to be tracked, too, because they could have switched plates."

Animation glinted in Dent's eyes, his drowsiness banished as he sensed Miller accepting and advancing his theory. "Exactly. They know how we work, Jane, how the Met work too. It's a simple trick, but effective. Their aim is to spread confusion."

"Any ideas where the white van goes?" Miller cut to the end point.

"I don't know exactly, but we've confirmed they are false plates. Not unusual in London, but a bit too coincidental in this case. What I do know is that the van doesn't reach the North Circular, because I sat up all night checking that junction, ticking off every white van that crossed it in the appropriate time frame. My hunch is that our van turns off the main drag somewhere between Archway and the North Circular, out of camera range. The fact that it hasn't been spotted by the Met probably means it's still in that area."

"Or changed its plates."

"True, but just about every police force in the land is now checking white van man's plates. Any false ones would be pulled over. I think they're holed up not far away."

"Still a big area."

"Yep."

"They may have switched vehicles again."

"Yep."

"You could have been up all night for nothing."

Dent threw her a look that could have cracked concrete. He knew well enough there was no certainty in the job of intelligence.

Miller headed for the door. "Tell you what, I'll go and make that cup of coffee."

36

On the surface, Emily appeared calm and composed. Underneath, her stomach churned. Her periodic table technique barely touched her anxiety as Katya set up the computer to show the video of Al.

They were in the television room, although *television* didn't do the enormous screen justice. It was fixed on brackets to the wall with seats set out in four rows on a gentle incline cinema-style. The room had no windows. Olga and Lily sat either side of Emily like prison guards, even though there was no prospect of escape.

"Anyone for popcorn?" Lily chuckled at her own quip. No one responded, although Emily thought she detected a frustrated sigh from Olga.

A couple of minutes later Smirnov appeared, dressed immaculately as usual. He sat to one side and signalled to Katya. The lights dimmed, the big screen flickered.

Emily had steeled herself for what she might find. From the still pictures she realised Al was badly injured, but even so the shock of seeing him struck her like a punch to the solar plexus. The camera was rolling before Al began talking, Olga having zoomed in to adjust the focus. His face appeared twice its normal size. The fractures were obvious, misshapen nose and cheek, the shut eye weeping blood and water, bruising already black or purple.

What must he have gone through? The pain, the fear, the worry. All because of me. I'm sorry, Al. I'm sorry. You don't deserve this.

"Oh, Al." She couldn't help it. The whimper escaped, natural and inadvertent as the guilt rose in her belly. She stemmed a trickle from her nose with a tissue. For a moment she could have lost it, succumbed to the horror of it all. But her training kicked in. By the time she saw Lily press the pistol against Al's temple, she had composed herself, concentrating her photographic memory to capture every nuance. *Information is a weapon.* She heard her tradecraft teacher's mantra.

The camera panned back, Al peering straight into the lens. He began to speak, although his lips didn't seem to move. The injuries had transformed the natural contours of his expression, almost as if he wore one of those latex masks robbers use to frighten their victims. The tone of his voice was similarly stretched, a rasp echoing the spasms of pain that accompanied each syllable.

He seemed to shiver, an anxiety in his body language that Emily had never witnessed before. His hands gripped his thighs as if attempting to stay in control. Yet it was still Al. Still the caring Al Emily knew and loved for his warmth and humour. At one point she thought she heard the sort of little hiss that accompanies a smile, although his facial muscles were no longer capable of producing that most natural of expressions.

"Hello Emily. It's Al here. I don't think I'm looking or sounding my best at the moment. But please don't worry about me. I'm in safe hands. Hope you are too. Hope to see you soon for a good catch-up. If you ..."

The message lasted no more than 20 seconds, at the end of which the screen went blank. The lights came on.

Smirnov immediately handed Emily a folded copy of that morning's *Evening Standard*. His voice was business-like, verging on stern. "You will have noticed the newspaper pinned to his chest. Read the headline."

Emily unfolded the paper. *Mortgage Misery For Millions*. The headline was identical. She checked the date on the newspaper. It was today's, proving the video was real, made within the last few hours.

"That concludes my part of the bargain," said Smirnov.

"Not exactly."

"What do you mean?" Smirnov removed his spectacles to clean one of the lenses with an anti-static cloth he lifted from the top pocket of his jacket. Without magnification provided by the lens, Emily was struck by his eyes, icy blue but not attractive. Too tiny and piggy.

"I said I needed to speak to Al via a live feed."

Smirnov's demeanour changed. Replacing his glasses, he smashed a fist on the arm of his chair. "No. You said you needed to see him breathing and talking. That was the deal. That's what I've delivered."

"But I ..."

"No." Rising, Smirnov held up his right hand, shutting off discussion. He fished an envelope from his inside pocket, offering it to Emily. "No buts. This is all you need. Forty-eight hours. The time starts now."

He stomped out. Olga accompanied Emily back to her room.

***

She was shaking. Not with anxiety, this time with anticipation. If Emily was right, then Al had said much more in that video than Smirnov and his henchwomen could ever have imagined.

The sight of Al, battered and broken, had tugged at every fragile aspect of Emily's psyche. She had always struggled with emotion. She wasn't good at sharing feelings. Always shied away from commitment and belonging because it demanded empathy. It was easier to stay isolated. Don't let anybody in. That way no one could hurt her. No one could exert control. It had been that way when she first met Al. She had liked him, regarded him as a friend. She enjoyed his jokes, the manner in which he drove social situations, for the first time in her life making her feel at ease in company. But it took many months for her to realise their friendship was becoming a relationship. One which required give and take, in feelings as well as physical aspects.

Al didn't want her to join SIS. Not that he ever said as much. But she knew he didn't relish being shut away from so many aspects of her existence. Never asking about work. Not able to meet her colleagues, or share the burden when she came home frustrated and agitated. When she floated the idea of working as a secret agent for specific missions she knew he was worried. But she also knew that he would do everything to help her realise her ambition. He was that sort of guy.

He had even helped her practise perfecting several aspects of the spying business, one of which was the skill of silent, covert communication. As a cryptographer, Emily was steeped in all manner of coded deceptions.

Which was why she sat at the desk in total silence, clearing her mind of any peripheral concerns, concentrating her photographic memory on the 20-second video she had watched. *I'm in safe hands*. That's what Al had said. An odd thought for a hostage, except that it was designed, Emily was sure, to concentrate her mind on his hands and what he had done with them. The thought triggered a wave of excitement.

She closed her eyes, picturing Al's hands, fingers outstretched, sliding almost imperceptibly up and down his thighs. They had not practised this routine for many months, but she trusted it as a simple, effective technique.

It was her idea, but Al had helped refine it. Each finger or thumb represented the letters and numerals on a qwerty keyboard with four positions on the thigh allowing every character to be accessed. So if the hands were by the knee, the little finger on the left hand would represent the number one, the next finger two, and so on, with the left thumb representing five, all the way to the right little finger and the symbol for nought.

By sliding hands, a fraction further up the thigh, all 10 letters on the next row of a keyboard could also be represented, the left little finger becoming Q and the right little finger becoming P. The nine letters on the next row and the seven on the lowest row of letters could also be represented by sliding the hands further.

Emily and Al had spent many surreal evenings sat opposite each other in the sanctuary of their Camden flat relaying messages, enthusiasm child-like, but knowing one day the game may be for real. Most of Al's messages amounted to nothing more cerebral than *bring me a beer*, but they always laughed when the solution was revealed.

Even at the painful epicentre of his predicament, Emily was certain Al had tried to send her a message, knowing she was bound to see the video and that her memory, which he described as supernatural, would retain it.

She replayed the video in her mind and there it was. The first twitch. With hands a fraction above central on his thighs Al twitched his left thumb, a momentary jerk, the sort easily attributed to anxiety. Emily mouthed the letter G.

A couple of seconds later Al's hands slid to the top of his thigh, the forefinger on his right hand twitching, denoting the letter M.

Hands slid down almost to his knees, denoting numbers. There were four more distinct quivers. Left second finger. Right little finger. Left little finger. Right thumb. All virtually imperceptible to anyone not searching for them. Together they amounted to 2016.

GM2016. That was the entirety of the message, all Al had time for. Emily marvelled at his capacity to think calmly, planting a clue under such pressure. But what did it mean? A date? A reference number? A co-ordinate? For half an hour she mulled over the six characters, checking she had identified them correctly, sifting her practices with Al for anything relevant. Nothing transpired. She trawled through the memory of the video, searching for other clues. The space where he was imprisoned was sparse, bare stone walls, dirty and cobwebbed. No distinguishing characteristics. Could be a disused cellar or a lock-up garage. Could be anywhere, although, judging by the speed the video was created, she realised it must be close.

She reached for Smirnov's envelope, taking out the Letter of Last Resort. A copy of the one she had seen in Chelsea. Now she had two codes to decipher. One could save her life. The other could save Al's. Emily had never doubted her code-breaking ability. It had never let her down, a gift so natural that she could never understand why others regarded it as extraordinary. Yet, as she held the paper, her hand shook and her heart pounded.

Can I crack the code in time? Even if I can, what then? I can't betray my country. But I can't let Al die.

The phrase, *a rock and a hard place*, came to mind. Emily had never fully appreciated the meaning of that saying. Until now.

37

Lieutenant Commander James Stark hunched shoulders against a biting breeze slicing off the North Atlantic.

He was half-way along his daily 10-mile jog and regarded the ringtone in his backpack as an irritant. Stopping, he rummaged in his bag, sucking in salty sea air, taking in the view below of His Majesty's Naval Base Clyde. Otherwise known as Faslane. A sprawling mish-mash of unimpressive, industrial-looking military buildings, warehouses and cranes, all shoehorned alongside an enormous quayside designed to house and service the UK's biggest submarines.

One of the vessels sat by the quay, body grey with rusty stains, scaly like a floating flounder, conning tower with communication mast reaching to the sky. HMS Vital.

Stark was a communications and weapons expert. It had taken a decade and a half to arrive at his present rank following his training as a midshipman at Britannia Royal Naval College.

In the main, he had endured rather than enjoyed his job. It wasn't for everyone. Three months or more at sea. No windows. No sun. No light. Working at a depth of 250 metres or more. Scant, or no communication, with family or friends. Cramped conditions. Nine bunks to a bedroom. Average pay.

It had already cost him a wife, Jenny struggling with the frequent absences, but the Navy was all he knew. His wife could leave him, but he couldn't leave the Navy. The day Jenny walked out was probably the day everything changed.

He'd never forget it. It was also the day of the big march, when thousands flew, drove, cycled or walked to the main gates at Faslane, staying for a week. They waved their political banners. *No Trident. NHS Not Trident. Books Not Nukes. Cut Warfare Not Welfare.* They shouted and sang their protest songs. At first, Lieutenant Stark curled his lip and cursed the weirdos from Hippyville. But as the week wore on a seed grew. Stark started to question his life, his job, his country.

"Hello."

"It's me."

"Oh. Is it about the new job?"

"Yes. We should probably speak."

"When does it start?"

"Soon."

"How soon?"

"Forty-eight hours."

"That is soon."

"Too soon?"

"No, let me check. I'll get back to you. I'm sure I can work something out, as long as we have all the right details."

"You will have."

"That's good. Excellent. I'll message you with the timings."

"Pleasure doing business."

Smirnov replaced the receiver. The plan had been hatched months ago when Stark finished his last shift at sea. It had been a trying mission. Ten weeks tracking a Russian sub, both aware of the other's presence. Both pushing boundaries, prolonged bouts of stealth mode, edging forward at two to three knots, eliminating superfluous noise, shutting down all non-essential services. No showers. No metal cutlery, talking in whispers for days on end. A nervy, tense shift. He used to find that exciting. This time it seemed sad and surreal. Little boys playing with pea-shooters. Except the pea-shooters aboard both vessels fired ballistic missiles capable of travelling 4,000 miles at 13,000 miles an hour, delivering an explosive payload that could wipe out London or Moscow.

Too much time to think. He'd hated that. Allowed him to dwell on his failed marriage. The fact that he never knew his father. Stark was the product of a holiday fling. Probably in Ibiza. At least that's what his mother had told him. It could have been Majorca. She'd done an island hop in the Balearics in her late teens. She was a headstrong woman with values and principles. He remembered her telling him about her time at Greenham Common back in 1981. She was from Swansea and had joined the Women for Life on Earth, a Welsh group who set up camp behind the perimeter fence outside the RAF base to protest against the government's decision to allow America to store cruise missiles there. She had stayed for months, leading the blockades, lying in the road when the huge lorries attempted to deliver their cargo. She died when Stark was twelve years old, hit by a bus on the way to another protest. She would probably have disowned her son if she knew what he did for a living.

His first contact with the Ivan Group had been by chance. At least, it seemed that way. Six months after his wife's departure he had taken a month's annual leave to walk Spain's Camino de Santiago by himself, a bucket list journey to complete the Way of St James, his namesake.

On the 26th day, blistered, sore, but full of satisfaction at a triumph almost complete, he had met Victoria, another lone walker, a few hours from entering Santiago de Compostela. They had strolled the dusty final miles together, taking photos, enjoying a meal and a carafe of rose wine when they reached the city. Victoria was from Belarus, spoke fluent English and reminded Stark of his mother. Vibrant. Idealistic. Opinionated. They drank, laughed, sharing talk of life and adventure. He even spoke of his work deep under the ocean. Not the dangerous bits, but even so Victoria seemed entranced. Stark couldn't remember enjoying a day as much for years, if ever. They arranged to meet months later in London when Victoria was due to attend a computer conference at Earl's Court.

As often happens, the wonder of that first meeting in the warm air and heady hills of Spain, failed to survive the constant rush and toxic fumes of London, but Victoria introduced Stark to Katya, her friend from Minx. Katya took him along to the Rivoli Bar in the Ritz Hotel on Piccadilly, where a group of friends included a sophisticated middle-aged man who insisted on picking up the bar tab before inviting Katya, Stark and a few others to his suite.

"James, what an exciting life you lead. Tell us more." Smirnov had turned on the charm. A combination of Stark's disenchantment with his life, his job, his government, strong cocktails, a luxurious ambience, and Katya's female guiles, had coaxed him to tell more than the Official Secrets Act allowed. Much more, although he remembered little the next day.

Katya had furthered the friendship over the following week. On one dank morning, hours before Stark was due to return to his boat, they had taken refuge in Katya's room at The Salon.

Stark's gathering disaffection spilled out.

"Everyone thinks it's exciting. People talk of the brotherhood, the camaraderie, everyone depending on each other. That's true to an extent. But working on a submarine is deadly boring. It's repetitive. The jobs, the conversation, the food, it's Wednesday it must be curry, and it always is. The lack of sleep, the absence of privacy. No sex. The endless dripping."

"Dripping? What's that?" A puzzled frown crumpled Katya's face.

Stark smiled. "Moaning. Whingeing. The lads call it dripping. When there's nothing else to do, that's how lots of men fill their time."

"Sounds like you do your fair share."

Stark threw a sharp look. Katya shrugged. They laughed.

"I suppose I do, but at least I've not gone wibble yet."

"Wibble? Is that even English?"

Stark snorted, suddenly aware how ridiculous the language of men known in the profession as *deeps,* or *sun-dodgers,* sounded.

"Sorry, I meant crazy. It happens. We called into port unplanned last trip to drop off a man convinced he was Napoleon. He wanted everyone, including the captain, to obey his orders, to salute him. Quite how he thought Napoleon had arrived 300 metres under the Atlantic is anyone's guess. I suppose I'm saying living in the deep is not a natural existence. Not for humans. It plays with people's minds. And all for the salary of a primary school teacher." He gazed out of the window, his air of melancholy matching the raindrops as a weak rainbow attempted to light the London skyline in a golden hue.

Katya studied him. She perceived a troubled soul with issues personal and professional. A high-ranking, multi-faceted, nuclear submarine officer, disillusioned with his lot, dissatisfied with his income, on the edge of his sanity. In short, a vulnerable target, with access to all manner of classified information. An asset to be nurtured with a view to turning.

Which is exactly what happened over the next 12 months, Katya monitoring Stark's increasing disaffection while encouraging a relationship, a bogus one built on faux respect and artificial trust, rather than pure physical attraction, although on the infrequent occasions they were intimate the enjoyment was mutual.

At first, when Katya raised the subject of the Letter of Last Resort, she thought it was a move too far. Stark seemed hesitant. Distant. Dodging a reply. They made love, tender yet passionate too. Afterwards, he languished in the warmth of her embrace, secretly wishing the moment could last forever and he never had to return to the boat. She asked to see his submariner's badge, formed from two dolphins and a crown, feigning interest, looking for the right moment to ask again. For an instant, she thought she'd blown 12 months of preparation.

Then it tumbled out. The fact that his responsibility included servicing the combination to the safe in which the letter was kept. It was also his preserve, along with others under his command, to tend the computer that dealt with the arming of nuclear warheads and firing of ballistic missiles. All computer ware had to be checked and rechecked in the week prior to sailing.

"So you're the man who presses the button." Katya teased him, an admiring trill in her tone.

"No, I'm one of the men who makes sure the rotator code is smoothly inputted, so when the captain presses the button, it actually fires. It's not a button by the way, it's a trigger, like the control on a games console. Button, trigger, who cares, the only thing the captain wants to know in a nuclear war is that his missile is not a dud."

At last, the subject was in the room, swirling unseen but heady, laced with sweet and sour intention, like the tangy perfume from Katya's exotic diffuser.

"Have you seen the letter?"

"I've seen the envelope."

"Have you never been tempted to open it?"

"No."

"What's the rotator code?

"No idea, except that without it, firing a nuclear missile is impossible."

"I know people who would pay the Earth and beyond for a glimpse of that letter."

Stark fixed her with a steady gaze. It was neither accepting, nor admonishing. In the few unsettling moments that followed, she tried to read his mind, uncertain which way his mood might fall.

"If the Earth was … say five million, put a price on beyond." Stark's voice was little more than a whisper, but deadly serious. There was no doubting his direction of travel.

"Twenty, at least."

He bent his neck, kissing her hard on the lips.

38

The computer screen flickered and Emily's spirits rose. Most triumphs start with small victories. She had won one.

Smirnov wanted her to work on the code locked in her basement room with little more than a pencil and notebook. Emily laughed in his face.

"It doesn't work like that. Even the most basic code is a language? Have you ever programmed a computer? It's complex. Have you ever thought how much work goes into what everyone takes for granted? Python. Java. Ruby. PHP. SQL? There are so many ways to code. The coding that cracked DNA took three thousand, three hundred billion lines of code. Do you think they did that with pen and paper? In forty-eight hours?"

"All right, all right." Smirnov's tone was sharp. He knew nothing about coding. Neither did any of the others, but he realised Emily's request for a computer made sense. It meant she would have to work at ground level as her room contained no electricity points. Emily also insisted access to the internet would be required.

Which is why she was sat in front of a laptop in the office overlooking the garden, where two magpies squabbled over a chunk of carrion.

Olga sat opposite, having fallen for the job of chaperoning Emily at all times. She also faced a laptop, the two screens synched so Olga could monitor any searches. She fingered the trigger of a pistol, a reminder of the stakes involved.

While the computer fired into life, Emily glanced around the office. One wall featured a library, full of classic novels, a section reserved for oversized medical textbooks. Artwork adorned another wall. Abstract, geometric shapes and vivid colours. Emily couldn't place the artist, Kandinsky her best guess.

On the wall opposite hung a framed oil painting of the mansion. At least that was her assumption. The eight pillars she had noticed on arrival were distinctive. Ionic, like some of those holding up the Parthenon in Athens, with ornate spiral scrolls. Except one of the volutes on the central pillar was broken, forming a semi-circle, rather than a full spiral. Emily stared at the picture. The house seemed familiar, although she couldn't place why. Maybe the pillars. She had always been interested in Greek and Roman architecture. Perhaps she was confusing it with images she'd studied of the Parthenon.

"Time's ticking." Olga's warning was polite, but firm.

Emily gazed at her over the laptops, striving to keep her temper. "Is Al really okay? He looks in a bad way. Why did you have to hurt him like that?"

"I didn't."

"Someone did."

"He'll be okay, I'm sure."

"Where is he?"

"I can't tell you that."

"He must be close by. Didn't take you long to check on him."

"Enough of the questions."

"But why hurt him? You've got guns. He hasn't. There was no need ..."

"Lily doesn't think like that."

Olga had supplied the information. Emily had known the group no more than a few days, but the dynamics were already rooted. Katya the intelligent organiser. Olga the techie with a robotic nature, a naïve outlook, but a tender heart. Lily the mean-spirited maverick, not to be under-estimated. Lily had been chosen to man Mario's café close to The Salon as a look-out post, for that is what it was, giving the group early warning of anyone posing a danger. The fact that Zofia had not mentioned Lily to Emily, or even been aware of her presence, suggested that the CIA agent may have been suspected early in her mission, the Ivan Group feeding her selective, perhaps spurious, information.

There was no doubting how far Lily was prepared to go for the cause. The nonchalant execution of Zofia was proof of her commitment, the fractured mess of Al's face further evidence. In Emily's estimation, Lily derived pleasure from inflicting pain, suffering and humiliation. A sadist. She would not hesitate to kill again.

Such thoughts trawled through Emily's mind as she unfolded the letter Smirnov had given her, searching for connections.

At once she pondered a Caesar cipher, in which each letter in the text is substituted for a fixed number of positions down the alphabet. With a right shift of three, the letter A would become D, B would become E, and so on. Julius Caesar is thought to have used the rudimentary code in correspondence to his generals in the battlefield. An effective, if simple coding, yet Emily immediately dismissed it. Without knowing the shift key, the permutations in a letter of some length were astronomical. She knew of an artificial intelligence programme which might have provided a short cut, but not in the time available. Anyway, she needed a code that would turn letters into numbers.

She tried other obvious ciphers, punching letters and words into the computer, all the while Olga mirroring her work.

After almost three hours, she sighed, stretching arms, working shoulders, striving to loosen concentration-induced stiffness.

"Any luck?" Olga's query seemed genuine.

Emily shook her head. "No. Sometimes, it's easy to make the mistake of looking for something too complicated. The best codes are simple. Sometimes, the key tumbles unexpectedly."

"Like opening a safe."

"Yeah, I suppose so. I'd not thought of it like that."

A train of thought trundled. Emily walked over to the window. Olga immediately intervened. "Away from the window. Who knows who's out there?" She waved the pistol.

Olga's nervous reprimand, perhaps fearful of police drones, confirmed to Emily that they had not travelled far. They were still in striking distance of central London.

Emily returned to her reasoning. She knew she was searching for an embedded code in the letter. One that required letters to turn into numbers to form co-ordinates which in turn would be inputted into the submarine's computer to facilitate the firing of a missile. She also knew, under the two-person integrity protocol, that two submarine officers had to hold a different key, each inputting a separate sequence at the same time. Two halves making the whole.

Simple logic told Emily such a code must be symmetrical. The words must be completely different, but possess similar characteristics.

She returned to the desk, isolating words with the same number of letters, those beginning or ending with the same letter, those with the same number of syllables, stripping down the letter to its component parts. Writing salient facts in a notebook.

She referred to her training that insisted the prime minister alone wrote the letter. She now realised that couldn't strictly be true. The PM may concoct the letter. The thoughts and words may belong to the PM, but for a code to be embedded it must have been inserted on completion with meticulous precision, checked and rechecked to avoid human error. The chances were that the key words contained the same number of letters and had been inputted by the Ministry of Defence. The two officers on board would be privy to the secret, having memorised the key words, but they would be able to access the crucial coordinates only on reading the letter.

"Don't you find all this stuff boring?" Olga's query accompanied by a yawn.

"What stuff?"

"Codes. Figuring out secret stuff."

"No. Knowledge is power. The key to power lies in unlocking secrets. I thought you lot would have recognised that by now. History is full of code-makers and breakers. Haven't you heard of hieroglyphics?"

"Yeah, they're from Egypt, but I don't really know what they are."

"They are beautiful, iconic characters that baffled everyone for centuries, until Napoleon's troops discovered the Rosetta Stone, the key which led scholars to match the characters with well-known Greek words. It allowed humanity to understand the culture and language of one of history's great civilisations."

Emily couldn't help it. The enthusiasm poured out. Codes were her life-time passion. "And there's the Enigma machine."

"Okay, I've heard of that. Enough." Olga raised her hand.

Emily chuckled. "I'll give you one thing, Olga. A code is like a joke. Best when it's short, to the point, and when you don't have to explain it."

In another world, Emily reckoned she and Olga could be friends. She recognised a like-minded fragility in Olga, as opposed to the composure of Katya and the meanness in Lily. Or maybe it was the early throes of Stockholm syndrome, when a kidnapping victim or hostage has feelings of affection for their captor. An old and trusted psychological ploy to make it more difficult for those holding the gun to murder. Not that she had time to dwell on any of that.

They sat at the desk for the next two hours, breaking for sandwiches and a bottle of beer that Lily brought from the kitchen. There was no sign of Smirnov or Katya.

"Look at me, back to being a waitress. Who would have thought it?" Lily's voice was light and frothy but there was a sinister film behind her eyes, as if harbouring evil thoughts. Emily could barely bring herself to look at her, skin crawling at the memory of Zofia's execution and the thought of the violence she had meted out to Al. Thankfully, Lily did not join them to eat. Emily wolfed down the sandwich, but took a couple of sips only from the beer. She needed to retain a clear head.

When they returned to the computers, the day was growing long. A black cloud was depositing its payload, a stiff wind dancing playfully with the branches of two huge oak trees growing uncomfortably close to the east wing. Emily worked for an hour and a half, distracted by the weather, wondering whether Al was safe and warm enough in his cellar, or lock-up.

As dusk fell, with no warning, Olga called an end to proceedings. "That's enough for today."

"But it's not late. I can still work. There's not much time."

"You can carry on downstairs with your notes."

Olga had risen, making it plain she wasn't changing her mind. Collecting her notebook and pen, Emily walked to the door, stopping in front of the picture of the mansion, as if appreciating the splendour.

"Great place, isn't it? You could imagine the King living here. Or a president. Or a Russian oligarch." Olga could see only magnificent perfection.

Emily had eyes only for the flaw. The crumbling spiral at the top of the pillar.

Looks familiar. I'm sure I've seen this before. One of the properties we used to pass when searching for the houses of princes and rock stars.

39

Like a jarring light in the darkest hour, pain exploded in his brain.

Black floaters and coloured shrapnel raced across his vision. Little detonations behind his eyes sent showers of sparks cascading. He could hear ringing in his head. Feel vibrations. Church bells tolling.

Al didn't realise, but the tolling was real, bell-ringing practice at nearby St Michael's Parish Church, not far from the cemetery's highest point.

The rest were symptoms of the damage caused by Lily's baseball bat.

Al knew his condition was serious. The left side of his head and face felt numb. It was more than the bruising, more than the fractures. His mouth sagged as if it were drooling. He tried to reason, but his concentration wavered, a fret of confusion enveloping his thoughts. Much easier to stare into blackness, allowing his mind to transport him to safer places. Most of them included Emily and Uncle Sebastian's clifftop sanctuary where they always fled in times of trouble. He remembered watching white racing yachts tacking, jostling for position on sunny afternoons in Portland Bay. Licking ice creams on the promenade in Weymouth. Observing sand art. Exploring Nothe Fort. Buying fish 'n chips from Bennett's, eating them sat on the harbour wall amid screeching seagulls.

But then another explosion inside his head dragged him screaming back to the present, the desperate theme of recurring pain and welcome unconsciousness entering yet another cycle.

Somewhere in the middle of his torment, he was aware of doors banging, artificial light and blurry figures. Lily and Olga checking on him.

"God, he's a mess, Lily. I don't think he'll last the night. He needs medical treatment. Now."

"What do you suggest? Popping along to the nearest hospital, kidnapping a nursing team? Good luck with that. They're thin on the ground these days."

"No, but …"

"Twenty-four hours. That's all we need. Then, he'll either be gone along with his girl, or it'll all be over one way or another."

Olga dropped to her knees, lifted Al's head, offering him a drink of water from a straw. She'd noticed the day before his broken jaw had rendered him incapable of drinking normally. Sucking hard on the liquid, the soothing trickle down his throat into his stomach tasted sweet.

"Easy tiger. There's plenty more." Olga had noticed the two bottles left the day before were untouched. Al was obviously severely dehydrated, probably adding to his confusion. She allowed him to drain the bottle, opening another, sticking the straw in the top, leaving it by his side for later.

Al's head began to clear. He tugged at Olga's sleeve, his voice no more than a croak. "Emily. Is Emily okay?"

"Aw, bless." Lily mocked Al's concern.

"Shut up, Lily." Olga spat the command before adopting a softer, caring tone. "Emily's fine. She's helping us, but you should be able to see her soon. Another day or so, that's all."

Olga rearranged the blankets. Al was shivering, the stone floor, damp air, enforced inactivity, inducing the first signs of hypothermia. She pulled the top blanket tight around him, tucking it inside his jacket to fashion a makeshift sleeping bag.

"There, that's better."

"Thank you." Al's grateful groan.

Lily shook her head, tone scathing.

"I don't get you, Olga. You're happy to rob banks, kidnap strangers, take hostages, flaunt your fancy gun around, but a few bumps and bruises, you go all soft and soppy. You're either full on in this game, or not at all."

Olga gritted her teeth, sucking in a calming breath.

"We may have to be savage on occasions, Lily. By God, you're good at that. But we don't have to become savages."

The scrape of metal on stone, together with a keener waft of air, interrupted the sniping. Someone, or something, at the outer door. Lily killed the light. The blackness smothered them, the only sound the muffled peal of church bells in the distance.

Maybe some busy-body, having seen them turn into the temporary entrance, had phoned the police, although that didn't seem likely. The east and west sides of the cemetery were bisected by a narrow public road with one-way traffic and few domestic properties. Only the odd dog walker would be out at this time of night. They had been careful, cutting the van's headlights as they approached the temporary entrance. Lily reached for her gun, edging towards the inner door, feeling her way along the stone wall before inching up the steps. She stopped to listen. Another scrape, this time almost certainly a boot, followed by scuffling, as if someone was dragging a foot. Two options. One, hide, hoping whoever it was would move on. Not Lily's style. She took the second option, bursting into the passageway between the chambers, pointing the torch beam along with her pistol.

"Don't move." Lily's command laced with threat.

Staring back at her was a man, hunched shoulders, straggly brown hair, unkempt beard. His trousers were torn at the knee, his skin sallow, eyes wild with surprise and fear. He shouted something, slurred, unintelligible. His arm jerked up to shield against the light as he staggered forwards.

The gunshot in the stony confines of the mausoleum was ear-splitting.

***

"What's wrong with you? What in the name of holy crap is wrong with you?" Olga bent over the man, panic, disbelief and anger in her voice. The man's eyes were open, but fixed. Blood oozed, forming a messy stain on the crumpled shirt over his heart, the air heavy with foul body odour and the acrid stench of stale alcohol.

"He pointed something at me. I thought it was a rifle or a shotgun. He was going to shoot." Lily spat back.

"You probably blinded him with your torch. He must have been terrified. Could you not smell him? If someone looks, acts and stinks like someone on the streets, then he's probably someone on the streets. Just a homeless old man looking for somewhere dry to spend the night. Must have got through the hole in the wall." Olga picked up the stick with the metal arm rest that had made the scraping noise. “A crutch is a crutch is a crutch. It doesn’t look anything like a shotgun.”

“Okay, we all make mistakes. Shoot first, ask questions later, that’s always been my philosophy. It’s how you stay alive in this game. The old man just happened to be in the wrong grave at the wrong time.” Lily’s flippant reply contained not a hint of remorse, even though the defenceless old man’s accusing death stare seemed to track her.

“Check there’s no one else out there, and put that safety catch on.”

Lily did as Olga suggested, returning a few minutes later. “All clear. Must have been by himself.”

“Okay, let’s get him back inside.”

They dragged the old man’s body into the inner chamber, a clatter of boots on the steps as they descended. Parking him on the opposite wall to Al, Olga threw down the crutch and a bag they had found beside him. She looked inside. A spare pair of shoes, a few rags that doubled as shirts and underwear, a pipe, a tobacco tin, half a bottle of rum. Wrapped in an old jumper, a photograph frame featured a couple on their wedding day. A handsome couple with fresh faces radiating the lure of youthful innocence, the hope of exciting, fulfilling, lives ahead of them. The woman, angelic in a beautifully embroidered white dress, hair in ringlets framed by a wispy veil, the man standing tall, proud, wearing white gloves as part of a sailor’s uniform complete with shining medals. It could have been the homeless man. Probably was. There was no way of telling. For a couple of seconds, a wave of overwhelming sadness engulfed Olga, as if she regretted the violent turn that life had forced upon her. She squeezed her eyes tight, steeling herself to carry on.

“Sorry, Al, afraid you’ve got some company for a while.” Olga shone the light on Al, who appeared to be asleep, but in reality had captured the gist of recent proceedings. The water had revived him. Even so, Dante’s nine circles of Hell infected his hallucinating mind, concentric spirals of sin reaching deeper and deeper to the core of humanity, punishing those afflicted for all eternity.

Lily quipped. “Actually, you could say I did the old boy a favour. Probably didn’t have long to go anyway. Got him a plot with the high and mighty, in a cemetery that costs forty grand a grave.”

Olga ignored her. “Come on, let’s get out of here.” This time Olga went first to check the gunshot had not alerted anyone, while Lily ensured both inner and outer chambers were locked.

Al heard the doors slam, succumbing once more to blackness and silence, broken only by the occasional splutter of gas escaping from the corpse opposite. The added horror of sleeping with the recently dead awaited. The church bells had stopped ringing. Al yearned for them to toll once more.

40

"You know the chances are she's probably dead already."

Jack Easton did not have time, nor inclination, for pleasantries or platitudes. His entire career in special forces had programmed him to deal with life and death in its harsh reality. Dent respected that. He knew Easton would give an honest appraisal, which is why he had summoned him to his office, along with Miller. Despite expecting the worst, Easton's words still gnawed at Dent's spirit.

"We appreciate that, Jack, but until that is confirmed we'll move heaven and earth to find her."

Easton nodded. He had a soft spot for Emily, ever since they had worked on the Tinman case when she was a trainee. Her photographic memory and capacity to think clearly had left a big impression. But he had led the team that stormed the empty nail parlour. What he had witnessed did not encourage optimism. The Ivan Group had out-thought them. Smirnov's team had demonstrated a degree of preparation that Easton admired. He applauded the swiftness and decisiveness of their escape, as well as the complexity in evading technology in one of the most scrutinised areas in the Western world.

"Where are you up to?" Easton's question was typically direct.

Dent pointed to a map of a large swathe of north London on the big screen. "We've identified this area as the most likely point of interest. We tracked one of the white vans here and there's no evidence that it left. The Met have been on the case. The Ivan group will know that. My hunch is that they are laying low to let the heat cool."

"There's a lot of open space and woodland in that area." Easton's tone was grave.

"I hear what you're saying, Jack. If they've dumped a body, it could take a while to discover. I agree. We've got drones up. The Met has been conducting discreet searches so not to alarm the public."

Easton contemplated the map for a minute, little trenches of wisdom forming around his eyes.

"What are you thinking?" Miller was first with the question.

"That I would concentrate on the posher areas."

"Why?"

"Everything about the salon in Chelsea pointed to leaders who gravitate to the finer aspects of life. We know the Ivan Group has wealth backed by Russian oil, endorsed by the Kremlin. The chances are there are properties, maybe owned or once owned by Russian oligarchs, that would make perfect hideaways."

Miller flicked a couple of computer keys. A list of properties emerged. She scrolled for several seconds, amounting to hundreds of addresses. "We're already pursuing that line of enquiry, but there are so many. I didn't realise how much Russian money is parked in London, even after big players such as Roman Abramovich were drummed out by sanctions at the start of the Ukraine war. I'm surprised parts of Hampstead aren't called Little Moscow."

Easton turned to Dent. "Does Emily have any covert communication, any way of getting in touch?"

"She had a small burner phone. One we found on Nina Volkov. It's slim, easily hidden. It was her emergency option, but we have to presume Ivan has discovered it, or surely she would have called."

"Maybe not."

"Pardon."

"From what you know about Ivan it seems they had sophisticated monitoring devices. Emily would have been reluctant to use the phone close to the salon. From my experience of SIS agents, emergency option means only to be used in the direst of circumstances. By the time that has arrived, it's usually too late."

"What do you suggest, Jack."

"Keep looking. Concentrate on Hampstead and surroundings. I'll prime my elite fast-response team to be ready any time in the next forty-eight hours. If we've not heard anything by then … well, I think you know as well as me what that would mean."

"Okay, thanks Jack. Hopefully, we'll speak soon." Dent offered his hand. They shook. Easton nodded to Miller as he left.

Dent stood at the window watching a couple of tourist boats chugging up the Thames, lights shimmering on the river, flags dancing on a gusty wind, the varied shapes and towers of the illuminated cityscape forming a dramatic backdrop, although all he saw was Emily with a gun to her head. Miller joined him.

"What is it, Miles? You look pale."

"If Emily is still alive, then, one way or another, we'll know soon enough."

"Why do you say that?"

"There are only two reasons why they would risk switching HQs with her on board."

"Go on." An anxious catch in Miller's voice.

"One is because they want her as a bargaining tool in some prisoner swap. Not likely to happen. We have some would-be spies, all low-level, but we don't hold any of Russia's high-value agents at present. More's the pity when you remember the Salisbury poisonings."

"The other reason."

"The admiral's letter. The rotator code. For all we know, the one crucial for the arming of nuclear warheads. As an expert cryptographer, Emily is one of the few people who could be of use to Ivan in that regard."

"But we, or to be precise, you, found the letter behind the Nelson portrait. Volkov didn't find it. The Ivan Group don't have it." Miller was sceptical.

Dent's cheeks reddened. A scenario of impossibly evil proportions had crossed his mind.

"We've underestimated the Ivan Group on a couple of occasions already and paid the price. Get on to the MOD. Let's find out the state and location of our nuclear submarines. If the rotator code and Shelkunchik are one and the same, then the nation's security is in imminent danger."

***

Katya marched Emily into the lounge, gun pointed at her back. Smirnov sat in a fireside chair sipping a drink. Amber fluid. Ice clinked against the glass as he raised it to his lips. Emily detected a faint aroma of malt whisky.

"Would you care to join me?" Smirnov showed her the glass. Emily found his charm more disconcerting than his steel. He could switch between the two in an instant, but his charming alter ego was creepy, a veneer to the psychopath Emily was certain lay behind. She shook her head.

He motioned for her to sit. "How are you getting on?"

"I told you, forty-eight hours is too tight. There are no clues. No key. Nothing via frequency analysis. No common words or letter pairings that I can detect. Cracking codes is all about maths. Simple maths. Subtraction and addition. Spotting patterns. If it's super-complex, you wouldn't expect to be able to crack a code in so short a time. I'm still thrashing around in the dark."

Smirnov raised a hand. "I don't want to hear negativity. We have an agent in place. He has put himself in jeopardy. It's up to you to deliver."

A sudden surge of anger consumed Emily. "I couldn't care less about your agent. What about my fiancé? What about Al? I need to see and speak to him."

"We've been through all that. You saw him earlier. He spoke to you. You'll get to see him for real when you deliver what we want."

"I need more information. I need a clue. At the moment they're just words with no connection." A desperate edge distorted Emily's voice. Her eyes darted around the room, taking in the artwork, the fine porcelain, the majesty of a thick Turkish rug, full of gentle swirls and rich shades of pink, brown and cream. She eventually alighted on an aerial photograph of the mansion, hanging in an alcove, not as big or as splendid as the oil painting in the office, but full of detail. Her attention immediately piqued. The distinctive eight pillars were impressive, as were the landscaped gardens. The image concentrated on the mansion, not dissimilar in design from the White House in Washington, although the photo included the edges of the neighbouring plots and a stretch of road running in front of the property. She had to squint to read the small inscription underneath the picture: *The Bishop's House.*

Now she was certain. Her frustration with the code replaced by excitement. The photo had confirmed the familiarity of the painting. This was one of the roads she had visited as a child with her parents when they had pretended the houses were owned by emperors, princes and kings. She even knew the name. The Bishops Avenue. A road connecting the north side of Hampstead Heath to East Finchley, nicknamed Billionaires' Row, with properties registered to companies in tax havens such as the British Virgin Islands, the Bahamas and Panama, allowing most of the owners to remain anonymous. Many of the mansions were unoccupied, some even derelict, their purpose simply to park the wealth of their foreign owners. The plot, many centuries ago the home of the bishop of the London diocese, was no more than eight or nine miles from the city centre.

As with Al in the cemetery, the coincidence of knowing her whereabouts didn't change her predicament, but somehow the knowledge offered hope.

"Tell me, Emily. Why do you work for SIS?" A pitch of genuine curiosity in Smirnov's question.

"Because there are people like you in this world who will do anything for money."

"You couldn't be more wrong, Emily. I don't work for money. I have enough money to last many lifetimes. I do what I do because the survival of my homeland is paramount."

"No one's threatening Russia."

Smirnov laughed. "The strengthening of our nation is interpreted as authoritarianism. Every time we strengthen, NATO responds with threats, stirring up fears in its people. Lashing out for no good reason. America criticises us. We don't have human rights, it says. Russia doesn't have a free society. Nonsense. It's America, the land of the free, where people are imprisoned. Imprisoned by the lying and duplicity of their leaders. Where presidents don't accept the results of their own elections and encourage the mob to take up arms against congress. Russia is part of the democratic

European culture. It's time the UK embraced us as friends, not enemies."

"Stop invading your neighbours then."

Katya threw a wary glance. She had experienced Emily's acid tongue before and had warned her not to bait Smirnov. An uneasy pause followed, but instead of rising to Emily's jibe, Smirnov raised his glass, sinking a generous measure of spirit.

"Okay, I've heard enough. Twenty-four hours, Emily. Not a minute longer."

He waved a dismissive hand, a sign for Katya to return Emily to the basement.

As they descended the steps, Katya asked the question that had grated since she'd met Emily.

"Why do you upset people? Why do you always goad and try to provoke him? Whatever you're doing, it won't work with Smirnov."

"It's my fiancé who looks half-dead with a shattered face. I'd say Smirnov was doing the provoking, not me."

Katya sighed. "All right, have it your own way. But don't say I didn't warn you. And, whatever you do, come up with the solution to that rotator code before this time tomorrow."

"Pardon."

"I said make sure you come up with the code within ..."

"No, before that. What did you call the code?"

"The rotator code. At least, I thought that's what it was called. Why?" Katya had picked up the phrase from her liaison with Lieutenant Stark. She didn't understand the relevance, but it seemed to twitch Emily's antennae.

"Oh, nothing. I'd not heard it called that before." Emily tried to sound flat calm but her heart leaped. This could be the connection she required. Maybe she could crack the code, after all.

41

Emily sat at the desk and wrote the word *rotator* in her notebook almost before Katya had slammed the door.

No more than a few hours troubled sleep in the last three days, but Emily's mind felt strangely lucid. She had been trying to turn the letters in the Letter of Last Resort into numbers. With 26 characters in the English alphabet, the permutations were endless. Even with the aid of the computer and various programmes essential to cryptography her searches had turned up nothing.

But *rotator* gave her something tangible to work with.

Someone not steeped in analysis would probably have concentrated on the meaning of the word, trawling through propellers, fans, Ferris wheels, rotor blades and clocks. Even planets and heavenly bodies, the entire universe being full of rotators at the mercy of gravitational forces.

Emily cut through the endless possibilities, dissecting the word itself, immediately spotting the connection.

To make sure, she wrote *rotator* again, but this time from back to front. It spelled *rotator*. A palindrome. A word or phrase reading the same back to front.

"Just like Otto and Hannah." Emily mouthed the names of two classmates she remembered from school, both of whom were teased because their names formed palindromes.

She grabbed the copy of the Letter of Last Resort, studying it for many seconds.

This letter has been the hardest I have ever undertaken. I must level with you. If you are reading it, it means I and many of my colleagues are dead and our nation is under threat of extinction. In these circumstances and in the knowledge that I will never forgive myself for allowing these events to occur on my watch, I direct you to my final instructions. My civic duty. Meet force with force. retaliating with every means at your disposal. Further to that, forwards or backwards, you should sail to an ally closest to your location and put yourself and your boat under their command.

The letter was imprinted on Emily's memory, but she wanted to see physical proof. Hold it in her hands, feel the weight of the revelation. Just as she thought. Two words leaped out at her. *Level* and *Civic*. Both palindromes, a password each, for that is what she was certain they were, for the two submarine commanders entrusted with complying with the letter's instructions.

Logic told her the commanders would have been furnished with the passwords. Their job on opening the safe and extracting the Letter of Last Resort would be to convert their password into numerals. How would that be done? Emily had no doubts. In all likelihood, for Emily had converted many such codes, each individual letter in the password would correspond to the numeric position of its first or subsequent use in the PM's note.

Thus, reading forwards, *level* would convert as 05-06-31-09-52, with the second use of letters l and e reverting to subsequent use in order that numerals were not repeated. Using the same logic, civic would become 07-09-139-45-48, this time reading the letter from the end, starting with the d of command. The order within the letter, *forwards or backwards*, would be implemented.

To many, such a code would seem overly complex. To Emily, it was routine, the reasoning rational. The code-breaking process required a measure of thought and consideration, supplying a brake to any knee-jerk reaction, the last thing required in any nuclear conflict. Prior to sailing, each commander would have received a briefing, enabling the numerals to be extracted in a safe, efficient, fashion. Neither would know the other's password, thus complying with protocol for TPI (two-person integrity).

Emily wrote the numbers in her notebook, trembling as she did so. If she was right, she held the trigger to the UK's nuclear missiles. The only thing she needed to decide now was when, or if, to tell Smirnov.

***

On her way to the MOD office in Whitehall, Jane Miller encountered one of those daily occurrences on London's teeming streets. A car crash. More of a bump than a crash, but the middle-aged lady driver of the Mini involved stood by the side of the road, her body shaking.

The lorry driver who had carved her up, turning left at the junction on the north side of the western end of Westminster Bridge, by the statue of Boudicea, pulled hard on a cigarette. His face was round and ruddy, features containing not a trace of concern. A small crowd had gathered, not too close, at a distance where they could linger, observing without becoming part of the action. A police car arrived. Two officers alighted, the woman officer immediately comforting the lady driver, while the male officer directed the already long queue of vehicles and frustrated motorists around the obstruction.

"Come on, everyone, move on please." The policeman appealed to the onlookers, but no one took notice. Miller stood for a few moments scanning the scene. A group of foreign tourists gawped as they passed. Two young lads took snaps on their phones. What was it about human misfortune, even on this basic, unremarkable level, that was so intriguing? Why do people feel compelled to stare at the aftermath of accidents? Miller's mind asked the questions. She didn't have answers, but pondered that people were wired to ask themselves what would they do in the same situation. She had done as much herself on numerous occasions.

What would I do? How would I respond? Would I be a hero, or would I run away? Would I have the strength to cope, or would I just stand and watch? She thought of Emily, wondering if the same thoughts had gone through her mind.

Thankfully, there was no blood, little damage, apart from the Mini's wrenched front bumper and deformed side panel. Everything seemed under control. The crowd thinned. She crossed the road, heading for Whitehall.

When she arrived at the MOD, a porter escorted her to a poky office with no windows. It could have been a store cupboard in another lifetime. Two people were present. She recognised Roger Williams from the MOD, who had attended the original meeting with Dent following the news of Sir Robert Bellingham's death. They nodded to each other and Williams introduced Lieutenant Commander Cresswell, an officer in the Royal Navy submarine service.

"The lieutenant is representing the Commodore today." Williams motioned for Miller to sit.

"I'm sorry. I was expecting the Commodore to be here."

"He's a very busy man. He's in Scotland. He couldn't be with us, but the lieutenant should be able to answer your questions."

Miller's heart sank. She had attended many such meetings with men who appeared to listen, nodding and making notes, primed to report back, but without the executive capacity to make decisions. The intelligence network was full of such individuals, characters who observed, like the onlookers at the car crash, but who excelled only at obfuscation, melting into the background at the first hint of actual responsibility.

"What would you like to know, Jane?" Williams's first question was an open invitation to test the value of the meeting.

"We, or I should say, SIS, needs to know the whereabouts and current status of the UK's ballistic submarines."

"Why?" The lieutenant's eyes narrowed, his demeanour defensive.

"I can't go into details, but we have reason to believe a terrorist group may have targeted parts of the nuclear capability."

"You'll have to be more specific. We have heard many such threats in the past."

Miller sucked in a deep breath. "From information we found in the possession of Sir Robert Bellingham, supported by what we have gleaned from our agent in the field, we believe a code, essential to the firing of ballistic missiles, may have been compromised. Right now, an enemy agent may be aboard one of your submarines."

"That's a lot of maybes."

"How many ballistic submarines are at sea?" Frustration rose along with bile in Miller's throat.

"That's classified information."

"Tell that to the enemy agent who's probably already aboard."

Sensing the temperature rising, Williams intervened, signalling to Miller. "I think it would be useful if your concerns could be put to the Commodore. Would that be in order?" He turned to the lieutenant.

"Of course, but, Miss Miller, everyone knows the UK nuclear deterrent is not predicated on a code. That is for the Americans, or fiction. The UK relies on military discipline."

"Bollocks." That's what Miller yearned to say. Instead, she contented herself with a withering look. "So you can't tell me the current status of any of your submarines?"

"As I'm sure you know, the submarines, Vanguard, Victorious, Vigilant and Vengeance, form our nuclear force. All are equipped with Trident 2 D5 missiles. I can confirm that one of them is on deep sea patrol to comply with the policy of Continuous At-Sea Deterrence. Others are on manoeuvres. One is being serviced."

"My hairdresser could have got all that from Google."

"All I can say is that your hairdresser must be well informed." In cricket parlance, the lieutenant was adept at playing a straight bat, his expression barely changing, dismissing Miller's questions with no detectable emotion.

"How about the submarine on patrol? When is it due back in port?"

"I can't give precise timings, but with a fair wind and a following sea, I can say its current mission is almost complete."

"Is the replacement CASD submarine due to takeover at sea, or is it at Faslane?"

"That's operational and classified."

"What about HMS Vital?" Miller had been researching the UK's nuclear deterrent and the fact that HMS Vital appeared to operate out of Faslane on a regular basis intrigued her. She'd checked with an SIS contact in Clyde. It was in dock right now. At 150 metres in length it was smaller than the Vanguard class, officially categorised as an attack submarine, but naval literature boasted it could perform silent and deep like the Vanguards, with enough capacity to circumnavigate the world 40 times without surfacing. That was the equivalent of a submarine capable of firing nuclear warheads. It would make sense to hold a ballistic missile-capable craft in reserve for covert missions. Keep the enemy guessing.

"That's not officially classed as one of our ballistic missile carriers." The lieutenant's dead bat descended again, but Miller detected a slight frown, as if she had touched an operational nerve.

Williams interrupted. "I think we have an idea of what information you require, Jane. I suggest we schedule another meeting with the lieutenant when he has had chance to consult with the Commodore."

A frustration of murmured platitudes followed. Miller recognised she was getting nowhere fast and was unlikely to do so with the office's present incumbents. The meeting broke up, Miller retracing her steps, the Mini lady and lorry driver having moved on from their own unscheduled encounter. The bronze statue of Boudicea on her chariot, carrying a spear, remained, resolute and immoveable. Not unlike the UK's naval commanders, thought Miller.

42

Emily spent much of the next day at the office computer, wrestling with the code.

Not the rotator code, although she pretended that was the case, but the short coded message Al had sent. *GM2016.* At first she thought the letters must refer to their position in the alphabet, making the actual number, 7132016, G being the seventh letter and M the 13th.

Juggling the numbers proved to no avail. There was no pattern, no connection to be made.

All the while, Olga sat opposite, one finger on the trigger of her pistol, the other hand doodling in a notebook, sketching a magpie that posed on a tree branch outside the window.

Emily leaned over to check her progress. "That's good, Olga. Who taught you to draw? The perspective's perfect."

"My father was an artist. Only an amateur, but he used to paint the factories and skylines of Brasov in Romania. He taught me perspective as a youngster. It has been my way of staying calm ever since."

"Al's a good artist. Not as good or as precise as you, but he brings things to life through colour."

The concern in Olga's eyes at the mention of Al did not escape Emily. "What is it? Is Al all right? Tell me, Olga. Please tell me."

Olga held up a hand and listened for a moment. She could hear Lily banging around in the kitchen, clumping metallic thuds. Sounded as though she was cleaning weapons, heavy weapons, while Katya was in the lounge plotting with Smirnov. "Al's not well. He needs a doctor. I'm not sure …" She paused, biting her lip.

"What? What are you not sure of, Olga?"

"He needs a doctor now. To wait may be too late." Olga's words were measured, but there was gravity in her tone. If it were Lily, or even Katya, Emily would have suspected a ruse to concentrate her thoughts on the cipher requiring decoding. But this was Olga. Plain, sweet Olga. Misguided in her choice of profession, but honest and straightforward. At least, that was Emily's summation, which was why terror swirled as she contemplated the practicalities of Olga's revelation. Olga was warning her that Al was close to death. By the look on her face, Olga believed he may not last another night. Emily had to do something. She owed Al everything. He had taught her to believe in herself, transforming the young girl with a feisty mouth and an anxious nature, who once swore her way out of a job at a call centre, into a confident woman capable of measured thought under intense pressure. One whose analytical genius protected her country on a regular basis. Emily's cheeks flushed. A sensation of loss almost overwhelming, but she pushed the feeling down, stemming the flames of helplessness as a fireman quells a raging fire. She knew then she had to save him.

The only weapon she possessed was the code. In that moment of brutal clarity, Emily decided to give Smirnov what he wanted.

She didn't tell Olga. Instead, she asked to be escorted back to the basement for a couple of hours, claiming she was suffering from a thumping headache, requiring a lie-down to clear her mind.

"But you only have a few hours left. Think of Al. Smirnov won't extend the deadline." There was genuine concern in Olga's voice.

"I am thinking of Al, but a scrambled mind is no place to decode. Much better if I reset and have one last session."

Two hours later, Olga returned. The sun was dipping as Emily again strode into the office. Her eyes were drawn to the big window. A huge crane working at the property opposite had tipped its hanging arm for the night, safety light already twinkling against the darkening sky. She sat at the computer. For the next hour, she strove once more to make sense of Al's numerical message. Nothing transpired. Worried about Al, she judged the time was right.

"Okay. That's it. Done. I've cracked it." She announced her progress regarding the rotator code in the manner of a funeral director. Solemn and halting.

"Really?" Olga seemed surprised.

"Really."

"Okay, let's go tell the boss."

They marched through to the lounge where Smirnov reclined in a leather armchair. Katya and Lily were at the other side of the room, sorting through rucksacks as if planning a journey. A couple of folding submachine guns, propped against the wall, acted as an incongruous reminder that the plush surroundings were not all they seemed.

"Emily, I trust you have something to tell me." Smirnov rose, anticipating news on the code, although Emily's expression gave no clue as to which way it might go.

"I have what you want."

"Excellent. Never doubted you. We heard you were the best cryptographer in the UK."

Smirnov's outstretched hand hung limp in the void between them. Emily shook her head.

"No games, Emily." Smirnov's demeanour hardened.

"It's in here." Emily pointed to her right temple. "I'll give it to you when I know Al is alive and safe, and when you tell me the target. I won't be responsible for the killing of millions of people."

Smirnov pondered Emily's demands in silence for around 20 seconds, although it seemed longer. He motioned for Emily to sit. When she didn't, Olga placed a hand on her shoulder, pushing her onto the seat of an armchair.

When Smirnov spoke, his tone was earnest. "All this is not about killing people. How would that benefit anyone? There is no target. Not New York, or Washington. Not Kyiv, Berlin, Paris, certainly not London."

"What then?" A wave of bemusement crossed Emily's features.

"Are you familiar with Faslane?"

"It's where the UK's nuclear submarines are kept."

"Correct. Down the years, Faslane has become a symbol of the nuclear alliance between the UK and America. The UK provides submarines, the US services its nuclear warheads. Yet both of them talk as if Russia is the aggressor. As if Russia is the only nation prepared to use nuclear missiles as a threat. The public believe the lies."

"That's not true. There have been dozens of protests at Faslane. Police have arrested hundreds of people, most of them women. No one in Scotland wants ballistic missiles on their soil. There's even a permanent peace camp only a few miles from the base."

Smirnov snorted. "Peace camp? What good does it do? The UK and US don't want peace. They want to chip away at Russia. Make us out to be incompetent and dangerous. Turn our allies against us. At every opportunity, they try to belittle our great heritage." He took a deep breath, regaining his equilibrium. "But we digress."

"You're deluded." Emily had told herself to stay calm, not to provoke Smirnov, but she'd had enough of his warped reasoning. She clenched her fists, spitting her riposte. "Russia lies to its own people. It's not democratic. You don't allow women into positions of power because they may bring reason, caring and compromise. Your heritage is full of violence and genocide. Russia is a dictatorship, run by paranoid mad men, most of whom are too frightened to live in the real world."

"Have you finished?" Smirnov was icy calm.

Emily didn't answer, realising she had deflected Smirnov from the crucial conversation.

He continued. "You asked about the target. Simple. To show those who have campaigned against the warmongering of the UK and the United States that they were right. That unstable nuclear weapons have no place in Western Europe. Their governments can't be trusted. After today, that will become blindingly obvious."

"My God, you're going to blow up Faslane." There was a tremor of incredulity in Emily's voice.

"That's right, Emily."

"But it's forty miles from Glasgow. Any explosion at Faslane will cause devastation."

"Exactly what the peace protesters have been saying for years. Which is why it will put paid to nuclear weapons on UK shores, making Europe, the world even, a safer place. And the chances are no one will know we had anything to do with it."

"Of course, they'll know. Don't you think British Intelligence knows precisely what you're planning?"

"No, Emily. I don't. Are you familiar with the term, *broken arrow*?"

"Yes." Emily's face creased with curiosity.

"Happens all the time. A missile goes rogue. Misfires. Goes off course. Hits the wrong target. There are countless examples, although the public rarely hear about them. A Ukrainian missile, probably supplied by the UK, turned west instead of east, taking out a poor farmer minding his own business in Poland during the war in Ukraine. A broken arrow." Emily detected a trace of smugness in Smirnov's tone,

"At least it wasn't a nuclear missile. That's the difference. Can't you see that?"

"A strategic strike. A single warhead. Faslane is isolated. Nothing around but sheep."

"It's forty miles from Glasgow. Have you been listening? It's even closer to the Navy's armaments depot at Coulport where nuclear warheads are stored."

"Exactly. Two birds with one stone. I think that is the English phrase."

"You're mad. Completely mad."

"Enough. The code." Smirnov's raspy Slavic hiss told Emily his temper was fraying, but she held her nerve.

"When I see Al is still safe. Where is he? I know he can't be far away."

The silence that followed could have gone either way. But Smirnov perceived resolve and determination in Emily, the sort that did not respond to threats. He turned to Katya and Lily, nodding his approval. They picked up their weapons and disappeared.

43

The air was icy. Katya and Lily's wispy breath rose in the torchlight as they entered the vault. Immediately, the women gagged, the stench striking them like a punch to the nose.

Coughing and spluttering, Lily dragged a scarf around her face, Katya put a handkerchief to her nose and mouth. They took a step back, pushing open both iron doors to allow the worst of the putrid aroma to escape, sucking fresh air for a few seconds before re-entering.

Katya spun the light beam around the stone walls.

"What the fuck!" Her startled shriek echoed in the tiny chamber. For a moment she could hardly breathe, shaking with shock as the torch alighted on the shrivelled face of a bearded old man, propped in a corner, dead eyes staring straight at her.

"Oh, yeah. Sorry, forgot to mention him." Lily shrugged. "He wandered in drunk. Had to take care of him."

Katya sized up Lily as if working out where the screw was loose. She spun the beam to the opposite corner, picking out a black and red blanket covering a still figure. Concerned, she strode over, pulling back the blanket to reveal Al. A shake of his shoulders. Nothing. Alarmed, she shook again, this time harder. He stirred, a faint whimper escaping his shattered mouth.

"Thank God." Katya reached for the water bottle with the straw, offering it to him. He sucked, out of instinct rather than reason. His good eye was shut. His skin pale and drained, accentuating the purple bruising around his nose and cheek.

"Al, we've come to let you speak to Emily. You'd like that, wouldn't you?" Al said something, but the words were slurred, too indistinct to decipher. In his head, the mention of Emily sparked a train of thought. The early morning phone call. The last time he'd seen her. The secret trip she had to take for a few days. Something was wrong, terribly wrong, but his brain wouldn't connect the clues. He drifted.

"No, Al, we need you to stay awake." He felt warm, soft hands, brushing back his hair, rubbing his hands and arms to promote circulation. Gentle whispers urging him to think of Emily.

He was aware of brightness, his good eye opening a fraction. It looked like the harsh light from a phone camera.

"Okay, Al, listen to Emily, she's talking to you."

And she was. Her voice soft and comforting, an edge of concern but he was grateful for the familiarity, his spirits lifting. Everything would be all right. That's what she was saying and he wanted to believe her. Oh, how he wanted to believe. He tried to speak but the pain in his jaw sent a rush of nausea through his body. He teetered on the edge of consciousness, clinging to the sweet sound of her voice, refusing to succumb, not wanting this connection with warmth and happiness to end.

He strained to focus with his good eye and while the image was little more than a blur he could make out Emily's cascading hair, natural prettiness, the way she tilted her head slightly when concentrating. He thought of the day in two months' time when they were due to get married. How he longed for that day. A simple ceremony for close family and friends. Emily had her dress, he'd bought his suit. The ring was a surprise. A simple gold band passed down from his grandmother, Anna. Every detail taken care of, apart from the music. A small tear came to his eye, emotion welling.

He tried to say something. "You can …" His voice cracked. Emily urged him to try again. This time he steeled himself against the pain, willing himself to concentrate, summoning shreds of lucidity. "You can have your song." The light went out and for a moment pitch blackness filled the vault.

***

Olga yanked the phone from Emily's vision, clicking the off-button.

Smirnov fixed Emily with cold eyes. "As you can see, he's alive and well. If you want him to stay that way, I suggest you give me your numbers."

There was no way Emily would describe Al as well. Seeing him again had confirmed her worst fears. He required urgent medical treatment. Yet she faced a dilemma. Once she had delivered the code, she only had Smirnov's word that Al would be freed. The word of a man who had ordered the callous execution of Zofia in front of her so recently. If she didn't deliver, the chances of Al surviving the night were slim. She had no choice.

"You'll need a pen." Emily tossed a glance at the desktop and Olga signalled her to fetch one. As she approached the desk she spotted a small paperweight, the shape of a snow dome. She stretched over the desk with her back to Olga and Smirnov, scooping up a notebook and pen while the fingers of her other hand wrapped around the paperweight. In the motion of recoiling, she deftly secreted the paperweight in her trouser pocket.

Emily adopted a business-like tone. "There are two sets of five co-ordinates. The first five need to be entered, followed by the second set. That should gain access to the arming mechanism if the code is correct. Only a technical expert would be able to make sense of them."

"Don't worry, we have a technical expert in place," said Smirnov.

Emily proceeded to recite the sets of numbers, Olga recording them in meticulous order, reading each one back to ensure accuracy. When the task was finished, Emily asked the obvious question. "What happens now?"

"You will need to stay with us a while longer. We need proof that you are as good a code-breaker as your people say. It won't take long. Everything is in position. We'll let you know in due course. In the meantime, relax."

Smirnov motioned for Olga to escort her back to her basement cell. It was a trek they had repeated several times, Olga keeping her pistol trained on Emily's back, although not as conscientiously as she once had. A certain trust had developed between them. Emily saw Olga as misguided, rather than evil. Olga regarded Emily as someone she could talk to. Not a friend exactly, as that would be absurd in their present circumstances. Not someone with personal empathy either, as Emily had always struggled in that department. Yet someone who appeared to understand how difficult it was to fit in, or be accepted in a team environment. She detected a kindred spirit.

They descended the first flight of stairs, Olga telling Emily she had done the right thing, that Al would soon receive treatment. They could be reunited. Whether Olga believed her own words was debatable, but as they reached half-way Emily appeared to trip, tumbling down the last six steps, landing in a heap. A manoeuvre learned at tradecraft school, but never performed with more aplomb.

Seeing Emily lying motionless on her front, Olga bounded down the stairs, kneeling down, placing her pistol on the bottom step, attempting to roll Emily. As she spun, Emily used momentum to sneak the paperweight from her pocket, bringing her arm over in an arcing motion like a fast bowler, solid marble crashing into Olga's temple, the resounding thud muffled by the depth of the basement. Olga slumped unconscious, blood streaming from her head.

Seizing the pistol, Emily had another decision to make. Creep upstairs to capture Smirnov, or search the basement for an escape exit. She chose the second option. Taking on Smirnov was a gamble. He was a ruthless murderer in a house full of weapons. If she failed to capture him, then Al's life was in the balance. Escape and she could save him. It was an easy decision.

Emily made her way along the corridor, past the cell where she had been held. There were doors either side but all of them were locked. She headed for the big door at the end of the corridor, praying it would give. The handle turned at the first attempt. She entered what appeared to be an old kitchen, probably dating back to Victorian times when banquets would have been prepared in the basement alongside the servants' quarters.

There was no door, but she could see dusk falling from a set of rectangular windows, high up near the ceiling but at the house's ground level. They were no more than two feet wide, 18 inches tall, but would be easy for her to clamber through if she could reach them. She scanned the room, alighting on a set of wooden chairs. Setting one of them on a worktop she clambered up, standing on the chair. Still not quite high enough, but she strained, clutching the window's handle, pulling and pushing. Stuck solid. Locked. She knew it was no good trying the others. They would all be the same, probably screwed shut as a security measure.

With haste essential, there was only one thing for it. She swung the pistol. The glass shattered. She chopped at the edges, stripping it of shards. Jamming the pistol in her belt, she grabbed the window frame, shinning her way up the wall. A blast of cold air tugged at her hair. Spots of rain felt sweet against her lips. The taste of freedom. Pivoting on the frame, she sucked in a lungful of oxygen, summoning one more effort to haul herself the rest of the way. Something or someone grabbed her trailing leg. She looked down. Olga, face streaming with blood, but a determined set to her jaw.

Emily kicked her trapped leg. It wouldn't budge, Olga's grip too tight. For several seconds there was a surreal impasse, Olga pulling on the leg, Emily straining to wriggle out onto the flower bed she could see before her. The mantra of Emily's SIS trainer came to mind. *Let surprise always be your friend.* She reversed the forces. Instead of straining upwards and out of the window, Emily kicked her free leg down with the full weight of her body behind it. Her heel smashed into Olga's face, shattering her nose, sending her spinning to the ground, Emily landing on top of her. Leaping back onto the chair, a rush of adrenalin surged Emily through the window into the garden.

She ran like never before, heading for the main gate, but not on the gravel drive, instead along the lawn under the cover of mature maple trees, keeping her hidden. Even so, at any moment, she anticipated the crack of a gunshot. When she reached the gate, her heart sank. It was electrically operated, made of steel, 10 feet high, smooth, offering no purchase to anyone trying to scale it.

The lights came on at the front of the house. She detected movement. The trees and shrubs were dense on one side of the grounds, probably kept that way to reduce maintenance. She ran towards them, hugging the steel perimeter wall, seeking gaps. There were none.

Dusk had given way to darkness, the only illumination reflecting from the mansion and the sparse streetlights on the main road.

Emily found a spot where she could observe the house, lying flat under a holly bush, thick foliage offering the perfect hiding place for the price of a few scratches. She slipped the pistol from her belt, digging inside her trousers, grasping another object. The burner phone. Anticipating her latest visit to the lounge could be her last opportunity, she had retrieved the phone from its secret compartment in her sponge bag.

The relief when she turned it on, spotting a signal, was huge. She punched in Dent's office number at SIS. He answered immediately, sending a giddy sensation, as thrilling as it was unexpected, coursing through her veins.

"Emily. Where are you? Are you okay? Are …"

"Shut up, Miles, and listen." Emily had no time for pleasantries, protocols, or the expectations of rank. "I'm in a walled garden in The Bishops Avenue, off Hampstead Lane. I'm hiding from armed pursuers. I don't know what number, but the house has eight pillars. There's a huge crane opposite."

"I'll get a chopper there right away."

"Miles, there's a Russian agent aboard a British submarine trying to explode …" The line cut off, the battery dead. "Shit … shit … shit."

Emily saw a figure emerge from the front portico. Olga, carrying a submachine gun. The security beams burst into life, flooding silvery fingers of light over the lawns. Olga took a few moments to sum up the situation, turning towards the dense foliage, marching directly towards where Emily was hiding. As she did so, the front gates slid open allowing a black van to enter. Emily was around two hundred yards away, but she could hear barks and snarls echoing in the back.

44

Four dogs jumped out of the back of the van. Emily's knowledge of dog breeds wasn't extensive but from their large heads and robust frames she settled on Rottweilers.

Two men wearing black weatherproof jackets controlled the dogs on long leads as they strained towards the lawns. Olga ran over to the men, arms signalling as she spoke, pointing out where Emily might be hiding.

One of the men headed with two dogs to one side of the dense foliage, the other man led the remaining dogs to the opposite side. Smirnov had called in the dog van and heavies, probably on the Ivan payroll. The plan was obvious. To search the wooded area end to end, meeting in the middle. No escape. None that Emily could think of. She could see Olga, weapon at the ready, scouring the wood from the middle of the lawn, waiting for her to break cover when she would be easy to cut down with a single burst of machine gun fire. She could also see the main road, the gate having been left open when the dog van arrived.

The rain lashed heavier than before, dripping through the holly bush, streaming its way under Emily's collar, down her back. She barely noticed, her entire concentration on Olga and the sounds emanating from left and right.

"Kill, kill." The handlers chanted, encouraging the dogs to search, harsh voices prompting a frenzy of growling and snarling, each side closing in fast. Nearer and nearer, until Emily imagined she could feel dog's breath on her face. A man's shout came from the front of the house. Olga turned, jogging towards the pillars.

Emily spotted her chance. A slim one, but the only one available to escape being mauled. Bursting out of the bush, she sprinted for the open gate, slipping at first on the wet grass, her leg muscles weakened after days of inactivity. Her survival instinct fought the panic and pain in her chest. For a few heady seconds, she thought she would make it.

Around half-way, about 70 yards from the safety of the road, she heard the dogs break the cover of the wood. She dared turn her head and wished she hadn't. The lead dog was closing rapidly, baring yellow fangs, a terrifying growl emanating from a mouth drooling with the thrill of the chase. Emily contemplated swivelling and shooting it dead with Olga's pistol, but logic told her by then the three others would be upon her. An image of tearing flesh and crunching bones came to mind.

She stopped, raising hands in the air, admitting defeat, hoping against hope that compassion would prompt the handlers to call off the dogs.

***

Two explosions blew Emily off her feet. For many seconds she didn't realise what was happening. Her ears hurt. Her brain refused to work. The air was filled with acrid smoke. She could smell cordite, wet grass and exposed soil. A whirlpool wind swirled, swamping her senses, but she was alive and breathing. That was all that mattered. The dogs had gone. No more barking and snarling.

After many seconds her ears detected the distinctive pulsing of a helicopter's rotor blades. She looked up and saw a figure dressed in black, automatic gun at the ready, winching his way down to the lawn. She had never been happier to see Jack Easton. He unbuckled his straps almost before he hit the ground, draping a protective arm around her. At last, Emily felt safe, although gunshots popped all around, some of them emanating from the helicopter, aimed at the house.

She saw Olga disappear into the front of the black van along with one of the dog men, the other ushered the dogs into the back, jumping in after them. The van sped down the drive and out through the open gates.

Easton signalled to the helicopter to land. He had been on duty with his G Force squad, parked at RAF Northolt in West London, engine warming, when he received the call from Dent. They took off immediately, covering the nine miles to Hampstead in a few minutes. The security lights meant to flush out Emily proved the perfect beacon from the air, leading them to the scene. When they arrived, the chase across the lawn was in full swing, calling for swift intervention. Which is why the pilot swooped low, allowing Easton's men to drop a couple of stun grenades to deter the dogs. It worked perfectly.

"Jack, we've got to get Al." Emily screamed in Easton's ear. "He's seriously injured."

"Where is he?"

"Just up the road, not more than a mile away. Highgate cemetery."

"How do you know?"

"Never mind, it's a long story." She prayed she was right. The code Al had relayed via the video recording, GM2016, had foxed her for some time, mainly because the rotator code also occupied most of her waking thoughts. Al, despite his horrific injuries, had the presence of mind to supply an extra clue. "You can have your song." Emily had thought about that phrase many times. She was sure Al was referring to the last conversation they had together at the flat in Camden as she was leaving for her secret trip. *You and I*. By George Michael. The song Emily wanted at their wedding.

Knowing that, GM obviously stood for George Michael. 2016 the date of the singer's death, after which he was buried in the same plot as his mother in the west wing of Highgate cemetery.

They piled into the helicopter, Jonesy and Spike, Easton's right-hand special forces operatives, helping to haul them in.

The helicopter wheeled away into the night sky, taking an evasive route to avoid the giant crane, the city's lights in the distance proving a spectacular backdrop. Easton brought up a map of the cemetery on his tablet.

He shouted co-ordinates to the pilot. "Head for the west entrance off Swain's Lane. Be careful, it's tight with trees and wires, but you should be able to put down in the front courtyard." The pilot raised a thumb.

Easton turned to Emily. "Anything else we should know?"

"I think Al's being held near George Michael's grave. In some sort of vault. It looks like a cellar or lock-up. Quite roomy. I saw it on a video and Al used GM as a coded sign."

"Okay. Anything else?"

"Probably two Ivans guarding Al, both with multiple weapons, including machine guns." She grabbed his arm and squeezed. "Jack. They won't hesitate to kill."

Easton smiled. "We're in the same business then. They've chosen a perfect place to die."

45

The Royal Navy chose Faslane as its nuclear submarine base for good reason. It is moderately isolated while Gare Loch on which it sits provides a natural deep seawater harbour with protection from prying eyes and the worst of the Scottish weather.

The route to the Atlantic is also fast and smooth. Down the loch, turn right past the Isle of Bute into the Firth of Clyde, past the Isle of Arran on one side, the Antrim coast on the other, before slipping out into the vast Atlantic.

Lieutenant commander Stark had done the journey on many occasions. But this night, as the boat disappeared beneath the waves after entering Atlantic waters, he was nervous. HMS Vital was completing its final at-sea preparations to take over as the CASD submarine from HMS Vanguard, which was due in port in a week's time.

As well as Stark being responsible for weaponry and communications the captain had also tasked him with overseeing a number of training scenarios to ensure the stealth submarine was abreast of all eventualities.

One of them included the protocol and launch of one of the boat's ballistic missiles, known as *boomers*. Not unusual, but a job entrusted to the most experienced. The hope was that *boomers* would never be required but, in the event that they were, better to be well prepared. The drill preceded every stealth mission. A missile launched 50 miles off the coast of one of the most isolated parts of the UK. No nuclear warhead, of course, and programmed to self-destruct shortly after launch over the sea.

This drill was particularly important. HMS Vital had struggled with the previous test. The missile tanks had inflated, the pressure levelled and the missile shaft gradually filled with water, but a problem had occurred with the explosive charge used to vaporise the water into steam to drive the missile out of its launch tube. The missile had failed to emerge at 40mph, the speed required to clear the water's surface, to allow the missile engines to kick in.

Engineers had rectified the problem, but it was Stark's job to test.

Shortly before the boat sailed, as Stark was finalising paperwork in the harbour master's office, he had received a call. The conversation short and staccato.

"Yes?"

"I have some numbers for you."

Smirnov proceeded to reel off the two sets of numbers Emily had recited.

"Are we sure?" A nervous edge to Stark's query as he jotted down the numbers.

"As sure as we can be. What's the timing?"

"Can't be precise. Sometime tonight."

"Excellent. Pleasure doing business." The line went dead.

For a moment, Stark's mind went numb. This was it. The defining moment of his unremarkable life. He thought of his activist mum, singing protest songs outside the Faslane gates all those years ago. She would be proud. She had spent 10 years of her life battering on doors, writing letters, waving banners, cajoling MPs. For nothing. Not a single missile rescinded or rehoused. Not even a polite reply from an anonymous civil servant in the Ministry of Defence. Yet, in the next few hours, Stark could be instrumental in wiping the UK's nuclear deterrent off the face of the Earth. As he strode along the gangway onto HMS Vital, he held his head high. He didn't feel like a traitor. He felt like a warrior.

After the boat set sail, Stark busied himself overseeing procedure for the test firing of a Trident 2 D-5 ballistic missile. A routine exercise before every mission known as Demonstration and Shakedown Operations. He checked mid-boat where the missile tanks were housed, the missiles stored in vertical tubes, reporting back to the captain that all appeared in order. Weather conditions were calm. When Commander Dove's call came, the hairs on the back of Stark's neck stood on end. His stomach twisted.

"Ready, Lieutenant?"

"Yes, Sir. Beginning input data. Nine minutes to launch."

The captain's voice resounded around the boat. "Action stations, missiles for strategic launch."

Each missile houses an instrument compartment for control and guidance, requiring precise data entry for variables such as flight telemetry, target location, safety devices, and warhead detonation. Which was why a team of technicians sat at display panels in front of Stark in the control room.

A launch sequence was always a source of nervous excitement. It broke the tedium, reminding the crew of the fire power they controlled and why they were away from family and friends, sometimes for six months or more.

The plan was to enact a scenario to launch a ballistic missile carrying a nuclear warhead, using fictional codes, before physically testing the launch gear by firing a conventional missile programmed to self-destruct.

Stark, sitting in front of the master control display, provided the target co-ordinates, which in a live scenario would be classified and secret.

"Are you sure, Sir?" The submariner in charge of inputting the data, a lad called Stewart, with acne cheeks and thick black glasses, who looked 18 but was probably 10 years older, questioned the location, although his cheeky grin suggested unusual target locations for such practice drills were not uncommon. Red Square in Moscow was a favourite. It was the first time Stewart had inputted co-ordinates for HMS Vital's home base at Faslane.

Stark nodded, grinning as if it was his little joke. The drill continued. When it came to the codes for arming the warhead, Stark reminded everyone that in reality these would be provided by two commanding officers, not including the captain, who held passwords to access the Prime Minister's instructions. To maintain two-person integrity the codes would be inputted separately. For the purposes of the drill, Stark informed them he would input two fabricated codes.

He slipped a small piece of paper from his trouser pocket, holding it under the desktop. Glancing down, he read the numbers he'd taken from Smirnov, inputting them one by one into the computer. Access confirmation flashed on the screen. Weapon live and armed. The team, all fitted with headphones, went through a series of checks.

"Telemetry?" Stark queried

"Roger that, Sir."

"Target?"

"Aye, aye, Sir." Stewart confirmed.

Stark lifted the receiver to access the Commander. "All systems fine, Captain, clear to fire."

The submarine's nuclear trigger looked like the slightly battered red handle of a pistol. It was modelled on the Colt 45 Peacemaker hand gun, but could easily have been the retro control of a games console.

Captain Dove felt the smooth grip in his hand, played with it for a few seconds, before his forefinger wrapped around the trigger. As always, he imagined what he would feel if this was for real, when he would, in all probability, be operating against a backdrop of panic and confusion, not knowing the precise target, nor the extent of the devastation an enemy's strike had already caused.

He wasn't a religious man, yet he always said a little prayer, even during a drill with fabricated codes meaning there was no chance of actual launch, praying that this moment would never arrive in reality. That mankind would never reach this level of inhumanity.

Captain Dove, unaware that the codes were real, expecting nothing more than a click, pressed the trigger. All Lieutenant James Stark could hear was the clang of doom.

46

The Circle of Lebanon lies at the heart of Highgate's west cemetery, close to its highest point.

It comprises 20 large vaults, each holding as many as 15 coffins, built around the roots of an ancient cedar tree when the cemetery was designed in 1839. Standing with your back to the tree in those days, the industrial vista of Victorian London would have been visible.

Sixteen more classical vaults, most with Egyptian pediments, were added later as an outer circle, the space between the two circles forming an architecturally pleasing and atmospheric walkway.

Like the incumbents of the vaults, the cedar of Lebanon tree succumbed to rot and decay, replaced by a sapling cedar that yearns for maturity.

As the helicopter circled, searching for a landing point, Easton studied the map of Highgate's main mausoleums and vaults, readily available on the cemetery's website, along with the positions of celebrity graves. He noted the Circle of Lebanon's location, a short distance from George Michael's final resting place, deeming it the perfect place to hide a hostage with the cemetery shut for renovation.

Easton's gloved hand jabbed the circle on the map, showing Emily where his team would start their search.

"You wait with the chopper. I'll let you know when it's all clear." He shouted over the whir of the rotor blades.

Emily screamed her reply. "Not a chance I'm waiting. I'm all out of waiting. Jack, I'm coming with you. End of."

Easton was not accustomed to having his orders flagrantly dismissed, but he also recognised Emily's anxiety to find Al.

"Okay, but do exactly as I say. Clear." He fixed Emily with a stony stare. She nodded.

The pilot took care to avoid phone wires as well as the cemetery's outer wall and front gates as he eased the helicopter on its tight descent. Before they clambered out, Easton handed Emily a pair of lightweight image-intensifying night-vision goggles and a bullet-proof vest. "These should give us an advantage. It's as black as coal around here."

He helped Emily strap on the goggles and vest, debating whether to wait for back-up. On the way, he had alerted other members of his team, as well as the Met counter-terrorism unit, but deemed Al's predicament too urgent to wait.

Spike and Jonesy gathered around, both carrying machine guns. Easton laid out the map. "Okay, you two approach from here." He pointed to St Michael's Church, raised above the Circle of Lebanon, cutting off escape from the rear. "We'll approach from below. Let me know if you spot anything."

"How many are we expecting?"

"Two, perhaps three tangos, although it's unlikely the one in the black van came here. Probably half way up the M1 by now."

Spike and Jonesy tracked up the right side of the cemetery, along the uneven Faraday Path, making good time, heading for the spire of St Michael's. Easton and Emily took the easier, tarmac route along the Colonnade path, onto the main drive, sculptured headstones forming sinister silhouettes in the haze of their goggles. When they reached the Egyptian Avenue, an arched passageway formed of eight small vaults either side, they stopped. Easton listened for around 10 seconds. He could see the Circle of Lebanon vaults 40 yards in front, the double-fronted iron doors, rusted and flaking in places, glowing red in his goggles.

Animals rustled in the undergrowth, twigs snapped, the distant scream of a fox sent shivers through Emily. The drizzle was heavier now, compromising their vision. Easton cursed. Entering the enclosed Egyptian Avenue was precarious, the perfect site for an ambush.

Emily tapped Easton's shoulder, pointing to the left. A van, parked up against the wall by the open gates at the avenue's entrance, covered by overhanging branches, virtually invisible. Easton checked. No occupants. Engine not hot, but not cold either. Been there an hour or two at most. He whispered, hand signalling his intention. "Stay here. I'll check things out, give you the thumbs up."

Machine gun primed, Easton edged along the stone-walled incline, boots scraping on slippery gravel, betraying his position, expecting a firefight at any moment. None came. On reaching the top, he peered around the corner, listening again. This time he heard a thud, metal on stone, emanating from one of the vaults, no clue as to which one, or whether it was in the inner or outer circle. He knew the vaults were either locked or sealed.

He waved, beckoning Emily to join him. Taking a Sig Sauer hand gun from its holster, he handed it to Emily. "Hope you know how to use this."

"Squeeze the trigger. That's all you need to know." She had been brought up to speed on special forces armoury only months before.

"No safety catch, remember. Stay here and guard this escape route, until I give you a sign." She nodded.

Easton's headphones crackled. "In position, Jack. At the top of the circle by a bloody great chapel." Spike didn't know it but he and Jonesy had positioned themselves either side of the Julius Beer mausoleum, the largest and grandest of all the cemetery's privately-owned monuments, perhaps even the biggest private memorial in London. Beer made his fortune on the London Stock Exchange in the 19th Century before becoming proprietor of The Observer newspaper. Little did he know his Portland stone resting place would provide the perfect cover for a firefight.

"Okay, Spike. You two cover us from above. I'm going to check out the vaults. They've no place to go but around in circles, unless they want to climb the steps at either end. If they do, they're sitting ducks. Oh, and Spike, any sign of movement, shoot first."

"Music to my ears, Sir."

***

Katya and Lily froze. They both heard the noise at the same time. Boots on gravel. Above them. Not the harmless scrape of a homeless man this time, but vigorous, scurrying footsteps, then silence. Followed by more of the same. The sound of soldiers taking up positions, covering each other. Katya had been on enough training missions back in Belarus to recognise the subtleties.

The vault housing Al was in the outer circle, almost directly below the Beer mausoleum.

Katya immediately killed the torchlight, her mind racing. They had been waiting for Smirnov's call to tell them all had gone to plan in Faslane, but had heard nothing. The stench in the vault was foul and at Lily's insistence they had left the doors open to let in fresh air. A mistake. There were more than 50 vaults in the immediate vicinity. Some were bigger than others. Some, like that of controversial poet and novelist Radclyffe Hall, containing sculpted inscriptions, *...and if God choose, I shall but love thee better after death.* Yet most looked identical, cold and impenetrable, some having been shut to the world for more than a century. The open door was a giveaway.

Easton spotted it, half a dozen vaults away, as he edged along the gravel path. Dropping to one knee, he raised his gun, swivelling to check Emily's position at the top of the Egyptian Avenue. In the momentary distraction of that turn, two grenades exploded, one of them a smoke bomb, shrapnel and gravel hurtling into stone, Easton and Emily saved only by the curve of the circle and the fact they were hugging the stone wall. The rat-a-tat of machine guns echoed in the night air, indiscriminate firing, designed to disorientate, the tracer flash of bullets transforming the Circle of Lebanon into the hell fire of Highgate.

47

In the vault, Katya had edged through the darkness to the doorway, Lily close behind. The stone and metal of the sacred circle had caught the faintest whispers of Spike and Jonesy, magnifying and transporting them like a telephone line. Nothing definite, except *Tango*, the phonetic alphabet word often used by the military to mean *Enemy*.

A pause at the doorway had also detected movement to their left, the metallic shift of the safety catch sliding on a machine gun, a sound familiar to both women.

The vault was surrounded. At least that's what Katya and Lily concluded, although the considered nature of the advance suggested a small force. There were two options. Surrender and spend the rest of their days in a prison cell. Or fight. With no time for considered debate, they resorted to warrior instinct.

Lily felt in her rucksack, grabbing two grenades. She whispered. "Fear and surprise, Katya. That's our best weapon. You with me?"

Katya squeezed Lily's arm, a gesture of assent. Lily immediately charged out of the doors, flinging her grenades in Easton's direction, Katya close behind, a prolonged burst of machine gun bullets fired into the smoke that Lily knew would negate the advantage of any night goggles.

The women turned right, away from Easton, the smoke cloud tracking their way, masking their escape dash from Spike and Jonesy.

Katya and Lily sprinted along the vaults, following the circle, passing steps on the right that led to the upper level. The Egyptian Avenue, where they had left the van, was their best escape route. If the van had been discovered, then at least there was the option of the many paths through dense undergrowth.

***

In the noise and confusion, Emily's peripheral night vision captured two fleeing figures to her left, but she hadn't expected anyone from that direction, the circle's curve meaning they were past her and heading down the Egyptian Avenue before she realised.

Recognising Katya and Lily, she fired a warning shot from her handgun, but they didn't break stride. Emily gave chase, rapidly gaining on the women as they struggled with the extra weight of cumbersome machine guns.

At the bottom of the avenue the women split, Katya wheeling left, Lily heading right.

"Go right, Emily, go right." Easton screamed the instruction from behind, his boots sliding on the wet gravel as he swerved left to chase Katya.

In the motion of weaving right, the strap holding Emily's goggles snapped. The night suddenly turned black. She could have stopped to find and retie them, but knew Lily would be long gone by then. She ran on, the pace dropping as both she and Lily struggled to see. They reached the end of the gravel track, the road now smooth tarmac, Emily pursuing almost by sound alone. The rain fell heavier, sporadic gunfire from Easton and his team echoing through the trees.

Emily's night vision, without the goggles, kicked in. The scudding clouds picked up a glow from the surrounding area, reflecting a fraction of the streetlights and headlamps, enough for Emily to make out silhouettes of crosses and memorials, but little detail.

Lily was around 40 yards in front when Emily sensed her stumble, going down in the undergrowth. A crashing fall. Emily stopped and listened. Nothing but the shouts of Spike and Jonesy in the distance, obviously still on the hunt for Katya.

Emily edged forward, gripping the gun in both hands, trigger finger poised to shoot. Reaching the spot where Lily had fallen, she wandered off the path, brushing through wet ferns, trousers rapidly becoming sodden. A realisation struck. No longer was she afraid or anxious. No longer did she feel traumatised by the events of the last few days. Maybe it was the adrenalin of the chase, the thrill of having escaped her captors, but at last she felt truly free. As if, whatever the outcome, the next few moments were meant to be. Rounding a bush, she held her breath, again pausing to listen under the spreading branches of a sycamore tree. The patter of raindrops. She turned to make once more for the path.

"Don't move." The chilling command sliced through the darkness. Emily couldn't tell from which direction, but it sounded near, containing a snarl she recognised as Lily. "Drop the gun."

Emily's heart sank. To drop the gun would allow herself to be held hostage once more. If she could see Lily, even if she could have sensed her position, she would have pulled the trigger, firing into the forest until all bullets were loosed with no care for herself, yet with one purpose. Bringing to justice the woman who had murdered Zofia and maimed Al. With no audio or visual clues, that would be suicide. Even in the midst of the darkest of nights, in a cold cemetery full of the ghosts of famous characters long gone, when life appeared cheap and nothing seemed real, it was logic that prevailed. Emily let the gun slip from her hand.

"Okay Lily, what now?"

"Smirnov should have let me finish you off, along with Zofia. Would have made our lives a whole lot easier. Once a traitor, always a traitor."

"I'm not one of you. I'm not the traitor. I didn't kill Zofia, or the man in the café. You're the one who goes around executing people for no good reason."

"Well, this time, I do have a good reason."

The shouting and gunfire in the distance having stilled, Emily turned around, her ears at last pinpointing Lily's location, stood against the sycamore trunk. Straining her eyes, she made out the shape of a machine gun pointed in her direction, sensing Lily favouring her left foot, the fall having sprained or broken an ankle.

"You're not going anywhere fast, Lily. It's over. Give yourself up." Emily tried once more to reason.

"Don't think that's a good idea. But you're right, I do need to get going."

Lily raised the machine gun, fingering the trigger. Emily's body braced, anticipating the end, remembering the ruthless fashion in which Lily had disposed of Zofia. With a single bullet. The blood, the death stare, the lack of compassion.

This time the shots came in a tight, short burst.

48

"Olga?" Emily's scream was charged with shock and disbelief.

The girl from Romania stood before her, nose smashed and bloodied from contact with Emily's heel, the torch she held in one hand lighting the widest of smiles. In her other hand, smoke rose from a gun barrel.

They stared at Lily, lying on the ground in a heap, bullet wounds in her neck and chest, face set in a curious frown, the yellow torchlight dancing on her diamond nose stud, her arms pointing towards a small mottled-pink obelisk that doubled as a gravestone.

Olga's torchlight picked out the inscription. *Alexander Litvinenko. To the world, you are one person, but to one person you are the world.* A framed photo of the Russian agent, who defected to the West but was poisoned by the Russians in 2006, lay against the headstone. Boyish smile, a picture of innocence.

An extraordinary serendipity, thought Emily. *Almost as if Litvinenko had led Lily to this place to exact his revenge on the Russian state.*

"Why, Olga? Why aren't you miles away?" Emily put the obvious question, for a moment even wondering if Olga, like Zofia, was a CIA agent. It soon became obvious that was a fanciful thought.

Olga's shoulders slumped. Her lips made to move, but no sound came at first, apart from a choking rasp. Emily thought Olga was going to cry, but she didn't.

"She shouldn't … have killed … Zofia." When Olga spoke, the words were slow and robotic, as if recent traumas had dulled her senses. "I never wanted any killing. I didn't want Lily to kill you."

Olga sat on her haunches, shaking her head, a dull thud sounding as her gun dropped to the ground. She had sped from the safe house towards the cemetery in the dog van, intending to pick up Katya and Lily. When the dog handlers spied the helicopter landing, their survival instinct kicked in. "Fuck this," shouted the driver, veering away from the cemetery's temporary entrance. Ivan paid well, but not enough to risk a firefight with special forces. Olga screamed at the driver to let her out. She followed the sound of gunfire towards the Circle of Lebanon, by chance intercepting the stand-off between Lily and Emily.

Recognising Emily was about to become another of Lily's victims, something stirred in the girl from Brasov. Where it came from, she had no idea. Maybe it was the memory of her artist father and his lessons in perspective. Perhaps it was the bond she had formed these past days with Emily. Whatever, something told her Lily had to be stopped.

Olga didn't try to escape when Easton came marching down the hill, Spike and Jonesy either side of Katya, whose hands were tied behind her back.

"Who's this?" Easton queried.

"Olga, the girl with the machine gun who jumped in the dog van at the mansion. She could have escaped. Thankfully, she decided to stay around." Emily explained Olga had saved her life, even though she was a member of the Ivan Group who had held her hostage.

"She'll have chance to explain everything to a judge in due course." Easton's tone was pragmatic as he tied Olga's hands, Spike collecting discarded weapons in the light from Jonesy's head torch. Emily didn't hear. She had no inside knowledge why Olga had returned to save her, apart from having formed a connection in captivity that seemed to amplify Lily's evil nature. Emily had no explanation for anything that had happened these past few days. Her head was numb with gunshots, fear, death, and overwhelming exhaustion.

Oh, my God. Al. I must go to him. Call the paramedics. Get him to hospital. Hang on Al, I'm coming.

Police sirens wailing in the distance, Emily grabbed Olga's torch and ran back up the hill towards the Circle of Lebanon, berating herself that despite her own traumas she could have forgotten, even for the briefest of moments, why she was here.

Please hang on, Al. I'm coming. Everything's going to be all right.

49

She turned into Egyptian Avenue, the stone vaults immediately shielding her from the growing hubbub at the cemetery gates.

Her lungs were bursting, leg muscles scorching with effort, torchlight dancing on the Egyptian pediments. At any other time, the historic surroundings would have conveyed an air of sanctity, yet dread is a powerful emotion. Emily's thoughts had no time for reverence, her face no concern for the stinging rain that sliced her cheeks.

All she could think of was Al. His welcoming smile, easy confidence, his ability to see the best in people even when they had betrayed his trust. His corny one-liners. Oh, how she groaned at his cheesy jokes. *"What's the best way to burn one thousand calories? Leave the pizza in the oven."* Somehow, when Al told them, they didn't seem so sad.

But the main reason Emily loved Al was because he never judged her when the character quirks others viewed as odd and unreasonable surfaced. Al didn't shuffle uncomfortably, or look the other way. He embraced Emily, with all her idiosyncrasies and imperfections, regarding them as special and unique. The memory prompted an infusion of warmth.

She worked her way down the row of vaults, calling Al's name, the torch beam picking out the details of those who had gone before, some of them dating back to 1839, the year of the cemetery's opening. When she reached the eighth vault, one of the iron doors was open.

"Al, are you there?" No answer. She pushed the door wide and sprayed the beam, illuminating coffins piled high either side. In normal circumstances, that would have been enough to send a shiver up her spine. Emily shied away from anything supernatural. She detested horror films, but her mind was numb to such emotion. She spotted the inner door, striding in, no thought of caution, throwing it open.

The first thing she saw was the bare stone wall, a cobweb caked in a century of dust suspended impossibly against it. She remembered it from the first video. Her torch tracked left, picking out the leering expression of the homeless man. A plug of vomit burned her throat. It was all she could manage not to throw up on the spot.

"Al." She screamed, the fear smouldering in the pit of her stomach having grown into a fire of such raging intensity that she felt she might pass out.

She swept around and at last there he was. Al. Caught in the yellow light, sitting up in the corner, red blanket pulled tight around his shoulders, his eyes at rest, a smile playing on his lips as if he had delivered one of his jokes.

"Oh, thank God, Al. Thank God I've found you."

She rushed to him, knelt on one knee, and shook his shoulder. Nothing. She shook again, this time harder. His head fell to one side. "Oh, Al, poor thing." In the complex considerations and intense emotions of the moment, she thought he must be exhausted. He must have slipped into a deep sleep.

She sat on the stone floor, took his head in her arms, stroked his hair, tender and comforting, rocking back and forth, hoping against hope, trying to convince herself. But reason, cold and miserable, kept interrupting hope. And as long seconds passed she was filled with a spasm of such intense loss that her whole body shook. Emily, the girl who never cried, sobbed. Rivers of tears ran down her cheeks, guilt pouring from her lips.

"It's my fault, Al. All my fault. I should never have joined. Never put you at risk. You always looked after me, kept me safe. It's my fault."

She buried her face in his hair, hugging him tight, as if the warmth of her body may somehow breathe life. And yet she knew he was gone.

Ten minutes later she felt strong hands gently prise her fingers from Al's shoulders. She heard a man's familiar voice, but her grief was too desperate to comprehend what he was saying.

"Come with me, Emily. It's time to let go. We can see to Al. I'll look after you." Jack Easton lifted her to her feet, the harsh light of several powerful torch beams bouncing around the vault walls, casting silhouettes, illuminating the horror and loneliness of Al's final hours.

"Jack, it's my fault," whispered Emily, as Easton half carried her to a waiting jeep that his team had used to negotiate the cemetery's dirt and gravel tracks.

"No, Emily. Don't blame yourself. You were doing your job. That's all. You did your best to save him."

"Remind me, Jack, what's this place called?"

"Pardon."

"Where we are now."

"The Circle of Lebanon. Why?"

"I just need to know."

Emily knew her photographic memory would preserve the precise details of the past few hours, some for days or months, some for eternity. She also knew, whatever Jack Easton said, she would never forgive herself.

This place of death would haunt her forever.

50

Emily sat between C and Dent. She had never attended the Joint Intelligence Committee before. This was no routine meeting. The big guns were present.

Opposite the SIS trio sat the Defence Minister, the Foreign Secretary, the Home Secretary, and the Metropolitan Chief Constable. For once CIA London chief Matt Jennings was early, while several junior ministers were also in attendance, as well as heads of the Armed Services.

Chairman Sir Ralph Short waved a copy of *The Times* newspaper in the air.

"I trust everyone is acquainted with this morning's headline."

For emphasis, he held the paper up again, twirling it around so everyone could see. The headline was stark.

NUCLEAR SUB OFFICER ARRESTED.

Sir Ralph went on to read the first paragraph.

"A high-ranking officer on HMS Vital, one of the UK's nuclear submarines, was taken into custody after apparently suffering a delusional episode. It is thought the officer attempted to launch a ballistic missile with the target unknown. In submariner's parlance, such episodes are known as a wibble. The officer concerned is currently under the care of mental health personnel."

The report quoted defence spokespersons, insisting no crew, or members of the public, were ever in danger and the officer had been arrested for his own safety. A sidebar demonstrated how the two-person integrity protocol meant a ballistic missile couldn't be launched by a single crew member.

Sir Ralph threw the paper down. "A wibble. Is that what you would call it, Giles?" Sir Ralph fixed C with a piercing stare.

C cleared his throat. "The truth is a little more sinister than a wibble. As you know, we have been monitoring a Russian-funded cell, called the Ivan Group, operating in London for several months. We took the chance to infiltrate this cell with one of our agents. It's not too dramatic to say we uncovered a plot to sabotage the UK's entire nuclear capability."

"Tell us more." Sir Ralph sat forward in his chair, as did most of the others, a disbelieving hush settling on the room.

"It's a long story."

"We're not going anywhere."

C took a deep breath, glancing at Dent. He looked at Emily, whose eyes were fixed on the desk, flicking from side to side. It was three days since the events in the Circle of Lebanon. Doctors had checked out Emily. They had diagnosed severe shock and recommended she take an extended period of leave. Emily had told them where they could go.

She didn't want leave. She didn't want time to dwell on the loss of Al. C, however, had insisted she take time off following her attendance at the committee.

The SIS chief proceeded to explain that the threat aboard HMS Vital had been real and imminent. That Lieutenant Stark had gained access to the Letter of Last Resort and required only to crack the codes embedded in the letter to take control of the submarine's nuclear warheads.

"But there are no codes. We all know that." Sir Ralph intervened, his tone mocking.

The Defence Minister swapped knowing, slightly embarrassed, looks with the heads of the Armed Services.

"What? Am I the only one who doesn't have the inside track on this?" Sir Ralph blustered.

Dent fished a piece of paper from his inside pocket. "Perhaps I can help. Here is a letter found in the office of Admiral, Sir Robert Bellingham, sadly murdered, we believe, by an agent of the Russian state. The letter was hidden, but reveals Sir Robert's concerns about the ease in which the UK's nuclear code could be compromised. The letter is titled, *A Child Could Crack the UK's Nuclear Code.* That is a simplification, but someone with expertise in cryptography could deliver the code in days."

"Never." A vice admiral, sitting at the end of the table, instinctively leapt to the Royal Navy's defence.

"I'm afraid the proof is in the numbers." Dent took another piece of paper from his pocket, waving it in the air. Two sets of five numbers. "This is the code required to arm the nuclear warheads on the UK's submarine fleet."

A collective gasp went around the room.

"Are you saying this officer was in possession of the code, seconds away from firing a ballistic missile with a nuclear warhead?" The vice admiral's tone was disbelieving.

"That's exactly what I'm saying." Dent's flat vowels somehow enhanced the gravity of the claim. "The target was the nuclear submarine base at Faslane and nearby armaments depot, the intention to take out the UK's nuclear capability."

"But my information is that this officer triggered the warning mechanism, all hell let loose in the control room, bells ringing, lights flashing. That was how he was apprehended, when it became clear he was jabbing in numbers, probably at random."

"Not quite." Dent glanced at Emily, a frown of concern, mindful of raking over harrowing recent events. "The truth is our agent here, Emily Stearn, an expert cryptographer, was coerced into supplying the code after her fiancé was taken hostage."

Another audible gasp.

Dent continued. "In an attempt to play for time and save her innocent fiancé, Emily went along with the group's demands. She supplied the code …"

"I tried to save him." Emily intervened, her voice at first faltering, but then strengthening as she gazed around the room, spotting men in sharp suits with comfortable lives, who made decisions, sipping tea and coffee, in wood-panelled offices. The contrast with the last days of Al's life was stark.

"I thought many times what would Al have done. I think I know. He would have told me not to betray my country at any cost. He was that sort of person. When I cracked the code and relayed it to Ivan, I changed one digit, the last digit. Instead of 48, I made it 49. I knew any false digit would trigger a warning mechanism, disabling any launch. That is standard procedure in this type of coding."

She studied the row of high-ranking officers and politicians, a steady gaze that fell a smidgeon short of accusing. She addressed Sir Ralph. "If whoever is investigating this incident looks at the last number that was inputted they will see it is 49, proving the officer was not jabbing random numbers, but inputting the code I gave to the Ivan Group. There is your proof."

Emily sat back, her eyes again reverting to the desktop. Nods and admiring glances around the room.

Dent hadn't finished. He knew the high offices of state moved at the pace of a disabled snail, but ever since Miller had reported back on her spiky, but unproductive, meeting with the submarine service, he had despaired at the arrogance of men who refused to believe their department could be compromised. If they had taken seriously the notion that an enemy agent might be aboard one of their nuclear submarines, then Al would still be alive. To emphasise his words, he stood.

"Sir Ralph, I should like to put on record the debt the nation owes to SIS operative Emily Stearn, whose bravery and expertise was instrumental in uncovering a plot to sabotage the UK's nuclear deterrent, perhaps saving the lives of millions of people."

"Hear, hear." Murmurings of assent rippled around the room.

"I should also like to call for an inquiry into the abject failure of this committee and parts of the armed services, in particular the submarine service, to cooperate with intelligence in the face of an existential threat. The fox was in the henhouse and the farmer looked the other way, sticking cotton wool in his ears."

Feet shuffled. An embarrassed silence descended.

"If you'll excuse us." Dent took Emily's hand and they walked out of the room, down the corridor, spilling out onto Whitehall where a clear, crisp day, painted London in a bright hue.

They ambled across Westminster Bridge, neither of them saying a word, Emily's melancholy and Dent's anger drifting undirected but side by side, like flotsam in the river below. Big Ben chimed. A group of tourists cheered, although it was unclear why. For a moment, all seemed safe with the world, except they both knew the world they inhabited was never safe.

The chances were Lieutenant Stark would now be exposed for his treachery. Katya and Olga would stand trial on a variety of terrorism charges. The London properties of the Ivan Group would be seized. As for Smirnov, he had vanished, his suite at the Ritz abandoned, his passport on the wanted list at every UK air and sea port.

Dent put an arm around Emily's shoulders as they gazed at the river. "Come back for a coffee. I'll see you home."

"No thanks, Miles. I just want to be alone for a while."

"Okay, I'll ring later."

Dent gave her a tender hug, before departing for his Vauxhall office, leaving Emily staring at the swirling waters, lost in her thoughts. After a few minutes, she spied a young woman with a jaunty stride and a welcoming smile making her way through the embankment throng, handing out fliers.

As she passed, she offered a pamphlet. Emily shook her head, but the woman pressed one into her hand, moving on swiftly. The flier was advertising an upcoming concert at Wembley. Emily was about to shove it into her pocket, with the intention of discarding it in the nearest rubbish bin, when she spotted a card stapled to the front. About the size of a business card. The word on the front caught her attention. *Shelkunchik.*

She tore off the card and turned it over. On the back, a number. She recognised the first three digits straight away. 007. It had always intrigued her that the first three digits of the international dialling code for Russia from the UK were fictional spy James Bond's secret identification number. The next three digits, 495, told her the number was somewhere in Moscow. The message alongside was typed.

Glad you are alive and well. We can always use a woman like you.

Emily shivered. The memory of Smirnov's dead smile came to mind.

51

Emily Stearn sat on the terrace licking an ice cream, watching yachts tacking, a generous breeze whipping up white horses on the English Channel.

It was late spring and already the sun on the south coast was warm enough to suggest summer was on its way.

Six months had passed since Al's death. Emily had moved out of London to the hilltop bungalow, once owned by her Uncle Sebastian. For much of that time, and in light of the message she had received on the embankment, a protection detail had been assigned to watch over her. She was no longer an SIS operative. She made that decision within a week of the JIC meeting. She didn't know what Al would have made of it, but she knew he would have supported her. Her heart was no longer in the business of treachery.

Al's funeral had been the hardest day of her life. Dent and Miller were there. C even turned up in a blacked-out limousine. Jack Easton, along with Spike and Jonesy, helped carry the coffin. They all walked into the church to Pachelbel's Canon in D.

Emily, flanked by her mum and dad, read a moving poem about love and loss, an understandable tremor in her delivery, while some of Al's teaching and football mates took turns to tell everyone why he was such a special colleague and friend.

When the service was over, Emily decided she wanted to stay in their Dorset hideaway, working from home on a special project for her father's publishing business. In her spare time, she could visit the Tasty Treat café on the promenade where Al used to work and where they had first met. She could sit on the harbour wall watching fishermen unload their haul or tinkle on the Steinway piano in the lounge overlooking the communications beacon on the Isle of Portland. She could do the things she shared with Al. Feel close to him, enjoying the present, with warm memories of the past and no thought to the future.

She read the newspapers, especially interested in the *Guardian's* report that security surrounding the UK's nuclear deterrent was being urgently reviewed, although the news report detailing the capture of several Russian spies, living in UK suburbia, passing defence secrets to Moscow, only suggested the Cold War of old was back, colder than ever.

There was a ring on the bell. Emily, tossing the remnants of her ice cream into the bushes, went to answer. Dent stood in the doorway, a brown envelope in his hand.

"Miles, how nice to see you. Come in."

"Don't mind if I do."

Emily smiled. The Yorkshire vowels always intrigued her.

They went through to the lounge and Emily made two cups of tea. Dent loved his tea.

"You should have phoned, Miles. It's a long way to come."

"Not at all. Remember that thing we were talking about? The memorial for Al."

"Of course." Following the funeral, after which Al was buried in a plot overlooking the sea, Dent had suggested SIS pay for a memorial stone in recognition of Al's sacrifice. C had agreed and Emily accepted.

Dent slipped a photograph out of the envelope, laying it on the table between them.

"For your approval."

Emily picked up the photo, studying it for several seconds. A single tear rolled down her cheek, but a wide smile lit up her face.

"It's perfect, Miles, just perfect."

They sat in silence for several minutes gazing at the photo of a mottled-pink marble obelisk, inscribed Alexei Andeyevich (Al Andrews), with a motto underneath that Emily had seen once before on that dark and feral night in Highgate Cemetery.

To the world, you are one person, but to one person you are the world.

Acknowledgements

During the course of writing this book, I was struck, not for the first time, at how fact is so much more unbelievable than fiction. Especially where Russia is concerned.

Yevgeny Prigozhin, leader of the mercenary Wagner Group, launched a mutiny, mobilising his private army to march on Moscow before turning around at the eleventh hour. Two months later Prigozhin's plane fell from the sky, killing him and nine others.

Alexei Navalny, Russian President Vladimir Putin's most prominent political opponent, was jailed for an additional 19 years on top of his original 12-year term in a special regime colony, the toughest conditions in Russia's prison system.

Sergei Karaganov, honorary chairman of Russia's Council on Foreign and Defence policy, kicked off a debate on the war in Ukraine with the argument that it was necessary to scare the West with Russia's willingness to use nuclear weapons. "In a war, the winners are not judged," formed part of his reasoning.

Meanwhile, five Bulgarian nationals, living in British suburbia, were arrested and charged with spying for Russia, while the UK continued to lead the European weapons support to repel Russia from Ukraine.

As Emily Stearn discovers in the pages of this book, the Cold War is colder and more dangerous even than the days of Kim Philby, Guy Burgess and Donald Maclean.

Thank you to the publishers, Sharpe Books, for having faith in the Emily Stearn thriller series.

Thanks also to the Friends of Highgate Cemetery, who have rescued a national treasure and preserved an oasis of architecture, sculpture and nature. May the restoration and conservation continue. My research in the east and west wings provided an informative and pleasurable stroll through almost 200 years of British social history.

Thanks to my son, Michael, for his support, as always. Most of all, thank you to my wife, Carole, for her proofreading, constructive criticism, meticulous front-line editing, and all-round inspiration.

Printed in Great Britain
by Amazon

31457623R00130